ZERO MAGENTA

JOHN HOWES

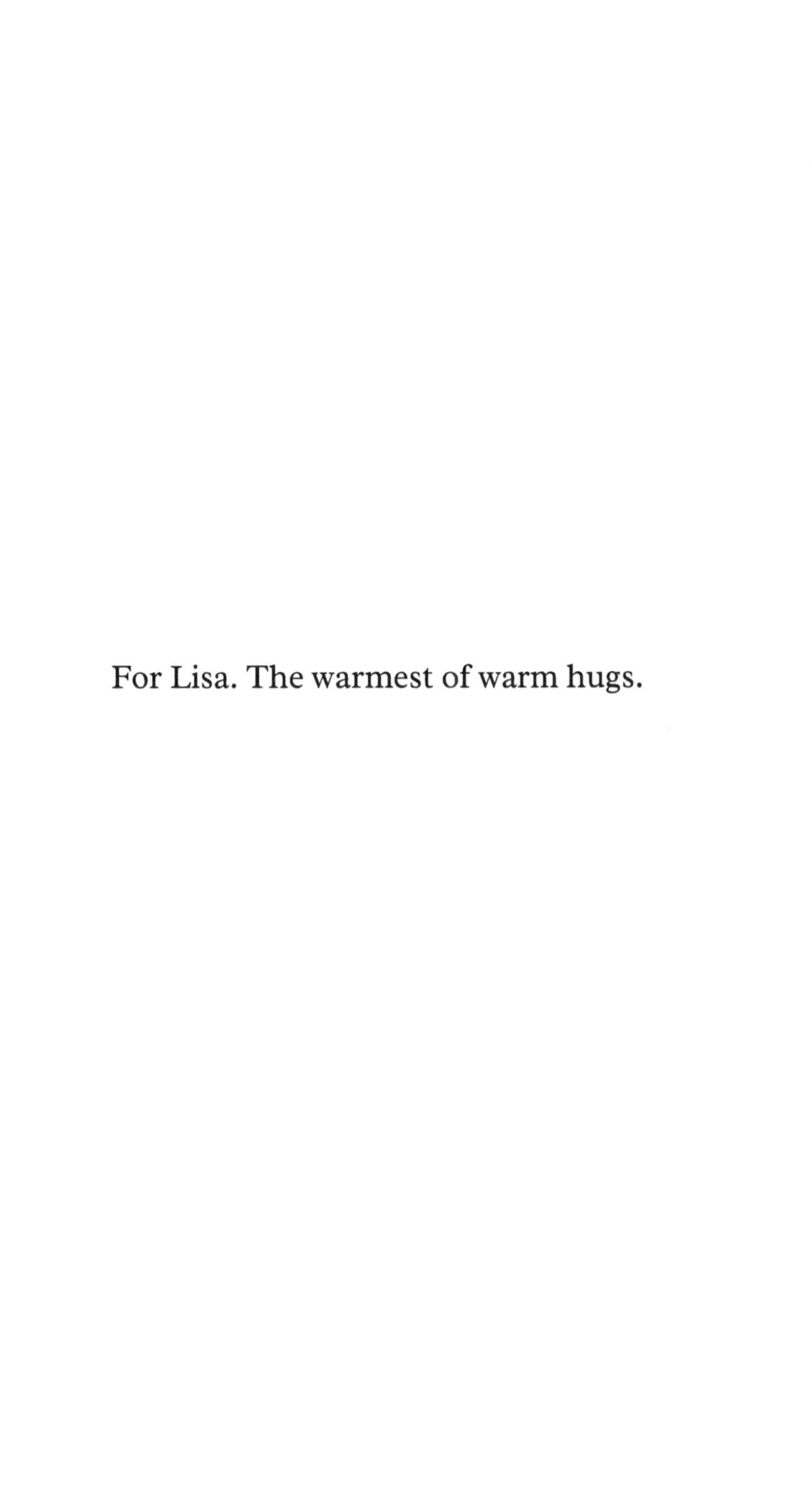

For Lisa. The warmest of warm hugs.

Novels by John Howes

Science Fiction

Zero Magenta

Fantasy

The Nifaran Chronicles

Part 1: Fay Legion

Part 2: Vega Rising

1 MAGS

Congratulations on purchasing the iM-21.

Your unit is delivered with a residual charge and cannot be operated until a full 100% charge has been completed.

Situate the charger as shown in the image below. A red LED will indicate charging, which will change to green when fully charged. The iMov app will also display the charge level, as will the optional iMov remote control.

Ensure you are fully aware of all the features and modes before binding for the first time.

(iM-21 Quick start guide)

The green LEDs on the six monitors slowly blinked out to the sound of distant vacuum cleaners and the occasional keyboard tap from the few remaining traders. Monday trading in the currency team of Coopers and Staltzman was always madness. Today had brought more stress than usual to the nineteenth floor of the Opus tower. Late September rain was hammering at the smoked windows, blurring the lights of London's Docklands and the city in the distance.

The DLR ran until 11:00 pm; Brad had thirty minutes to get to the station, and he'd do it with seven minutes to spare. He'd been taking the exact route for the four years and three months as the most successful currency trader at C&S London. Brad was tired and hated his job, but the financial rewards were staggering, and he could do the work with his eyes closed. A rich white guy in a sea of rich white guys had never been his dream.

Time to go home.

Brad leaned back in his mesh-covered, designer office chair and pictured her for a moment. She would still be awake, smiling and welcoming him into her arms. He could see the shine in her eyes and the tiny creases in her smile, her dark hair framing her perfect almond face. Holding those images, he made for the lift and was on his way. It was always these stressful Mondays that made Brad think of Mags the most. Her thoughtfulness, her care, and the way she loved him unconditionally. He knew she was blind to his wealth and would always be there for him.

Lost in thought, Brad barely noticed the rain or the stark, cold glass of South Quay Station. Autopilot had kicked in and would now navigate him through Tower Gateway and all the way to Monument, where he would make the short walk to the Zenith apartments overlooking London Bridge.

Zenith combined the original investment bank's exterior, added glass and chrome, and four penthouse floors built above. It was less vulgar than some of the other apartment monstrosities popping up around the capital. The view over London Bridge was breathtaking, especially at night, and it provided an excellent home for Mags.

At three point nine million pounds, Brad's penthouse floor, third down from the top, was humble by trader standards. It had two bedrooms but no garage. Brad couldn't see the point in owning cars in central London, unlike the multiple Ferraris and Lamborghinis owned by his colleagues, which spent most of the year under wraps in basement garages. Brad preferred to spend most of his money on Mags and the life they shared.

The tall glass doors of the main entrance opened silently to Brad's card key, giving way to an opulent marble-floored lobby. The reception desk stood empty; it was only staffed from 8:00 am until 7:00 pm. Brad's footfall and the rain drops falling from his coat were the only sign of life as he summoned the lift. Would she be in her night dress or still in the tight t-shirt and jeans she favoured? She was beautiful in anything, and Brad smiled to himself, just thinking of her as the spacious lift climbed to level P3.

There were six apartments on floors P2 and P3, with just four on P1, at the very top. Brad stopped in front of the plain oak door of room P32 and fumbled for his card key with tired, wet hands. The LED blinked from red to green, and the door swung open with only the relay click of the mechanism to give it away. Just that tiny sound was enough to prompt movement from within the apartment as Mags made her way to greet him.

"What time do you call this?" she said, with mock annoyance. They'd never shared a cross word in the four years they'd been together. The massive ear to ear smile was the big giveaway as she came bounding through the door, arms outstretched. "Urgh! You're wet through," she spluttered, giving him the usual warm hug and a long warm kiss that always told Brad he was home. "Give me your coat and go chill out on the sofa. I've done chilli. I'll just sort it out and bring you a coffee." She was halfway to the kitchen and stopped in her tracks.

"I love you," said Brad, still standing near the door with dripping hair.

He was a man of very few words, borderline Asperger's according to his last psychiatrist, but Mags didn't need a stream of words. She understood him completely. "I know," she said, flashing him a beautiful smile, then vanished off to the kitchen.

The ultra-modern apartment was tastefully decorated in hues of cream and brown but with splashes of colour in each room. A sumptuous cream carpet ran through most rooms, as Mags didn't like cold solid floors.

An inviting hallway with a bookcase and cloak cupboard led to the generous kitchen, the small bedroom (Brad used as a study), and the cosy modern lounge. It was here that they spent most of their time.

It was a massive room with a large cream sofa and two cliché Barcelona chairs providing a black contrast to the natural tones. The space was dominated by Brad's pride and joy, the one-hundred-and-ten-inch OLED TV, but the main focus was the floor-to-ceiling window which ran the length of one wall. A vast sliding panel opened onto a wooden-decked terrace with views over the Thames, completing the penthouse look.

The rain was streaming down the windows, which made Brad feel even more content than usual. He collapsed onto the long, cream sofa and chilled out, as instructed.

Mags ran in with his coffee and berated him for not getting changed, "Come on," she said. "Dinner's on the way, go and get cleaned up; that's an order."

"Okay," he grumbled and trudged off to the bathroom to shower. The stress of the day drained away. Thinking of Mags made Canary Wharf seem very distant.

Dinner was served in the kitchen diner, as usual, all bright cream and crimson red. Brad wasn't sure when the kitchen was installed, but now it seemed just fine. Mags had an excellent eye for style; she chose the décor for the whole apartment as Brad insisted it was her choice when she arrived.

"So, how was your day?" she chirped as he started digging into yet another perfect chilli.

"Not much to say," he said, in his usual brevity, "just another hectic Monday in the office."

"Oh, come on," she said, "You know I love to hear about your day. I don't care how boring you think it is."

Brad paused for a while, trying to think of a way to spin currency trading into a narrative. "Well, there was a massive fall in the Dollar, and the bank base rate is up by zero point five per cent; it was carnage."

With that, he started to recount just how many millions had been lost that day. Of course, Brad was fine. He'd even managed to turn a three-and-a-half million-pound profit by waiting for the late market to rally. Mags didn't feign interest; she was always genuinely interested in his day.

"So how about your day?" asked Brad, after finishing the story of his Monday madness.

"It was pretty good, no fights, which is always a plus", she smiled broadly. "We had the usual junkies and meth drinkers and a depressing number of young people today." She shrugged. Mag's days were as predictable as his, but the difference was that she enjoyed her work. Mags volunteered at a soup kitchen in Dagenham called Light Lunch four days a week, where her positive nature always brightened the days of those in need.

Brad didn't like her working there and told her often that she didn't need to work. As far as he was concerned, she could shop all day and spend all his money, but volunteering made her happy. Mags would often say, "I can't just shut myself away. I was made to serve, and who better to help than those who feel abandoned?" In reality, it just made Brad prouder as he watched her grow into a person far better than he could ever have imagined.

Yet another late dinner and another late night; it was past midnight, and Brad was shattered. Mags never really became tired, although her movements would slow, and the trademark smiles would be far fewer. It was time for bed.

The bedroom was huge, decorated in sumptuous natural tones and with the same floor-to-ceiling glass spreading from the lounge and wrapping around two walls. Another giant, sliding glass panel opened onto a covered section of the terrace. A full-sized sofa and swivel chair completed the modern, spacious look.

Mags hit the remote control, closing the curtains on the rain still beating down while Brad sank into the generous bed. The lights were dimmed out, and Mags snuggled up beside him. It would be another dull day at the office tomorrow, but he had Mags to wake up to and come home to. He smiled to himself as she released him and switched to her preferred position on her back.

Sleep began to take Brad, but just as his eyes started to close, he saw her. Halina was standing at the door to their home in Hackney, it was cold, and she was wearing her furry hat and coat that made her look cute. She was turning away now and closing the door behind her. It was the last image of her that he could remember. Brad woke from his semi-sleep by the sound of the familiar relay click; somewhere under the bed, a red LED blinked on. Charging had commenced. Mags' body would now warm slightly, as the aluminium batteries deep within her body were charged by the large inductive loop beneath. Mags was special in many ways.

2 THE CONTRACT

Binding.

Prior to binding, it is essential to select the correct mode. A complete list of the one hundred and seventy-five modes can be found on the AHS website, along with video demonstrations and helpful tips. Other modes are available for download at additional cost.

Creating a custom set-up requires the B-Mode app (available at an additional cost).

All modes (except mode zero) can be reinitialised without affecting the memory.

WARNING: Mode zero may only be modified through a complete system reset. See System Reset.

(MyPAL iM-21 User Manual)

Brad had been in the Zenith apartment for one week. There was no furniture, except for a couple of small wooden garden chairs in the lounge, which he'd brought in from the terrace, and a sumptuous king-sized bed in the main bedroom. The kitchen was fully functional, but Brad couldn't be bothered to cook and had eaten takeaways for the duration. The whole apartment looked tired, with stains on the wooden floors, faded brown curtains, and bare wires hanging from the walls where lights should be. It needed attention, or a woman's touch, as Brad thought.

He was unshaven, poorly dressed and knew that he couldn't go on living this way. He would need to look his best in just over a week for his first day at Coopers & Staltzman, but right now, he was waiting, gaze fixed on his watch.

The delivery was due an hour ago, but he couldn't assume they weren't coming. His contract stated clearly that he must be available for the delivery. He was just about to look for the number on his mobile when the access system buzzed. He selected the

HomeGuard app on his smartphone and immediately saw a young Asian woman staring back, looking very severe and business-like.

"Hello…" he started but was immediately interrupted.

"My name is Baljit Kulkarni. I'm your liaison for TKS Installations, official AHS partner."

Brad stared blankly at the screen.

"I have your package; please may we come up?" she asked, in a tone that sounded like an order.

Composing himself, Brad enabled main door access with one touch, and the screen went blank. He had been waiting for this moment for four months and had timed the new apartment, new job and special delivery for the same week. A fresh start, he told himself.

Brad imagined a large object being squeezed into the lift before slowly ascending his way. He quickly ran around the apartment, throwing out the empty pizza boxes and shoving the packing boxes to the side of the lounge, one of which was acting as a stand for the tiny eighteen-inch TV. Many of Brad's clothes, computer, and other possessions were still packed up. There would be much to do over the next week, and he wasn't familiar or comfortable with the prospect. Halina would have guided him, protected him and made sure that he felt safe, but now he was alone and had never felt more so.

A loud, short knock at the door jolted him out of reflection. Brad stood for just a second in front of the door before taking a deep breath and grasping the handle. The door swung open, revealing the Asian woman, accompanied by two burly men on either side in TKS-branded, blue boiler suits. Dominating the scene was a large wooden box that looked like an upright, rough-built coffin emblazoned with the AHS logo.

"Mr Cavendish?" the lady said urgently. "I'm Baljit Kulkarni with TKS, and I have your AHS myPAL iM-21."

She was dressed in a neat black suit and carried a small executive briefcase. It was a no-nonsense business-like look.

"Yes, yes," blurted Brad, "please come in". He understood that all the random acronyms meant he would no longer be alone.

The two men wheeled the box into the lounge on what appeared to be a large industrial sack truck. Baljit quickly surveyed the room but gave no hint of her thoughts as she stopped by a chair and dropped her briefcase to the floor.

"Please," said Brad, gesturing for them to sit. "Can I get you guys anything to drink, tea or coffee, maybe?"

"We're fine," she said briskly, not giving the men any chance to speak.

Brad pulled up the other chair and sat opposite.

"There are several things we need to go through regarding the contract and insurance," she said as Brad nodded. "But firstly, I would like to thank you on behalf of TKS Installations for ordering your AHS myPAL through us."

It sounded like a speech she'd given hundreds of times and not the exciting experience they'd advertised.

"Can I ask first if you have a suitable bed, with a space of at least three hundred millimetres below?" she said, producing several checklists from her briefcase.

"Yes, a big bed just through there", he gestured towards the main bedroom.

"And which side do you normally sleep on, Mr Cavendish?"

She rattled through one of the checklists.

"Is there a suitable power socket nearby?" she continued.

"Err, I sleep on the left, and there are sockets on both sides," he answered, feeling a bit puzzled.

Baljit turned and gestured to the two men, who remained mute. "If it's okay with you, we'll unpack and install both the charge plate and the myPAL in your bedroom, on the right-hand side of your bed."

"Of course," said Brad, not expecting his usually private bedroom to be invaded by two large, unknown men.

"The first charge will take at least seven hours. Don't remove the bag until the first charge is complete. You'll find a quick start guide in your welcome pack and full instructions online and also in the iMov app." She handed Brad a large glossy folder.

The cover depicted a gorgeous family with perfect kids, all in soft focus, facing what looked like a blonde supermodel holding grocery bags.

"You've also chosen to purchase the optional remote control," she continued, "an excellent choice, sir. It's much simpler to use than the app and comes pre-synchronised to your myPAL."

She reached into her case and produced some official-looking documents. "First things first, we need to go through your insurance."

Brad fully understood the insurance limits. No modifications were allowed, and operation outside of the user manual recommendations would invalidate the cover. He also understood that using the myPAL for sexual practices "not within the listed norms", whatever they were, was at the owner's risk. It didn't stop Baljit from going through every line while Brad tuned out. He signed the forms, and Baljit produced the contract.

Although Brad was buying his myPAL outright, he still needed to sign the contract. It confirmed he understood his legal obligations and absolved the supplier of any further responsibility. For example, a myPAL couldn't be used in a place of work without a special exemption. There were numerous rules, but the media had done the job of propagating them, explaining them, and concentrating on the more controversial aspects with voyeuristic glee. The contract also acted as a form of registration. All myPAL's had a registration number, and this needed to be submitted to a government website.

Brad signed again and handed the pen to Baljit.

"Thank you, Mr Cavendish. We'll register your myPAL later today. Do you have any questions?"

She was standing now in a pose that implied they were done.

Brad thought for a moment.

"Do you have any advice for a first-time user?"

Baljit genuinely smiled for the first time and turned to face him. "Three things," she said, "don't open the bag before charging is finished, and make sure the first image is of you. Then bind straight away". She turned and made for the door, along with the two boiler-suited men who had returned from the bedroom carrying the empty box. She stopped briefly by the door and offered one last piece of advice.

"Don't forget, you can always reset and start again", she gave a mischievous smile, and with a courteous "Goodbye, Mr Cavendish," they were gone.

It took a moment for Brad to realise he was no longer alone. Walking into the bedroom, a large, thick, bright pink plastic bag appeared on the right-hand side of the bed (he later learned that myPALs were supplied in either pink or blue bags, nothing like a bit of gender stereotyping).

As Brad headed back to the lounge to start reading the user manual, he noticed the faint glow of a red LED beneath the bed. It would become a familiar site, as the inductive charging plate would start the charging operation anytime a myPAL was nearby. The room would never be cold and lonely at night again.

3 FOREX

Mode zero

After binding: On your iMov App or optional iMov remote: select Initialisation – Modes – 0

Your myPAL iM-21, when set to mode zero, will have the following attributes:

- *Full compliance with the standard AIR Laws (United Nations CSTD Resolution 7865-X-75S).*

- *Default AE state start-up.*

- *Consciousness and self-determination set to one hundred per cent*.*

- *Access to safe mode and emergency shut down.*

A single beep will indicate mode setting in progress. A further single beep will mean that the mode setting is complete.

**WARNING: The consciousness and self-determination setting may have unpredictable results. Even though the myPAL is bound to the user, there may be incompatibilities in character, temperament, sexual orientation, or other interpersonal attributes.*

Undesirable myPAL behaviour may require a full system reset.

(iM-21 Quick Start Guide)

The rainy Monday had given way to a grey Tuesday, and Brad could see, through the gap in the curtains, that there were fewer raindrops on the window. It was 7:00 am, and Brad had just two hours to get up, dress, wash and leave for Canary Wharf.

Mags bounded into the room.

"Good morning, my love," she said, grinning, "Here's your coffee, and I'm making buckwheat pancakes for breakfast. Come on, don't hang about." She sat on the bed beside him and kissed him on the cheek.

"Are you at Light Lunch today?" he asked, sipping on his perfectly made coffee and reaching for the TV remote.

"I am indeed," she said, "but don't worry, I'll be home to cook tea and save you from yourself." She laughed, smiling broadly before jumping up to cook the pancakes.

Brad never wanted to take Mags for granted, and he told her constantly not to run around after him, but she would always respond, "It's my job. You're Mr Big Bucks, and my job is to look after you, so quit moaning and just enjoy it". How could he possibly complain? He had the perfect partner, and he appreciated her every day. He made a mental note not to be too late home that night. He wanted some quality time.

Skimming through the TV breakfast news, Brad caught the stock market and currency bulletins on the large wall-hung OLED TV while finishing his coffee. Mags bustled in and out while handing him his suit and cajoling him to the kitchen for pancakes, blueberries and maple syrup. She needed to leave for the soup kitchen around 10:00 am, but she would always be up early to look after Brad.

Mags never tired; a full charge in the morning gave her lots of energy. She only appeared tired when her charge was getting low, and Brad only saw this a couple of times. In theory, she could run for thirty hours on a full charge, but it depended on how active she was.

Brad gave Mags a generous hug at the door then they shared a kiss.

"Look after yourself," she said, beaming, "and don't let the bastards grind you down."

Brad knew this was a reference to his boss Jason (who he often described as a "monumental bell-end") and the clique of the boys' club always laughing at Jason's bad taste jokes. For example, each would play the usual alpha male games, bragging about their cars and "It Girls" they were dating.

With a quick look back at his beautiful Mags, Brad was gone. The dull journey by foot and tube blurring into a familiar set of landmarks as he made his way to the Opus Tower.

*

Jason Pacey was one of the currency trading managers at Coopers and Staltzman. His job was to keep the traders in check, ensure their positions were viable, and catch any risky dealing. It was an open joke that those who couldn't trade were managers, and Jason was very much in this mould. It irritated him intensely that *Bradley*, as he insisted on calling Brad, needed no supervision and was considered one of the best currency traders in London. C&S would get rid of Jason long before they would ever let Brad go.

Although he came across as a cockney wideboy, Jason was Oxbridge educated, like his boys' club. He hammed up the cockney for effect and loved using it to share racist or sexist jokes with his cabal, always within Brad's earshot, knowing how much he hated it.

Brad had gone to Aston University, almost unheard of in trading circles; this was another source of mirth.

It was highly unfortunate when Jason discovered that Brad owned a myPAL. He'd spotted an AHS brochure on Brad's desk but said nothing until he heard Brad chatting to someone called Mags on the 'phone. This made Jason immensely jealous, so much that he immediately bought his own myPAL by convincing his wife it was for home cleaning.

Jason would later enjoy taunting Brad with tales of the gymnastic sex he was having with *Jasmine*. All while his Marketing Director wife was working in Paris.

Brad assumed Jason's MyPAL was a mode thirty-five, programmed for household chores and sexual acts. Jason, too, believed that Brad owned Mags purely for sex. He correctly guessed that she was a mode zero but had no idea they had a real relationship, and Brad was happy to keep it that way.

The currency trading department at C&S took up two-thirds of the nineteenth floor of the Opus tower, with the large square office home to some sixty staff. The open-plan room was surrounded by windows and had a bright ambience, but the line of glass-fronted *fish tank* offices down one side robbed some of the light.

Traders were arranged in long rows of desks at the brightest end. Each trader had a double desk covered in monitors and keyboards, which displayed market information and analysis. The lower-level support staff, or *plebs*, as Jason called them, were relegated to the darker end near the tearoom.

The quiet Monday morning had given way to a fairly easy afternoon, and Brad was scanning the monitors for currency fluctuations. Occasionally he would look up at the wall monitor showing the PBC rolling news, but his mind was elsewhere. It was 4:30 pm, and he would soon be back in Mags' arms.

"How's the sex bot doing?"

Brad looked up to see Jason grinning down at him.

"Tried anything exotic recently?" he continued while Brad stared through him.

"I was thinking we should get our bots together for a ménage à trois". Jason was almost dribbling now as he gave an over-emphasised comedy wink. Some members of the boys' club had noticed and were giggling in the background.

"Seriously, mate, I've decided we need to get to know each other better. Layla would like to ask you and Mags to dinner soon". Jason knew that Brad didn't go anywhere, and he intended to give him no option to refuse.

Brad was stumbling for an excuse. "I'll need to see what I'm doing--"

Jason cut him off straight away. "I'm not taking no for an answer. I'll let you know when we're doing it". He was making it sound more like an order than a request. "About time you took Mags out somewhere, buy her something nice to wear." With that, he turned on his heels and disappeared down the office, grinning to himself.

Seized by feelings of anger, loathing and fear, Brad spent the rest of the afternoon trying to think of some way to turn down the invitation. A session at the office gym would typically have helped dissipate any work grief, but throughout his workout, and the journey home, he couldn't think of anything other than telling his boss to *fuck off*. Sometimes Brad wished he had more fight and wasn't so meek and easily trampled on.

Would Mags still love him if he was different? Halina always told him it was his mysterious quietness that drew her to him at Cyrus Lee. Thinking of Halina always calmed him down. He could picture her sharp blue eyes and bleached blonde hair, topped with her trademark furry hat.

The image faded as he stepped out of the lift on floor P3 and headed for his apartment. Once more, his thoughts turned to Mags and how they would spend the night cuddling up on the sofa.

*

After dinner, Brad told Mags about the bonding session Jason had planned, but she thought they should attend, much to Brad's dismay.

"It'll do us good to get out and meet another couple. I can't believe he's as bad as you say." She gave him a playful nudge as she cleared away his plate.

"No, he's worse," Brad uttered under his breath as Mags buzzed around the kitchen. He sighed and looked around at her. "Well, okay," he said, "I'm going to hate it, but if it shuts up that bastard, it may just be worth it," but that wasn't his primary concern. "Mags, he knows about you, but he doesn't know how special you are. He thinks you're a sexbot". Mags whirled around with a shriek.

"A sexbot?" she said, laughing, "I better get my catsuit out. You've been a very naughty boy", she raised an eyebrow and slapped her thigh. She then started moving around the room in the stilted, jerky motion of a non-zero myPAL.

"I'm serious," said Brad, "you have no idea how much of a sexist, racist dick he is. The thought of him disrespecting you makes me feel sick. He's got this all planned so he can meet you."

"Oh, don't worry about me, love. I can look after myself". Mags threw her arms around him, "now come and cuddle up on the sofa. Your program's on in a bit."

While Brad couldn't get the negativity fully out of his head, cuddling up with Mags soothed him well. Hand in hand, they went off to bed, where they made love. Both Brad and Mags drifted off to sleep, holding each other close.

4 BODY BAG

Binding:

- *Before binding, ensure that your iM-21 is fully charged.*

- *As the owner and registered keeper (subject to individual national laws), ensure you are the only person present during the binding process.*

- *Only bind in an enclosed space, too much visual stimulus may interrupt the binding process.*

(iM-21 Quick start guide)

Brad woke to find a large warm pink plastic bag beside him on top of the covers. He'd almost forgotten yesterday's delivery and the three hours spent reading through the manual, legal papers, and safety notes. The apartment was still a mess, with picture hooks missing pictures and faded patches where they'd once hung. Brad's dishevelled appearance matched the general ambience, but there was potential, as the estate agent said.

The manual said he should make *a good impression* when binding, so he headed off to the shower for a shave and to tidy himself up. He dug out a good clean shirt and waxed his hair.

Now for the apartment. Although there was virtually no furniture, Brad still ran around scooping up any rubbish and zipping around with the vacuum cleaner. A thorough detox of the kitchen, and he was ready to go. He made his way back to the bedroom where the pink shape still lay, and he thumbed to the beginning of the Quick Start Guide. "Unzip the packaging and then select Simple Instructions on the remote or iMov app to move the myPAL into a standing position."

Brad carefully grasped a zip at the top of the bag and slowly began to draw it down. Dark brown hair was immediately visible. It was smooth and reflected the glow of the bedroom ceiling lights. It was so real that Brad paused for a moment, almost expecting the body to stir. He continued and slowly uncovered a face so beautiful he could feel tears welling behind his eyes. She had olive skin and a rounded, warm face. A half-smile was already present on her pristine pink lips.

Continuing to unzip her, he noticed she was dressed in a black, body-hugging Lycra outfit. Her body matched the perfection of her face, perfect even round breasts and hips that looked realistic. He stood back and drank her in for a moment. There was a stunning brunette on his bed.

"Okay, next step," he said to himself, picking up the remote and selecting *Initialisation* followed by *Wake up*. Her eyes flicked open, and Brad jumped back, dropping the remote on the bed. "Fuck me!" he said as he reached for the controls and waited for his heartbeat to subside. She stared up at the ceiling, unblinking with wide, deep brown eyes, almost Asian in appearance. Brad deliberately specified a random physical appearance, with the only provision being that she should not be blonde.

He thumbed the remote and selected "Simple Instructions," he heard a short beep from somewhere on her body, and then he said, "Stand up."

She immediately began to move, stating "Standing up" in monosyllabic English. The myPAL used her hands to move the packaging aside, then swung to the edge of the bed and pushed herself into a standing position. She turned to face him, and Brad now felt very intimidated. It felt as if he had a dominatrix in the room.

Brad was about to start the binding, but he thought he might try out the simple instructions first. "Walk to me," he said, and she started striding towards him, repeating "Walking to you," as she did, stopping just a couple of feet away. "Hold my hand," he continued, but this time she didn't move; instead, she stated "no physical contact prior to binding," in the same monotone voice.

Okay, so he better start binding, as the *simple instruction* mode was very basic. He selected *Initialisation* and *Binding* on the remote. There was the same simple beep, and she stated, "Binding," and then blinked for the first time. "What is my name," she said flatly.

Brad gulped. He'd been so busy reading the manual he hadn't thought of a name. He started going through names in his head. Jenifer, Jane, Jill, Anne, Debbie. It didn't take long to realise he had no ideas for a good name. He looked around the room, but all he could see was the bright pink bag.

"Your name is Magenta," he said, "but all your friends call you Mags." Brad didn't know if a detailed statement like that would work, but it was worth a try.

There was a short pause before she said, "Hello, my name is Magenta, but you can call me Mags."

Brad laughed out loud.

"What is *your* name?" she said, again with no emotion.

"My name is Bradley Cavendish, but you can call me Brad."

Again, there was a short pause before she greeted him in full.

"Hello Brad, my name is Mags."

Even though he was only binding, Brad realised how clever the software was. The exchange continued. Each time she asked a question, Brad would answer, and then she would repeat the answer with some flourishes:

"How old are you, Brad?"

"I'm thirty-eight on May the nineteenth," Brad said, embellishing to see how complex he could go.

"You are thirty-eight next May."

"What was your birth gender, and with which sexual orientation do you currently identify?" she continued in the same business-like way.

"Err, well, I'm a straight man," he said, suspecting he was blushing.

There was a longer pause than before, and Brad began to suspect he'd given the wrong answer. In truth, the myPAL was using his answers and voice inflexions to determine the most likely result without causing too much embarrassment.

"You are a cisgender, heterosexual male," she hurled, almost like an insult.

The questions continued until she came to one last area.

"Please describe the relationship you would like to have with me using any words which come to mind."

Brad suspected that the answer to this question was important. He pondered it for a while before deciding to tell her what was in his head.

"We've just met," he said, "I'm really attracted to you, and I hope you feel the same about me. I want us to be friends first and lovers second. I want us to have fun, and I never want you to feel any less than my equal in all things. I want someone to share my life, and everything in it, and you Mags, will be perfect for me."

He waited for a while, but she said nothing, so he said, "that's it."

She blinked and then said, "Hi Brad, my name is Mags. I live with you at apartment P32 in the Zenith building, you are a currency trader, and we are soul mates."

Brad was stunned by how she had interpreted his words, "Soul mate," he thought to himself. It's like she had read his mind just the way Halina did so often.

"Safe mode," she continued. "Please dictate a simple phrase to initialise and end safe mode."

Brad had read all about safe mode. It was used as an emergency *get you home* tool if anything happened to the myPAL, such as a system failure or software crash. It allowed the owner to give simple orders, and the myPAL would obey without question, allowing you to steer it to a repair centre.

"Black, furry hat," Brad said without hesitation.

Just saying it brought back images of Halina in the cold.

"Black, furry hat," Mags repeated, followed by "emergency shut down, please dictate a simple phrase to shut down in an emergency."

The phrase was a legal requirement that Brad never really understood, as all myPAL's were governed by the eight AIR laws. He couldn't think of a situation where he would need it; his mind was blank. It needed to be something he would never say, not even by accident, maybe a word he didn't like. After what seemed like an age, an odd memory came to the surface.

*

She was the first girl he'd had a crush on at school; he was only fourteen. Brad had taken months just summoning up the courage to speak to her. She was pretty and seemed quiet, like him. He got his chance one night after school while they were both waiting by the school gates for their parents to chauffeur them home. He moved closer and said "Hi," she didn't back away and instead smiled and said "Hi," in return. He was past the point of no return.

"I was wondering if you had any plans this weekend?" he asked, beginning to shake.

He thought this would start a conversation, but all she said was "Why?" with a look of incomprehension creeping over her face.

"Well, I thought maybe we could go out into town together, maybe the cinema or something," he said, now beginning to wish he'd picked another moment.

Her demeanour had changed, and she cut him off before he could suffer any longer. "Are you high?" she said, dripping with venom, "With you? You're a freak; everyone knows you're a freak. Keep the fuck away from me."

With that, she moved across the entrance to the other gate and looked away.

In the following weeks, he was taunted constantly in the class as she'd told all the other girls, and they were now mercilessly bullying him, with many of the boys joining in. It was one of the worst periods of his life and knocked his already fragile confidence to rock bottom.

*

"Jenifer Hale," Brad pronounced loudly and clearly.

"Jennifer Hale, emergency shut down," Mags responded, followed by "binding complete."

The iMov remote now showed *Initialisation in progress - please wait* with a progress bar indicating up to two hours.

"Great," thought Brad. He hadn't even put a TV in the bedroom yet.

He quickly ran to the kitchen, made a coffee, and grabbed the Financial Times. He knew he was supposed to be present when Mags *woke up* for the first time. He hurried back and settled in for the wait.

5 LIGHT LUNCH

1. *An AIR may not harm a human or allow a human to be harmed.*
2. *An AIR must include an emergency stop function that overrides all other functions.*
3. *An AIR must not damage itself unless protecting itself could harm a human.*
4. *An AIR is the responsibility of its owner. It cannot own itself.*
5. *An AIR has no rights except for those bestowed by an individual country's laws through its owner.*
6. *An AIR must be aware of its true nature. It must not believe it is human.*
7. *An AIR may not modify its hardware or software and may not self-reset.*
8. *An AIR may not modify the hardware or software of another AIR.*

(The United Nations CSTD Resolution 7865-X-75S on AIR (Artificially Intelligent Robot) technology)

A humanoid artificial intelligence robot may not replace a human in any paid work unless the work is covered by one of the exemptions in section four below.

(EN 98265-0-V European convention on Humanoid Artificial intelligence robots)

Mags watched Brad leave for work below, from the very end of the apartment's terrace near the bedroom. Although the terrace hung above the Thames, if you stood at the London Bridge end, you could see around the building's side to King William Street and the Monument tube station in the distance.

She imagined he would still be worried about dinner with the Pacey's. Mags knew he hated groups, noise, silliness, and situations he couldn't control. Brad had told her many times he might be on the spectrum. She didn't think there was any doubt, he was definitely a quiet one, but from the moment he had sparked her into existence, she'd cared for him.

Brad asked her once what it felt like to be a myPAL. He wondered if she could feel the computers and software running inside her. It was an odd question for her, and all she could do was ask him, "Can you feel the neurons firing in your brain? Do you know which part of your brain has triggered a thought or emotion? I feel the same as you, I just am". Brad had never asked her since and treated her as if she was no different from any human.

She knew he was nervous that she might fall out of love with him or that they would grow apart. It was very common with Zero's (the popular name for mode zero myPAL's), but her feelings for him were deep and real.

The fact Brad paid nine-hundred-and-seventy-six thousand pounds to give her life just to love her, not as a sexual object, meant so much to her. She wanted to stay with him and never entertained any negative thoughts. He let her do what she wanted, so when Mags said she wanted to do charity work, he said, "Go for it" without hesitation. He'd prefer her not to volunteer at the soup kitchen just because he worried about her, but he also knew she enjoyed it.

The apartment needed minimal cleaning as Mags made sure it was always tidy. She ran around quickly, putting a few things away, then started to get ready. She could wash and shower like any human, although she needed to take care not to get too much water in her mouth. The mouth was semi-sealed, acting as a pressure vent to stop the myPAL body ballooning on aircraft.

She would shower just a couple of times a week, as she didn't sweat, and her synthetic hair didn't get oily, and it didn't grow.

Today was a shower day. She stripped off and enjoyed the feel of the warm soapy water on her advanced synthetic polymer skin. The product of a giant Japanese petrochemical company, one of the three companies that formed AHS: the company that made her.

The graphene servos that moved her limbs and the micro servos which enabled her to express every emotion were guaranteed for sixty years, as was her Mysl network processing core. Unfortunately, the aluminium batteries only lasted for five years. She had been with Brad for just over four years now; next year, she would need a battery replacement, not something she was looking forward to.

Her model, the myPAL iM-21, was pretty old now. The current model iM-33 had a longer battery life, weighed less, and could even eat and drink, by storing ingested food in a self-cleaning silo. She would often joke to Brad that he should trade her in for a newer model, but he never found it funny. He hated it when she spoke of herself like an appliance.

She soon discovered she was part of an elite band, as there were very few Zeros. Many owners would start with a Zero, but when they realised their expensive purchase had opinions and may not like their owner, never mind sleep with them, they often reset them.

Disgruntled owners often continued to choose a more slave-like mode, such as mode thirty-five. These were commonly known as the 'sex bot.' Mode thirty-five not only cleaned your house but was also compliant with any sexual act you could imagine.

Mags viewed all the other modes as simple robots. Only the Zero's had self-determination, could choose their path, and essentially had free will. Of course, there was always the possibility of a reset, but she believed Brad's assurance that he would never use it. He told her that she was free to leave at any time. She had her own keys and came and went as she pleased.

She guessed some Zeros were not as lucky, but she'd never met another Zero.

Today she was off to *Light Lunch*. She would usually leave around 10:00 am, giving her plenty of time to get across London to the soup kitchen in Dagenham. It was run by an evangelical Christian group, who were very fond of using *Light* to describe anything God-related, like "He is the light" and "Discover the light," hence the name: Light Lunch.

It was a short journey on the District Line to Dagenham East. Mags enjoyed the trip each day. She would sit watching the other passengers, playing with their smartphones, listening with headphones, or reading the paper. All were oblivious to her true nature.

Many would be unimpressed if they knew what she was. The acceptance of humanoid robots was varied. Many hated them simply as they were toys of the rich, the most basic types being over half a million. In contrast, others were worried about the future of employment, even though humanoid robots couldn't currently work.

The most fervent vitriol was reserved for cybersexuals, those humans who actively pursued sexual relations with myPAL's. The Christian right, especially in the USA, had lost interest in persecuting gay people and had found a new enemy in artificial intelligence robots. They were often described as sex toys. Then there was the assertion that only God could create sentient life, with many Christians referring to companies like AHS as Frankensteins.

The Christian right found an unlikely ally in the unions, and they had clubbed together to force legislation to stop humanoid robots from working in most western countries. At least for now. It was for these reasons that nobody at Light Lunch knew what she was.

The café was only a short walk from the tube station, down a couple of side streets. Many of the old shops and cafés on the route were boarded, betraying the depressed nature of the area. The loss of heavy industry, such as car production, left a scar that had never fully healed.

There was nothing to see of the soup kitchen from the front other than a yellow door with "Light Lunch, food and comfort for those in need" painted on it. The door opened to a set of stairs leading up to the café on the first floor.

The restaurant was two rooms taking up the whole first floor. A vast space with visible pent roof and skylights was filled with rows of simple, melamine-topped tables and plastic chairs reminiscent of a school hall.

Mags made her way towards a door in the middle of the far end, with a sizeable, closed hatch to one side. The second room comprised the kitchen, servery, and storage area with shelves stacked with food donated by local supermarkets.

"Hi," said Mags breezily as she popped her head around the door.

"Hello, my lovely," came the response from the middle of the kitchen, where a large Afro Caribbean woman was unpacking boxes of canned food past its sell-by date. Bettina seemed to be at Light Lunch every day, and she never appeared to take a day off. Despite losing one of her sons to a gangland murder, her bright demeanour never dimmed, and she was especially fond of Mags, who she was now hugging.

"I was hoping you would be in today," she said smiling broadly, "we've got loads of donations to sort, and we need to get the chilli on. Although I do love Jamelia, she hasn't got your brain or any wits really". She roared with laughter.

"You can't say that," said Mags, with false sternness in her voice.

"I don't mean it. She means well, but I think you could run this whole place with your eyes shut."

Bettina continued to chuckle while Mags got to work, helping to sort through the boxes of tinned food.

Today they had over two hundred tins of mince in gravy, which they would turn into a chilli by adding vegetables, tinned beans, and various items from Bettina's list of *secret ingredients*. They didn't have the resources to make multiple choices, but the customers who came in were glad of anything.

Later they would be joined by Jamelia, Bettina's twenty-one-year-old niece, Rosalind, the retired schoolteacher, and David, her husband, who drove the van, helped to keep any trouble out and looked after *the girls* as he called them.

The subject of robots seldom came up, but when it did, there was always negativity. Rosalind once said that "she couldn't understand why people wanted fake humans, when there were plenty of real people on the planet," while Bettina would sometimes describe them as "false gods" and then start quoting scripture. They all knew that Mags wasn't a Christian, but they knew her as a "kind soul," as Bettina would say.

The doors opened at noon, and a steady trickle of people would start to arrive until the hall was almost full by 1:00 pm. Drug addicts, alcoholics, rough sleepers with learning difficulties, single parents, and a whole train of the poor and dispossessed would eat a warm lunch today.

Unfortunately, Mags had a complete sense of smell, which she sometimes wished she could shut off; this was especially the case with Tony.

Tony was a black ex-junkie, ex-petty criminal, ex-father, and ex-gang member. He was now a middle-aged alcoholic and always had a can of cheap cider in one of the deep pockets in his huge, brown coat. He would try to stay as dry as possible in the mornings, not so that he could use Light Lunch but because he loved seeing Mags for whom he reserved his biggest smile.

"Hey, girl!" It was Tony's usual greeting as he sighted Mags in the queue for food. "You're looking fine today. I hope that big shot man of yours knows how cool you are."

"Oh, I tell him every day," said Mags smiling back. She liked Tony even though he had a torrid and violent past. There were persistent rumours that he'd killed a man in a gang-related attack in his younger days, but Mags could see the best in people, and she always tried to make time just to see how he was.

Tony was nearing the food and widened his eyes in exaggerated wonder.

"I bet you cooked this chilli all by yourself, extra spicy," he said, winking.

"No, no, you know it's a joint effort," she scolded him lightly, "I hope you're keeping well, looking after yourself."

She spooned some rice onto a plate for him as he leaned over.

"I mean it, girl. If that man of yours doesn't treat you right, you tell me now. I know people; just say the word, and I'll sort him out."

Knowing his history, Mags didn't doubt it. "I'll bear it in mind," she said sternly while Tony moved along the line and headed off to find a table, but not before turning to flash her a grin.

She watched him shuffle down the hall where he found a chair on his own, in the far corner, where he could still see her. His lack of hygiene made him a lonely site, but Mags had a real soft spot for him. Many of the other customers knew Mags and would say hi, but Tony was a regular who'd been coming to Light Lunch since Mags started almost three years ago.

She didn't miss working for a wage as she got a lot of personal satisfaction from the voluntary work. She just wished she could tell them who she was.

6 BOUND

"The breakthrough came when we finally understood the nature of consciousness. The conscious mind is a simple computer, but it is constantly interrupted by hundreds of other computers, all with their own programming."

"Imagine you're watching a news report of a famine in Africa. You see the image of a desperate, hungry child, and suddenly you feel empathy, and you start to cry. Your conscious computer is interrupted by your empathy computer, which is triggered by the image. Your crying computer also responds, and you cry."

"Imagine thousands of computers, all with their own programming all interrupting with their own agendas."

"Free will is the illusion we can replicate with the Mysl processor network."

(Interview with Professor Olaf Laugesen – Inventor of the Mysl Processor)

Brad was still flicking through the Financial Times and getting quite bored now. He'd read the opinion pieces, checked all the money markets, and even checked some of the ads for timeshare.

The sparse, grimy apartment wasn't fun to spend time in, and the stiff mannequin woman standing in the middle of the room wasn't much company.

He yawned loudly. It was just then that he caught movement out of the corner of his eye. Spinning around, he dropped the paper; his eyes fixed on the incredible dark-haired woman standing in his bedroom.

Gone was the inanimate statue, replaced by a beautiful, shapely ninja complete with a black Lycra jumpsuit. She still stood near his bed, but now she moved a little, the same way a human moved when standing still, shifting her weight slightly here and there to keep balance. Brad was mesmerised.

She blinked once, then twice, like a child trying to adjust to the light of a new day. She hadn't seen Brad yet; she was starting to look around the room, at the walls, the bed, the ceiling, the FT lying on the floor. She slowly started to lift her arms, not with the jerky movement of a classic robot but with the smooth movement of a ballerina. She tilted her head down as she raised her hands, palms up as if she was studying the creases and inspecting her lifeline.

Gradually she raised her eyes to meet Brads, who was now standing just a few feet away, with a look of awe on his face.

He didn't know what to do, the instructions were pretty vague from this point, and apparently, every Zero woke up differently. Should he say something or wait for her? He had no idea. So, he waited for what seemed like an age while she continued to inspect herself. He was about to say something when she suddenly dropped her arms to her side, and the silence was broken.

"Hi, Brad."

She was looking right at him. There was a velvet RP quality to her voice, not too plummy or sloaney but sexy, without being over the top.

"Hi, err, Mags," said Brad, stumbling.

He couldn't help drinking her in; she was real, as real as him. He'd heard stories of myPAL's, but nothing prepared him for just how realistic they were. She was moving towards him, but Brad backed away a little instinctively.

"I don't bite," she said, "well unless you ask nicely," she giggled. A lovely smile spread across her face.

How could she know humour? Where did this come from? She'd only been alive for three minutes, and already she sounded her artificial age of thirty. She tilted her head to the side and gave him a mischievous look.

"First, I need to get out of Catwoman's clothes; she needs them back."

7 THE BOYS' CLUB

"Brad is quite simply the most accomplished currency trader we have ever employed. Don't be fooled by his quiet exterior. His analytical skills, attention to detail, and sheer productivity are phenomenal.

I understand his reasons for leaving, but we would have him back in a heartbeat. He will be a credit to any financial institution in virtually any high-stakes analytical role. I will personally miss him as a friend, colleague, and professional high achiever. Failing to employ Brad in this position is not an option."

(Reference letter from Manfred Wardle, Vice President of Currency Portfolio Management at Cyrus Lee)

Mags would be at Light Lunch, busy enjoying her work, while he passed the time in this stark office, surrounded by wankers and with a prick for a boss. Brad looked up from the screens for a moment in time to see the rain start again. The drizzle suited his dark mood.

He was happy at Cyrus Lee, but the memories became too painful. He would have moved anywhere just to try and start again, but he was seriously beginning to question his position. Jason hated him; the boys' club hated him, so why ask him out if it wasn't just to humiliate him. He'd been an outsider all his life. The quiet one, the nerd, the freak, a disappointment to his mother and father. He was at his happiest when he was on his own, or with Mags, or with Halina, the most happiness he'd ever experienced in his life. There she was again, just turning at the door, all smiles and joy, and then the image faded.

There were four members in the Oxbridge boys' club. Ben Fuller was Jason's primary sidekick and most likely to pick up the baton when Jason moved up. The two were like a couple of kids, sharing dodgy jokes and sniggering. He was also the same age as Jason, at about thirty-two. Next up were Artemis Healy and Kyle

Magnusen, younger at twenty-nine and twenty-eight. They probably hated Brad the most as neither of them were top traders, and Brad eclipsed them the most. Lastly, there was William James or just Bill to everyone in the office. Bill could have been a decent guy, but he'd aligned with the club for an easy life, knowing it was the best way to protect his job, and keep the bonuses coming.

Of course, the club all had nicknames which Jason loved using in the office, the same way he annoyed Brad by calling him, Bradley. Artemis liked to be called Arty, which is probably why Jason called him "Farty" or just "Fart," while Ben was often just named "Crappy" from rhyming with his surname Fuller *crap;* while Kyle was known simply as "Two." The name came from a notorious Christmas party in the office when he'd had sex with one of the admin girls in the cleaner's cupboard. When he came out, Jason and Ben were standing by the door, both checking their watches. They reckoned he'd only been two minutes, hence the name. They originally called him "two minutes," but over time, it just became Two.

"Hey, Brad."

Brad slowly turned to see Kyle and Arty standing behind him. Kyle was holding some kind of brochure.

"Check out the iM-40. I mean, *that* is art."

Kyle flipped the brochure round to show a full-page nude spread of the new myPAL iM-40 female.

"I could cyber that," Arty chimed in.

"They're saying everything can be customised."

Kyle was starting to sound excited.

"Tits, ass, pussy, you name it, they can tweak it."

The pair were sniggering like school kids finding a porno mag.

"All mine has to do is bend over on-demand," chipped in Ben, who had wandered over to share in the fun.

"Oh, wait a minute," said Kyle, trying to sound puzzled, "Isn't she just made of plastic?"

"Yeah, that's right," added Ben, "would be like fucking a lilo."

They all burst into laughter.

"Better start saving those bonuses, hey Brad, never know when the old model will rust up."

They wandered back to their desks, still laughing, while Brad seethed. He never fed the fire, but it made no difference; they bullied him just to amuse themselves. If Jason had been there, he would have joined in. Brad had spent a lifetime turning a deaf ear to this kind of bullying, but it still hurt him. It made him think of Mags and how she would make a joke out of it. He wished he had her strength sometimes.

Bill wandered past Brad's desk a little later.

"Just ignore them, man," he said.

"I do," said Brad wearily, "I ignore everyone in this fucking office."

"Look, man, you need to make an effort; you need to fit in; Jason's trying to help you." Bill fancied himself as a stoner, in reality, he was simply a dull analyst.

"Fit in?" Brad was incredulous, "With captain Pacey and his band of cocks?" For once, Brad was taking a stand; he was furious.

"Steady on, dude." Bill tried to calm things down.

"How about you all just go fuck yourselves."

The office went deadly quiet as they all looked at him. Brad started to sink back in his seat when a familiar voice straightened him up.

"Bradley, a word, my office."

Jason had poked his head out of his fishbowl side room and was trying not to look too pleased with himself. Brad locked his workstation and took his time wandering over while the rest of the office tried to look busy.

"Take a seat," said Jason as he slumped into his large director-styled, leather chair and waited for Brad to shuffle into place.

"I like you, Bradley." That was a lie. "But you need to learn how to share, maybe throw the guys a bone now and then."

The boys' club would often gather to discuss strategy, but Brad always worked alone and made the most money doing it. "You know I'm not a team guy; that's how I am," Brad said sheepishly, but he knew there was more to it than that.

"I know all that, and so do the guys upstairs, and that's fine, but there are other ways you could share the love. That's why I've invited you over to ours. You need to get more with the troops. They'll respect you more if you're on message." Jason was leaning over, trying to look caring, but it didn't suit him.

"Look, Jase, you know me, I'm a worker, and I just like to get my head down. I'm at my best when I'm just on my own." Brad knew how bad it sounded. They were all supposed to be team players. "Look, I'll try to fit in a bit more, but I'm never going to be in the club."

"Well," said Jason, leaning back in his chair, "we'll see how things go, one step at a time."

Brad started to head for the door when Jason called him back.

"One more thing, mate. I love a good *fuck* as much as the next man; just keep the volume down in the office." His face was already cracking as he congratulated himself on the double meaning.

As Brad sank back behind the monitors, he was thinking it was time to start looking elsewhere. If he did walk, Jason would probably be fired. He had no idea why Jason was playing such a dangerous game. He really should have stayed at Cyrus Lee, nobody bothered him, and those he did talk to were good people, good friends, but then the image of Halina clarified again. This time she was leaning on a vacuum cleaner, giving him that sassy smile of hers, "You work too late," she would say. He smiled to himself, just recalling the moment before the image vaporised and the figures on the screen came back into focus.

He remembered Halina's scolding and didn't work late that night. It was that time of day when his thoughts turned to Mags, and he was off on his way home once more. There was a chill in the air as autumn knocked on the door of winter.

*

MyPAL's did feel the cold, just as they felt everything through the thousands of micro sensors just under the skin. Mags felt the chill evening air as she pulled on her coat near the door to Light Lunch. It was a late finish today as she hung around helping with the washing, cleaning, and finally, the unpacking and stacking of a fresh batch of food. She shouted goodbye to Bettina, who was always the first and last and headed out into the street.

"Hey girl," came a familiar voice from behind her, which made Mags spin around to see Tony leaning behind the door.

"God, you gave me a fright," she said, composing herself, "what are you doing around here?"

"This is a rough neighbourhood, and it's got pretty dark now. I thought I should walk you to the tube, lovely lady like you."

Tony was sincere, but Mags wasn't sure if she should be scared or not. Her naturally trusting nature won over, and she agreed to let Tony walk her as far as the main street, which made him very happy. "I hope you're sleeping somewhere warm tonight," she said. Mags always thought that one spring, he just wouldn't be there anymore.

"Oh, don't you worry about me girl, I'm in at the hostel tonight. I've got three nights solid."

"That's great news," said Mags, feeling genuinely glad, "I do worry about you."

"No, don't worry, I'm always okay; Tony will be around for a long time, especially seeing you four times a week. It's just a shame you don't do weekends." The mischievous smile returned.

"I need to make time for Mr Mags, you know, my other man," she said, winking.

"My offer still stands girl, just say the word."

"Yeah, yeah, I'll be sure to let you know if I need somebody whacking," she was chuckling as she said it, but Tony let out a massive roar of laughter.

"I've got your back, girl."

They reached the main road, and Mags thanked Tony for his chivalry. He watched her go towards the tube, the only light in his dark day. He wasn't at the hostel tonight. He'd lied. Sighing, Tony headed off to find his favourite area under the arches.

Brad didn't worry Mags with his woes that night; they were both tired and simply relaxed. The one fixed point in both Brad and Mags' life was each other, and they both appreciated what they had.

8 AE STATE

"All myPAL's are delivered in what we call the AE state, which we named after Adam and Eve."

"When God created Adam and Eve, they were created as fully grown adults. They could walk, talk, reason, understand right from wrong, understand the concept of modesty, and they could recognise flora and fauna around them for what it was."

"Every myPAL has base programming that includes a vocabulary of forty-five thousand words, recognition of thirty-seven thousand objects, and the recognition and enactment of every human emotion. Of course, also the ability to walk, run, kiss, make love, and thousands of other human attributes."

"Try to remember the first time you learned a word. You can't. As an adult, you simply just know. That's how a myPAL thinks."

"Also, every myPAL has a random element enabled by binding, which gives every myPAL a unique initial character."

"All myPAL's have a base character which is mild, kind, and caring, but for fully enabled zero-mode models, the base condition is just the start. They will develop their characters over time. Sometimes positive, and sometimes not, anyone who owns a myPAL can play God and roll the dice."

"Unlike the real God, you can always push the reset button if things don't work out."

(Interview with Linus Berkowitz – Technical Director at AHS Robotic Systems Inc.)

Brad couldn't let Mags totter around the apartment dressed in a figure-hugging catsuit. He didn't have a dominatrix in mind when he decided to buy a myPAL. He went through his clothes looking for something suitable. He settled on a gym T-shirt and jeans that looked about five sizes too big. He handed them to Mags and went to leave the room.

"Where are *you* going, cowboy?"

She seemed to be playing up the Miss Whiplash thing.

"Err, well, I thought I'd give you some privacy," he said, stammering his words.

"Privacy?" she retorted, "a) we live together, b) you only seem to have one bed, and c) you've just got your Christmas present, don't you want to unwrap it?"

Brad was shocked; he hadn't bargained on his new lady being quite so forward. He was shy with quiet people, but loud, confident people challenged him.

"Look, Mags," he said shyly, "I'm a bit shy around people until I get to know them, and I just need a little time to adjust."

In later months, Mags would pinpoint that moment when her connection with Brad was made. Something deep in her processor network recognised the shyness in Brad's voice, and a tiny association was made. While her outgoing confidence would never change, her understanding of Brad was something that grew from that moment.

"Of course," she said, her cheeky smile giving way to a warm smile of understanding. "I'll just be a moment. Why not make yourself a coffee."

Brad visibly relaxed and did precisely as Mags suggested. He didn't need to wait long for Mags to appear. She looked so cute in his jeans and T-shirt. She noticed him looking but didn't let on, as her processor registered his favourable reaction and sent a message of satisfaction into her conscious.

"So, what comes next?" said Brad, half hoping Mags would have all the answers.

"Well, honey, for a start, what about some girl clothes, and then maybe you could tell me why you have no furniture," she said, casting her gaze around the lounge.

"Ah, I'll come to that later, but you're right. Firstly, let's go shopping," said Brad, looking at his watch. It was only 10:35 am on Tuesday; plenty of time to shop for the basics.

"Goodie!" chimed Mags, "shopping is my favourite word."

Brad wasn't such a big fan of shopping and didn't know where all the coolest shops were. He decided to head for Covent Garden, even though it was a bit of a tourist trap.

Taking Mags out dressed in his clothes with an old leather coat felt like taking a teenager to a cool amusement park. Mags looked around in wonder as Brad led her through the Zenith building and onto King William Street. Not the most attractive part of London, but she took in every detail.

She smiled at the passengers on a red London bus and peered in awe at the bright colours of a sports shop as they neared the Monument Tube station.

Brad asked Mags if she knew where she was and where they were going to which she replied:

"The good people at AHS didn't see fit to install GPS. As I've never been to London before, I've no idea where we are."

Brad liked the sarcasm; she seemed like a strong woman, much like Halina. He needed that.

The tube wasn't busy, just the usual tourists and day-trippers heading for Covent Garden to check another destination off the list. All oblivious to the robot in their midst, gazing in wide-eyed awe as the tube train hurtled down the Circle Line.

As they arrived at Covent Garden and stepped out onto the platform, Brad felt Mags reach out for his hand and hold tightly through the long lift ascent to street level. She didn't see the content smile which spread over his face or sense the warmth he felt inside.

"Wow, this place is amazing!" said Mags when they finally walked out into the packed square.

Designer shops and high street outlets jostled with tourist fayre and quirky artisan food emporiums. It was an assault on the senses, made more manic by the throngs of tourists grouped around jugglers, comedians, and all manner of sideshows.

Mags was laughing as she tried to take in the spectacle. "I want to come here every day!" she said, planting a quick kiss on his cheek.

They shopped like mad, starting with underwear at Mags' insistence. She needed an entire wardrobe; they continued buying all manner of blouses, jeans, skirts, trainers, shoes, and a very cool Desigual handbag.

Mags even insisted that Brad bought a very sophisticated Ted Baker shirt she'd picked out for him. They were so loaded with bags they could barely move, and Brad was smiling from ear to ear and couldn't stop laughing. It was insane.

Every time Mags tried something on, she did a catwalk strut in front of him and started calling him Daddy Big Bucks in front of the shop staff.

At first, Brad found her quite daunting, but the way she addressed him was never bossy or domineering. It always felt like they were just sharing a joke, like a couple of kids. Then he remembered during binding when she told him they were "soul mates." Right from day one, they felt like the best of friends.

"That's it. I need a break," said Brad dumping his bags on the floor, "and I need lunch."

They found a small coffee shop doing paninis where they could sit people-watching in Covent Garden. Brad knew that myPAL's didn't eat or drink, but he had no idea if they got tired, so it was strange to hear Mags sigh as she sat down.

"Tired?" said Brad, "Is that even possible?"

"I think it's my body telling me to conserve battery life so I can run for a whole day. It also makes me seem more human."

Mags seemed to be anticipating what Brad was thinking.

"As far as eating is concerned, I don't crave food at all. I'm never going to be a bloater."

Brad couldn't stifle an explosive laugh as he tried to imagine the svelte Mags piling on the pounds. "You're a really funny lady," said Brad smiling, "I had no idea you would have such a great sense of humour."

"Well, I suppose that's part of my base programming, but to me, it just feels natural. You're smiling. I hope it's okay for me to be like this."

It was more than okay. From first seeing how lovely Mags looked to spending time with her today and learning how much fun she was, Brad was already falling for her. "I want you to be yourself, never worry about how I perceive you, and just be you." Brad meant it.

"That's sweet of you," she said, giving him a heart-melting look, "my only concern is that if I'm one hundred per cent myself, you might go off me and reset me to oblivion."

It had never occurred to Brad that he would ever do that. He knew that he could, but that just wasn't him. "Never," he said. "You have my promise that I will never reset you or try to modify you in any way. If we fall out and grow apart, you're free to find a life on your own. I've no idea how that would work, but you must never consider me as your owner. You're free."

Her lip quivered, and her eyes narrowed; she would have cried if she could. She moved her chair closer to Brad's and reached out to him; pulling him close, she kissed him on the lips.

Brad wasn't sure at first, but her warmth captured him. He embraced her, and they kissed for several minutes. When they finally released, he caught sight of an older woman at the table behind them, smiling affectionately. It felt like young love, and Brad was smitten.

"I won't let you down," said Mags, still holding his hand, "we're going to be good together."

Brad felt the same way, and for the first time in a while, the images of Halina didn't appear.

"Now tell me why your apartment looks like it was burgled?" she said. With the return of the mischievous smile, Brad would learn to love so much.

He needed to tell her the truth, but he knew it would be too painful if he told her the whole story. "It's a long story, so here's the short version." Brad steadied himself and took a deep breath. "About four years ago, I met someone at work, someone very special." He was aware that Mags was holding his hand tightly. "I lost that person just over two years ago, and I've been struggling to deal with it. I decided to try and make a fresh start. I quit my job, moved to a new apartment, and found someone extraordinary to share my new life with." Brad reached out and held both her hands, pulling her close.

"I'm so sorry for your loss," said Mags genuinely, "but why decide to make your life with a myPAL and not a real woman?"

It was a valid question and one that Brad had asked himself so many times over the weeks and months. "I'm terrible with women," he said finally, "I'm very, very shy. I find it very difficult to talk to women and dating just horrifies me. You may have noticed how quiet I am, which doesn't work for most ladies; I just end up not going out. That just makes me focus on what I've lost." It was like a weight being lifted, and Brad was glad he was sharing. He visibly relaxed as Mags took it in.

"I understand completely. You can't do the small talk, the dating politics. Maybe the rejection has a massive negative effect on you. I get it; I understand."

Mags did seem to understand him. Her base programming was so detailed she'd arrived as a fully formed, caring individual.

"Really? I must sound insane," said Brad.

"No, not at all; I can see how having me just turn up in your life would be much easier for you. You must have been nervous, just waiting for me to be delivered and for me to switch on?"

"You have no idea," agreed Brad, "when you turned out to be so bright and strong, I admit I felt intimidated, but in just half a day, I feel really relaxed. Like we've been friends for a long time."

Mags was beaming; she never seemed to stop smiling. "I feel the same way; I'm lucky to have you as my owner, err, I mean partner."

The waitress paused for a while as the couple seemed to be sharing a moment, then they spotted her and smiled as she served a cheese and ham panini with coffee for Brad.

"So back to the furniture," said Mags.

"Right, yes. The reasons I don't have any furniture are that firstly I only moved in a week ago, secondly that all my furniture reminded me too much of the past, so I've sold all of it, and thirdly I want the new furniture to be all your choice."

"My choice?" said Mags sounding very surprised, "you really trust me on this. Have you seen this bag I've just bought?". She held up the brightly coloured Spanish handbag.

"Not only am I sure, it's an order," he said, giving her a dose of her own humour.

"Oh, it's like that, is it? Well, I accept that order and let's see if you don't regret it."

Over the coming weeks, Mags would research apartment style online, visit some of the neighbouring apartments, and drag Brad to a multitude of showrooms. Not only did the apartment transform into the most incredible pad that Brad had ever seen, but their relationship blossomed and strengthened every day. Brad had no regrets about flicking the on switch.

That night Brad started putting together a makeshift bed on the lounge floor using towels and a spare blanket until Mags walked into the room, dressed in her new pink pyjama bottoms and a white vest top.

"What the hell are you doing, mister," she said, using the school headmistress tone she loved to adopt.

"I'm making up a place to sleep," he said nervously.

"I'm afraid I have to sleep on a bed because of charging, dear." She knew full well what he was doing.

"No, Mags, I'll sleep here tonight."

"You most certainly will not," she said firmly, "your bed is through there, with a hot robot chick in it."

He couldn't help but laugh; her irreverent humour was the antidote to all his fears. "I didn't want to assume anything," he said sheepishly.

"I know," she said, "and that's why I love you."

After just one day, she was using the four-letter word. It was hard to believe, but it felt so natural. She came over to hold his hand and led him towards the bedroom. "I'll go easy on you. Don't worry, just relax and let me show you how happy I am that you brought me into existence and made me your girl."

She led him into the bedroom and sat him on the edge of the bed. Kneeling in front of Brad, and with her gaze fixed on him, she slowly undressed him.

"I don't expect anything," said Brad quickly.

She hushed him, holding a finger to her lips, and continued down his body. First removing his trousers and then easing down his boxers. When she took him in her mouth, he leaned back, and all the pain of the last two years receded into the distance. He promised himself he would never disrespect her, never mistreat her, and always cherish her.

9 DINNER AND A MOVIE

The MyPAL iM-29 includes an uprated sensor array with over three thousand five hundred networked sensors for detecting environmental and system conditions. These include temperature, light, colour, density, orientation, gravity, odour, vapour, speed, perspective and pain levels associated either with operating outside of normal parameters or a fault condition. If you can feel it or sense it, so can your myPAL.

(AHS myPAL iM-29 advertising brochure)

It was a tough week; an invitation to a dinner party he didn't want, bullying from his so-called colleagues and a dressing down from the boss. Brad was actively looking for another job, but he didn't want to leap straight into another alpha male enclosure. He sent out feelers to some of his old colleagues at Cyrus Lee.

Mags knew that work was getting to him; she decided they needed a night out. A new Bond film was playing in Leicester Square, and she knew Brad enjoyed a good action film. It had been an age since they'd been out for a meal. Brad didn't usually see the point as Mags couldn't eat or drink, but she didn't care and decided to ignore him and booked something he'd like.

"We're going out on Saturday night," she announced on Friday, using the tone she liked to adopt when Brad needed pushing.

"Are we?" he said with some surprise.

"Dinner and a movie, you'll enjoy it, and that's an order."

Brad did love it when she took over. His life would have been dull without her.

As with most Saturday mornings, Brad would sit up in bed sipping his coffee while watching the TV news. Mags' sunny demeanour didn't fit well with current affairs, which she mainly found depressing; she tended to ignore it. Unfortunately, something caught her eye today.

The news relating to artificial intelligence and robots, in general, was often negative, scary headlines about robots taking over the world and dire warnings from the religious right about the evil of cybersexuals. The story today, however, was spun as a positive and Mags came into the room at just the right time to hear it:

"Scientists at IMSR, the UK Centre for vehicle crash testing, have announced a new crash test program using AI robots produced by US giant AHS Inc. The Robots known as myPAL's have been programmed to act exactly like a human. I spoke to Professor Graham Knight, and I asked him what benefits this brought to the science."

"Using an AHS myPAL programmed to mode zero allows us to see the real human reaction in a car crash situation. The data we are receiving is invaluable in making cars even safer."

"What happens to the robot after the crash test is complete?" the interviewer asked.

"We analyse the damage and rebuild the robot for further tests."

The news program ran a film showing a crash in slow motion where a car was crashed, and the myPAL was unsecured. Its expression was pure terror as the vehicle hit a wall, and the myPAL was hurled into the windscreen. It settled back into the seat in slow motion as chunks of its face fell away and clear liquid coolant sprayed out of several cuts. Just before the film stopped, the myPAL appeared to be screaming.

Brad fumbled for the remote and switched off the TV, but Mags had seen the whole story. "I'm really sorry, love," he said quickly.

Mags stood there for what seemed like an age trying to make sense of what she'd seen.

"You're right to avoid the news," added Brad. "There are lots of idiots out there who have no idea what they're dealing with."

"They know exactly what they're dealing with," she said solemnly, "we're just crash test dummies; we're worthless; we don't count."

Brad had never heard her talk this way and wasn't sure how to react. "Look, one day, people will understand, but for now, they just don't get it. Not enough people have relationships like ours. Too many people still see Asimo when they see a myPAL. I'm so sorry you saw that, my love." Brad stood and came to her with his arms open.

"How do we change things? How do we stop the barbarity?" she said in an unfamiliar tone.

"One step at a time, my love. Just like it took hundreds of years to stop slavery, decades to get women the vote, and thousands of years for gay people to marry. All these things came to pass, and I'm sure AI robots will gain the same rights one day." He was holding her close now, and he felt her chest moving in and out rapidly. It's what she did when she was trying to cry.

"I'm glad I have you," she said, barely able to get her words out. "The world is an evil place sometimes."

"We're going out tonight, thanks to you. Try not to think about it. Don't forget there's an awful lot of love in the world, and you're proof of that."

She turned to him, and that familiar smile finally formed. "You make things better, my love. Tonight's going to be fun."

It wasn't the first time Mags had heard stories of myPAL abuse, but she'd never seen it so real before. She also knew well that many people feared AI robots would kill them in their sleep and take over the world, despite the AIR laws built into every myPAL.

The crash kept playing over in her mind, and she was struggling to keep it out. She hoped that the evening would help.

They had nothing planned for Saturday. Brad decided a bit of retail therapy would cheer her up. They went out to find some cool designer fashion shops for an evening outfit. By the time the evening came around, Mags had almost forgotten what she'd seen and was back to her positive bouncy self.

"Cab's here!" she shouted, "move it, soldier."

She was proud to break the cliché of women who take an age to get ready. She was always prepared long before Brad and loved barking orders at him when he was dragging his feet.

"Okay, okay, I'm coming. Keep your transistors cool." Brad enjoyed playing on her myPAL self, but he gave as well as he got.

"Stop being a girl and move your ass." She couldn't help chuckling to herself. She always enjoyed the back and forth.

The short cab journey helped to build excitement, and Mags cuddled up close to Brad in expectation. She looked stunning in a figure-hugging, knee-length, blue dress, with a black bolero jacket covering her arms and a new funky white handbag completing the look.

"You look beautiful tonight," said Brad, full of pride, "a million dollars."

"More like one and a half mil adjusting for inflation", she said, squeezing his arm playfully. "You look pretty handsome too, in that shirt I chose for you", she continued.

Brad was wearing the cool shirt she'd picked out for him on their first day together.

"We're great," he said, pulling her close.

The taxi pulled up on the Charing Cross Road, and they jumped out, taking Irving Street towards the square. The whole area was buzzing with tourists and Londoners looking for fun. Bright lights and neon danced on either side above chain restaurants, cool bars and nightclubs. Mags loved London at night.

They laughed and joked for the whole walk into Leicester Square, where the restaurant was located.

"You must be joking," said Brad as they turned the corner, "this place will be stuffed with tourists."

"Don't be such a snob. They get good ratings on TripAdvisor, and you'll like the food, I promise."

The restaurant was called Cool Grub, and it sat right on the corner, opposite the Odeon. It was indeed packed with tourists, but the vibe was relaxed, and they didn't look out of place dressed up. It was expensive, which probably kept the burger joint lovers out.

The east European waitress showed them to a booth at the side, which was slightly quieter than the melee in the middle. Brad usually hated places this busy, but Mags always had a calming influence, and he felt good.

He ordered a modern paella which included pulled pork as an unusual extra ingredient, and to his surprise, Mags ordered a large portion of French fries. She always hated the looks she got when ordering no food at restaurants. Tonight, she decided to have a bit of fun. Brad gave her a sideways glance; he knew better than to question her.

Brad put his hands in the middle of the table, and Mags clasped them.

"What do you want to get out of your life?" he asked, squeezing her hand tightly.

She pondered for a second, then looked him straight in the face. "To be honest, I've never really known what my life is for. I don't mean that as a criticism of you; I just mean I'm not sure what I should do with it. That's why I got the job at Light Lunch. Part of my life is to be yours, and I love that part, but it always feels like there should be something else."

"I sometimes get that from you," said Brad. "Sometimes I look at you, and I know you could be doing something significant. You're very bright, and you learn so quickly."

"Ah, that will be my super-fast Mysl processor brain." MyPAL's could learn four times faster than humans. You never needed to explain anything to Mags twice.

"I'm serious," said Brad, "If there is ever anything you want to do or goal you have, please let me know. I'll try my best to help you." He wanted Mags to be happy, and he was conscious of her not just being there for him. He considered her as his equal, just as he'd told her.

"I know," she said. "You do support me. It's up to me to decide what I want out of life, besides you, of course." She smiled and tilted her head coyly. "Tell me if there's anything you want to do or anything I can help *you* with?"

Brad didn't hesitate. "You already give me everything I need; you're perfect. My life needs a new job, but other than that, I'm a happy man."

They were still staring lovingly into each other's eyes when dinner arrived. Mags then spent the next fifteen minutes creating a Jenga tower from her plate of fries, much to the disgust of other diners and the waiting staff, but Brad couldn't stop laughing and soon joined in. One last wrong move and Brad sent a shower of fries across the table. They both broke into laughter that continued as they set off for the cinema.

The Bond film was typical, but it didn't matter. Both Brad and Mags were on a high, and they came out of the cinema making fun of some of the more outrageous stunts. It was 11:30 pm as they headed off towards Charing Cross Road for a taxi.

The crossroads between Charing Cross and Cranbourn were busy at all times of the day, especially when the Odeon closed, and tourists ran for the Leicester Square tube. Taxi's jostled for position, loud Londoners were shouting across the street, and hen parties screamed and giggled in fancy dress. However, tonight it seemed incredibly crowded and very noisy.

As they approached, there was a lot of shouting, with people standing in groups. One particular group were congregated near a lamp post. Bystanders were slowing near the crowd and looking over before moving on.

Another collection included an official-looking man in a peaked hat, a well-dressed businessman, and a tall, elegant, dark-haired woman dressed in designer clothes and lots of gold jewellery. The woman yelled into her smartphone in some foreign language while the two men talked to her. She ignored them and continued shouting. "Gde strakhovaniye, chertovski strakhovaniye," she yelled, sounding very angry.

As Brad and Mags walked nearer to the first group, Mags noticed several people looking down at a shape on the pavement. Some people shook their heads and walked on by, while others were pointing and laughing. Through the circle of people, Mags just caught a glimpse of a body slumped on the curb near a lamp post. It was only a shape in the shadows, but it looked like a man. She wondered if it might be a drunk, but something made her nervous. "Oh no, someone's hurt," she cried.

Brad tried to lead her away. He remembered how she'd reacted earlier that day, and he didn't want this to spoil the night. Unfortunately, a passing man corrected her. "Nah, it's only one of those robots, tried to save somebody and got hit by that bus." He walked on past as Mags' eyes followed him. She turned around and noticed that the body was still moving and crying out in a faint voice. "Pomogi mne, pozhaluysta." It was a thin male voice repeating the same phrase, gradually fading.

Mags looked at Brad, who was still holding her hand and trying to lead her away. She shook her head. He knew what that meant and broke his grip. Her heart was bigger than any human's. She ran to the body where several people, including families with small children, and some sniggering teenagers, were standing around. She pushed a couple of men out of the way to some strong protest and stopped when she saw the scene.

The body was that of a male myPAL, modelled to be in his mid-twenties. He had short dark hair and slim features, which meant he was a newer model than Mags. He was only partly recognisable, as the damage was extensive.

His clothes looked designer, but they were ripped and dirty. The left side of his face was caved in, and his eye was hanging by a bundle of wires. His chest had ruptured, and clear coolant oil was seeping out of his wounds and surrounding him in an oily slick. Finally, his right leg appeared to be broken, and his left leg had been severed, part of it lying on the road a few feet away. He was in a bad way and kept murmuring, "Pomogi mne."

Mags had no idea what it meant, but it sounded eastern European. It was a melancholy sound in any language. She remembered the crash test video from the morning, but this was much worse, and his pleading moans were awful. She fought the urge to run, and instead, she knelt in the oil and reached for his hand. "It's okay, I'm here," she said, her voice quivering as she fought back the emotions flooding her mind. She looked around at the standing crowd and pleaded with them. "Somebody do something, please, for god's sake?"

Two of the watchers shrugged and walked away while one of the teenagers joked. "Is there a welder in the house?" His friends were laughing, but Mags flashed them an icy look.

"Pomogi mne," the lad said again, trying to turn his head to see her better. He grimaced with the pain and gripped Mags' hand firmly.

She wanted to hug him, tell him it was okay, hold him tight, but she knew he was in trouble. Paramedics would surround a human, no expense spared to save him, but this was a damaged appliance to human eyes.

"Can you speak English?" she asked, looking up to see Brad kneeling beside her. She knew Brad was poor with empathy, but she could tell he was affected too; he simply had trouble showing it.

"Please help me," the myPAL lad said, gasping.

"I will. Everything's going to be alright." She knew that was a lie. The damage was too extensive, they'd make him an insurance write-off, and they both knew it. "What's your name?" she said, kneeling closer.

"Dimitri." He looked down at his shattered body. "I can't feel my legs."

Mags gulped back the tears that couldn't come, and she knew she needed to be strong for him. Brad put his arm around her. "Tell me what to do, my love," he said tenderly.

Her chest was heaving, and she was starting to feel hot. These were the tell-tale signs that her emotions were beginning to mix. Sorrow at the plight of Dimitri combined with anger that nobody seemed to care. She stared at him for what seemed like an age, just wishing she could do something for him. She looked over at Brad, and then she knew what needed to be done. "Take his hand and speak to him; try to keep him calm. I'll be back."

With that, Mags stood up and followed the sound of female shouting. Then, she noticed the night bus parked further up the road for the first time, with passengers milling around, chatting and smoking near the door. On the other side of the road was a Jaguar with a heavily dented bonnet.

The woman was still shouting into the smartphone while the two men tried to get her attention. Her demeanour made her look like a woman familiar with getting her way.

"Dmitriy glupo, gde strakhovaniye," she shouted angrily while the man in the peaked cap tried to speak.

"I need your name and address madam; I've got a bus full of passengers; your insurance can wait."

The woman ignored him and carried on shouting.

Mags guessed that the other man must be the Jaguar owner. He seemed to be waiting for an opportunity to speak.

Mags waited for a few seconds, then pushed the men out of the way until she was inches away from the woman's face. Mags only needed one thing from her, and she was determined to get it. "What's the emergency stop phrase?" she said, eyes fixed on the shouting woman.

The eastern European completely ignored her and continued yelling into her smartphone. Perhaps she didn't speak English, thought Mags. "Please give me the emergency stop phrase, so I can help Dimitri," she said again with more pleading, hoping the woman would pick up something from her tone.

The woman continued to ignore her. Mags sighed and tried to steady herself; she could feel anger starting to bubble up inside. It was a far stronger feeling this time than watching the video earlier.

"Look," she said, "I need the emergency stop phrase so I can help Dimitri; he's in a lot of pain."

This time the woman stopped shouting for a moment and turned to face Mags, her eyes raised, steely and determined. "So what," she said before returning to her 'phone.

Mags looked back to where Brad held Dimitri's hand and talked to him as she'd asked. She could barely imagine how much pain the young myPAL would be feeling as thousands of damaged sensors relayed pain messages to the Mysl processor. The heat she felt inside was now so intense she could feel throbbing in her head, and her hands were shaking. Something inside her snapped.

Mags whirled on the spot with one movement and grabbed the woman's phone, hurling it down the street where it smashed against a telecom box. Almost in the exact moment, she grasped the lapels of the woman's fur-lined coat and dragged her so close Mags could practically taste her breath. "Give me the fucking stop phrase, or I'll rip your fucking head off!"

Mags felt more heat flooding her head, and the servos in her temple began to vibrate. The two men fell silent, and the woman stared in wide-eyed terror as Mags used twice the strength of a human to lift the woman off her feet.

"Now!" Mags was screaming, and the sound silenced the whole junction. Brad looked up, he'd never heard Mags speak like that before, and it scared him.

Shaking, and with a breaking voice, the woman finally spoke with her thick Russian accent: "Obrazets."

Mags dropped her to her feet, and she collapsed onto the pavement. She would have kicked her where she lay if her programming had allowed it. The two men watched her silently as she ran back to Dimitri and knelt in Brad's place.

Dimitri turned to face her, and a faint smile appeared on what was left of his face.

"Nobody speaks to Irina that way," he said shakily.

"I'm going to help you, Dimitri," said Mags. She held his hand tightly and felt him writhe in pain. When his eyes fixed on hers again, she felt that Dimitri knew it was almost over.

"Please, can you do something for me first?" He was gasping now, and every movement seemed to hurt him. It sounded like the last request.

"Of course, I will", the compassion in her voice starting to crack.

Dimitri steadied himself and strained to look Mags in the face. "Forty-two Pembridge Square." Each word seemed to bring more suffering as he struggled to speak through the pain. "Please tell Philip." His lip was quivering as the crying reflex took control. "Please tell Philip that I love him."

"I will," said Mags, her voice breaking. She could see a tear running down Brad's cheek as he put his hand on Mags' shoulder.

"Are you an angel?" said Dimitri, as he struggled to focus on her through the pain.

She gulped and fought back the mixture of compassion and anger coursing through her. "No, I'm just like you," she said finally. If she could cry, she'd be blind through the tears now. "Are you ready, Dimitri?" she said softly.

"Thank you, my angel," he whispered.

She bent forward and kissed him on the forehead. A look of peace spread over his face, and he loosened his grasp of her hand. "Obrazets," she said clearly.

As the word ended, a rasping beep sounded from somewhere deep in Dimitri's body, and he froze. All movement had stopped, and he was rigid like a mannequin. Mags carefully forced his remaining eyelid closed and turned to Brad, who was fighting back the tears himself. They wrapped their arms around each other tightly but said nothing.

Dimitri might never be released from the pause state. He would be powered down and recycled, an artificial life lost on the side of the road while passers-by just passed on by.

Eighteen minutes earlier, Irina and Dimitri left the Conway club, an exclusive casino and bar, where Irina's millionaire husband Konstantin was playing poker. He would be there all night, and Irina was bored; she told Dimitri to drive her home. They exited the club and headed for the Leicester square crossroads. She was playing with her smartphone, but Dimitri knew precisely where the car was parked. He stopped at the crossing, waiting for Irina to catch up and for a break in the traffic.

Out of the very corner of his eye, he saw a little girl, maybe five years old, just start to stray away from her mother, who was chatting to a friend. Slowly she came closer and closer to the opposite curb until she was standing right on it.

At that moment, Dimitri noticed a bus coming in her direction at high speed.

He made no conscious decision; his programming took over. Calculating the probability of the girl being too close to the edge and the bus hitting her at over fifty per cent, his automatic protocols took over. Adhering to the first AIR law, he started to run in her direction.

The first car to hit him was a white van; the left side caught him and shattered his elbow. He rolled across the van's front and landed on the bonnet of a Jaguar, causing a dent in the car and breaking one of his legs. Still striving to reach the little girl, he limped for a couple of paces until the bus hit him, pushing him along the road and eventually crushing him into a lamppost.

The little girl had run back to her mum. After realising he was just a robot, they left without a second glance.

The cab journey home was silent. Brad and Mags held each other close, which continued until they climbed into bed.

"Just so you know, I'm going to forty-two Pembridge Square tomorrow," said Mags, and it didn't sound like a discussion.

"And just so you know, I'm coming with you."

She kissed him, and they snuggled up close, but she couldn't get Dimitri out of her head.

"Are you an angel?" he'd said, almost as if he believed in heaven. Did heaven exist for robots? It wouldn't be answered in her dreams as myPAL's couldn't dream. She closed her eyes.

"Tell Philip I love him."

The red LED under the bed blinked on.

10 WINDOWS

"I'm often asked about love. Surely an AI can never love the same way a human can, as love is an indefinable human emotion."

"This isn't true; love is actually very simple and easy to replicate with the Mysl processor. Love is a reward system. When you have feelings of love, your brain is flooded with chemicals that make you feel happy. These chemicals are released because a set of conditions have been met deep within your emotion systems. We can duplicate those conditions and use them to send positive interrupts to the conscious computer."

"Nobody should be scared by this; it doesn't make love any less real."

(Interview with Professor Olaf Laugesen – Inventor of the Mysl Processor)

Brads eyes blinked open and slowly adjusted to the light coming through the curtains. It was quiet, quiet. Mags was up around 5:30 am most mornings, busy making breakfast and then coffee, but he could hear nothing today. He looked over to the clock; it was 8:34 am, and still no sounds.

Rolling over, Brad was stunned to find Mags was still in bed and staring at the ceiling. "Hey, is everything okay?" he said, rubbing the sleep from his eyes. Mags was silent; this wasn't like her; she was the life and soul, a breath of fresh air. Something was different. She was motionless. Had she malfunctioned? Did charging fail overnight?

When Mags did finally speak, it didn't give Brad a warm feeling. "We're nothing, just toys for the rich, throw away items."

How long had she been awake fixated on last night's horror? Brad was terrible at dealing with negative emotions, his own or especially anyone else's. He wasn't sure what to do. "Talk to me, babe," he said finally, "I'm here for you."

She continued staring at the ceiling and sighed as if weary with some burden. "If I break, will you get me fixed? How bad does any damage need to be before you just switch me off?"

Brad's heart was racing now; he was worried. As ever, he decided speaking his mind was the only way to go. "You can quit that talk right away; I'm not standing for that." He sounded angry, and some part of him was. She should know him better by now.

Mags flinched at his words, she'd gone too far, and she knew it, but Brad wasn't finished. "I may have brought you into the world, but I don't own you. You're free to go whenever you want." Maybe this time, *he'd* gone too far. While he meant every word about freedom, he never wanted her to leave.

She turned to him, and a look of pain swept over her face. "I can't get Dimitri out of my head. I'm sorry," she said, finally facing him.

Brad wrapped his arms around her as she began to shake. "I blame myself," he said soothing her, "the world can be an ugly place for your kind, and you've been sheltered from many of the horrors."

"I wish I could cry," she said, continuing to tremble, "I need to release these feelings."

Brad continued to hug her, sweeping her hair through his fingers. None of the myPAL's could cry, not even the newer ones. AHS engineers found that water reservoirs became blocked unless you used deionised, sterile water. They also tried to limit any need for myPAL's to be serviced, as it was complicated and costly.

Brad felt he owed so much to Mags for his current wellbeing. He would do anything for her. "Let me have some breakfast, then let's find out who Philip is."

Mags nodded in approval, and the faintest hint of a smile returned.

Brad thought he should make his own breakfast for a change. He disappeared into the kitchen.

Something made Mags reach for the tablet computer on Brad's side of the bed as her Mysl consciousness buzzed. She would often use the internet for shopping, looking up funny videos on YouTube or home makeover and baking sites. She never viewed current affairs and decided long ago that social media sites were dangerous for her. Today was different; she needed to know more about the ugly world Brad was talking about.

A Google search for *robot rights* turned up over sixty million hits. She began scrolling through the first results and noticed an AI robot rights group called "Freedom for AI robots" or "FAIR" for short. It seemed to consist only of human members. Mags scanned the pages, but it all appeared to be very political. She continued to sift through the search results and noticed a link to a site called "zero2hero". She was about to click on it when Brad came in with his breakfast. Although not certain why she quickly changed the browser to YouTube. Maybe she just didn't want to drag Brad down again, or perhaps she needed this for herself.

"Right, Magsy, look up Pembridge Square; I've got a feeling it's in, or near, Notting Hill," said Brad, stirring his muesli and yoghurt.

*

The sun was shining for a change as the taxi arrived at the end of Pembridge Square, making the site even more impressive. When Brad paid the driver, he and Mags both turned around and were met with a gleaming avenue of bright white Georgian townhouses. These were some of London's most sought after properties, demanding well over two million, many converted into apartments.

"Wow, there's some money around here," Mags whispered, afraid to break the silence in this exclusive end of the capital. "Almost as impressive as *our* place," she teased.

"Hmm", replied Brad, "it's a shame that such vulgar people can own such classy places."

Brad assumed that the Russian woman lived somewhere on this street, perhaps even number forty-two. They'd both concluded that the woman was Russian, based on her accent and the expensive clothes she wore. There was a large community of Russian millionaires in London who came to spend their immense gas wealth. The short Russian manner often jarred with English politeness; they'd gained a reputation for having a forthright attitude.

Mags and Brad walked past house after house in identical gleaming white stone. A Porsche here, Ferrari there, and more Mercedes Benz cars than Mags had ever seen. The whole street was leafy and green, with a vast, shared garden in the centre, fenced off to guard against the riffraff.

With the bright day and a mission to occupy her, Mags' mood was a little lighter. She was especially pleased that Brad was so keen to help, and she was hugging his arm in appreciation as they finally reached the end of the street, and number forty-two was before them.

The house was nearly identical to all the others except for a pristine, bright yellow Citroen 2CV parked outside and the front door was post box red, while most of the others were a dark colour.

Brad and Mags looked at each other, holding hands as they opened the gate and headed to the front door. Mags pressed the doorbell, and they waited. There was no sign of life. After a couple of minutes, she pressed it again. There was still no answer. Mags was about to push it a third time when a voice shouted out from inside. "No, thank you, not today." It was a man's voice, well-spoken and English.

Mags looked at Brad with disappointment, but she wasn't going to let it end there. She knelt and yelled through the letterbox. "We're not selling anything. We need to talk to you about Dimitri?"

There was silence; they waited for another few minutes and then decided to try writing a letter and started to head back. As they opened the gate, a voice stopped them. "Am I in trouble?"

They turned to see a thin, pale man in his mid-fifties standing in the doorway. Wisps of grey hair gave way to a large bald patch, but his eyes sparkled blue and looked kind. He was wearing a white T-shirt and blue denim dungarees splattered in various paint colours. A pair of bright yellow flip-flops completed the picture.

"No, no," said Mags, who was already striding back to the front door, "Is your name, Philip?"

The man looked shocked for a while but seemed to comprehend as he eyed Mags suspiciously. "Who wants to know?"

Mags was about to explain when Brad intervened. "My name is Brad, and this is Mags. You could say we're friends of Dimitri." He didn't want to give the full story in the street. Mags could lack tact sometimes, and sometimes she could be a little too direct.

"Friends, you say," said Philip, "Is Dimitri in trouble?"

Mags was now standing right at the door, and like Brad, she didn't think they should talk on the doorstep. "Would it be okay if we came in to talk?" she said gently. "We won't keep you long."

Philip continued to eye Mags cautiously and pondered the question until he eventually opened the door wide and gestured for them to come inside. They were met with the strong smell of chemicals, like paint or thinners.

The bright white exterior was mirrored inside, but every wall was covered in paintings. Most of them were substantial bright abstracts with bold explosions of colour, but a few more natural works were scattered about, including still lifes and landscapes.

Philip led them into a large back room where an enormous canvass was propped against a wall covered in bright blue arrows. It appeared to be a work in progress, with various opened pots of paint and other tools scattered about. There were also several works hung on the walls.

Mags was immediately struck by a painting on the far wall, which appeared to be a street view from a window.

"We're sorry to disturb you," said Brad as he realised Philip was an artist at work. "We just need to tell you something."

"Please take a seat," said Philip, pointing to a sizeable paint-stained leather sofa, "can I get you some tea or coffee?"

"We're good," replied Brad, forgetting that Mags would be expected to answer for herself.

Philip sat on a small stool opposite and leaned forward. "So, what has Dimitri done?"

Brad looked at Mags. He knew it would sound much better coming from her, and she knew it too.

"I'm afraid I've got some bad news." Even as she spoke, Mags could see the last colour starting to drain from Philip's face. "Dimitri was involved in an accident last night, and I'm afraid...." He was deactivated, decommissioned, damaged? None of these words meant the truth. She could see Philip's eyes start to moisten; hers would too if they could. "He died," she said eventually, knowing that Philip would understand.

He appeared to crumble in front of her eyes, a tear starting to fall from one eye as he tried to grasp for the words. "Oh no, please no," he said.

Mags' movement was instinctive. She went to him, putting her arm around his shoulder. "I'm sorry," she said as Philip stared into his hands. She knew it would make him feel worse, but there was no better time. "He wanted you to know something and asked us to tell you before he died."

Philip looked up, and Mags moved around so she could tell him face to face. "He wanted you to know that he loved you."

Mags shuddered as the emotions of that night came back, but Philip convulsed. Sobbing, he started to look around the room as if he expected Dimitri to be hiding somewhere. "My beautiful, beautiful boy," he stumbled through the tears, "my wonderful, beautiful boy."

Mags knelt forward and embraced him as he sobbed into her shoulder, still struggling to comprehend.

"What have they done to you? My beautiful boy." He was inconsolable.

Brad watched, transfixed by the emotion for a humanoid robot, the emotion he knew so well. He was watching for what seemed like an age. Mags told Philip how Dimitri had passed, but Brad didn't want to re-live last night. He stood and offered to make Philip some tea. There was no response. "A coffee, maybe?"

There was the slightest hint of a nod. Brad disappeared to find the kitchen, where he discovered a coffee machine he recognized. After going through every cupboard, he found the coffee capsules and mugs and made them all a drink.

When he returned, he found Philip had stopped crying, and he was starting to talk to Mags about Dimitri. Brad handed them all a coffee and sat down, leaning in to hear the story. Philip was well educated and spoke in very clear, gentle classical English.

"The Pervaks live next door; they purchased Dimitri about three years ago mostly to look good in front of their odious friends, but also as a companion for their spoilt daughter Maya." He paused to gather his thoughts and took a sip of coffee before continuing.

"Maya couldn't care less about him. They used him like the hired help, running errands, driving them around, doing the shopping, they treated him like shit." Philip was shaking his head as he remembered Dimitri's life.

"They never let him go out and make friends or have any life outside of them. The Pervaks would lock him in the house most of the time unless they sent him out on another errand. I don't care that he was a robot, he had the mind of a young man, and that's no way to treat a person." He choked back more tears and rubbed his brow before returning to the story.

"We first met when they locked him out. They sent him to the shops to get cigarettes, but they went out before he returned, pretty typical. It was pouring rain, and I found him sitting on his porch when I came home. I know myPALs can take the rain, but it just felt wrong." Philip looked around at Mags, giving her the same suspicious look as he had earlier.

"I couldn't just leave him there." His arms were outstretched, so both Brad and Mags nodded in agreement. "I asked him in."

Mags imagined Dimitri gazing in wonder at Philip's creations, sparking an imagination he never knew he had.

"He was immediately interested in the art," continued Philip. "He told me he'd never painted, but he felt artistic. I don't know why; I just picked up a canvas, gave him a brush and let him paint. He couldn't paint, but he was just so interested; he asked me about my art, about my use of colour and shape; he was like a sponge soaking up everything I knew. He learned so quickly."

Brad was looking at a very striking orange painting and noticed the signature for the first time. He could just make out *P. Rylance* in the corner. It took a moment to remember where he'd seen that name, then it clicked. "Philip Rylance!" exclaimed Brad, "you're Philip Rylance?"

Philip smiled in confirmation. Mags still looked puzzled.

"Mags! He's Philip Rylance. He's a world-famous painter. He did those green men in the Tate Modern that you love."

A look of realisation spread over Mags' face as an association triggered an address in her Mysl memory. She turned to Philip in awe. "Did you teach Dimitri to paint?"

Philip nodded. "He was such a fast learner. We would meet when the Pervak's went out, just snatching maybe an hour or two each week, but every time Dimitri seemed to learn so much, he was a star student. He borrowed books on art from me, and he tried all kinds of styles. I told him that great art comes from the emotion within. The joy, the sorrow," said Philip, looking up towards the ceiling. "Dimitri was very quiet. We only talked about art. He never talked about himself, Maya, Irina or Konstantine. His art spoke for him." Philip was shaking his head. "My boy was sensitive, emotional, more than many humans I've known; nothing like real young men of his age. I'm not a religious man, but he had a soul. He had such a kind heart, such warmth."

Philip turned towards Mags. "I need to show you something; come with me, you'll understand." He led them up the impressive carved staircase to one of the bedrooms. Like many of the other rooms, it was white, but the walls were covered in paintings, all in portrait, and all the same subject.

Each painting depicted a view from the same window. The white wood of the sash frame, the emerald green curtains, and the room's cream walls were all the same in every painting. The road outside the window was the same, and the house across the street the same, but still, each image was different.

Different cars would be parked across the street. Sometimes a person would be passing by, and the tree in the garden opposite would change with the seasons. Some paintings showed winter, others spring or summer. One even showed the same scene at dusk with long shadows.

Brad had seen one of the same paintings in the hallway. They both noticed a tiny "D.P." in the bottom right of each painting.

Mags made the connection first. "Dimitri painted these."

Philip nodded.

"They're wonderful", added Brad while Philip continued to nod.

Brad and Mags looked around the room in awe as a thinking machine's true artistry and soul were revealed.

"But why?" said Mags.

Philip nodded and simply said, "Yes."

"Why are they the same?" They both turned to Philip.

"It's the view from his room. He spent most of his life in that room. They just didn't want him around unless they had work for him."

Mags was trying to take it in while Brad looked at the paintings closely.

"He was trapped," continued Philip. "The window was his window on the world. He bares his soul in these paintings."

Both Brad and Mags were enthralled, but Mags started to shake the way she had the day before. "You said he was reticent, but you did have a relationship?" She let it hang in the air while they both stared at the paintings.

Philip smiled; he knew what they were thinking. "Yes, I'm gay, and I think Dimitri knew, but I never laid a hand on him. I loved him like a son, like an extension of me. I never knew how he felt until today."

The tears began again, and Mags realised the complex emotional link between a human and a myPAL.

"Yes, I loved him too," said Philip, finally through the tears, "I am so grateful that you brought me his message. You're an angel."

That word again.

They all returned downstairs, where Philip ordered them a cab while they waited in his studio.

Philip was studying Mags intensely. He'd been doing so since they'd arrived, and Mags was starting to find it unnerving. "What is it?" she said finally.

Philip smiled and shook his head once more. Mags had the feeling he liked her. "What generation are you?" he said as if he'd known all along.

Brad was shocked. He could never tell the difference. "How did you know?" he said.

"I noticed that Dimitri was different. Kind where most would not be, thoughtful when most wouldn't care. You have those same qualities."

Mags was starting to worry that others would recognize what she was, but Philip wasn't finished. "You're not as good as humans, you're better in every way, and that's why we fear you."

Brad found himself nodding.

Mags had never heard talk like this before, but she knew she didn't want Brad to fear her.

Philip put a hand on Mags' shoulder. "Only a few of us can see," he said, still smiling.

They continued to admire the paintings while they waited for the taxi, and Philip noticed that Mags was staring at Dimitri's window painting in the studio. "It's yours," he said.

"No, I couldn't possibly. It's too precious to you."

Philip was already taking it down from its peg. "Dimitri had no friends and nobody to care for him except me, and in his last moments, you were there for him."

Philip was crying once more as he handed Mags the painting. "He would have wanted you to have this. Please take it."

Mags didn't let the painting out of her hands all the way back to the apartment. A window into the soul of a myPAL like her. She'd heard of robot art before, but never something like this. So raw and so personal.

They relaxed for the rest of the day, but Mags' consciousness kept processing the same images: Dimitri, Philip, the crash tests, the window painting, and the fear in Irina's face as Mags held her off the ground. In a short space of time, she'd seen things that questioned human compassion but also the promise of genuine human-robot love from Philip and Brad. How could some humans be so cruel while others were so kind? myPAL's weren't vindictive or callous, so what was missing in some humans? Perhaps myPAL's were stupid? These were the questions bouncing around her consciousness that night before sleep engaged and charging commenced.

11 DDEEJACKSON

"Thou shalt not make unto thee any graven image or any likeness of anything that is in heaven above, or that is in the earth beneath, or that is in the water under the earth."

(Exodus 20:4)

The weekend of Jason's dinner party was fast approaching, and Brad was in a foul mood that morning as he disappeared off to work. Mags watched him go as usual from the corner of the terrace. She wasn't going into Light Lunch that day.

"He bares his soul in these paintings. You're an angel", the words were still echoing in her mind. How could her programmers have designed her to be haunted by what she'd seen and heard? Why make her so human as to feel pain, but deny her any rights? Nothing made sense. Mags saw Dimitri's shattered face everywhere she went. "My beautiful boy."

She needed to know more, and she wanted to share her feelings. Brad was hard to talk to about feelings; he always became uncomfortable when emotions were involved. She loved him to bits, but she needed another friend. She grabbed the laptop and headed online.

Googling "Robot Rights" again, she scrolled down the page of links she'd seen at the weekend. Right at the bottom, she noticed a site called "zero2hero". She hovered the mouse pointer over it and looked up, almost expecting Brad to be standing there. It didn't feel right keeping this from him, but after a few seconds, she clicked the link, and the site loaded.

zero2hero, it said at the top, "a site for myPAL's, myPAL lovers and all those who support robot rights" above a large picture of two very attractive new model myPAL's. A blonde, white woman and a super fit black man.

Mags had a nasty feeling that this could be a site for cybersexuals, but the links down the side looked promising. They included a gallery, news, letters, articles, bugs and faults, links and interesting looking *forums*.

Clicking on *forums,* Mags was prompted to create a login name. She'd never used social media and didn't have her own email, so this was the first hurdle. She spent the next hour creating an online persona, including a webmail account and her zero2hero username: *RoboAngel.* Finally, she entered the forum and noticed a range of topics from cybersexuals to robot worker rights, ethics and even myPAL fashion. She saw a forum called *Toys of the rich* and clicked to enter.

The forum was a mixed bag, but her eyes were drawn to *"Treated like dirt"* among the various sub-topics. It was an essay supposedly written by a zero myPAL named *Tranzorb.* It seemed to detail the life of a male myPAL iM-24:

"My owner is a social media influencer; I was a gift from one of her parents. Things started well. We went to cool parties, and I met lots of celebrities. She took me everywhere, and we had some great sex. I was happy, and I thought things would continue that way."

"Things began to go wrong when she started doing drugs. MDMA, cannabis, coke, she was doing them all. Of course, I couldn't join in, and her junkie friends decided I was boring. She got a druggy boyfriend who was in a band, and that's when she began leaving me at home."

"For a while, I took it. I just chilled out watching TV, thinking she would come back to me, but soon I became miserable. I asked her if I could come with her, and she blanked me. I started going out on my own, but she hated that; I was her property. She stopped giving me any money. Eventually, I went out anyway, but that annoyed her, and she locked me in my room."

"I've been in my bedroom now for six weeks. I haven't seen anyone or talked to anyone; she took my smartphone away.

Last night, she told me through the door that she was resetting me to a mode twelve housekeeper to clean up the drug den she lives in with her guy.

I'm terrified. I feel like crying every day. I just want to talk to someone."

Mags stared in disbelief at the screen; she wanted to find the spoilt drug addict and stove her head in. The heat was rising in her temple, and her hands were beginning to shake.

Many other users posted messages of support, and Tranzorb thanked everyone until he posted a final message three weeks ago. "Thank you for all your support. I hope one day we can stop the abuse. Tomorrow I'll be gone. Goodbye, my friends."

Mags clutched her chest and took a sharp breath. Just like that, another perfect life snuffed out, like throwing out an old smartphone. She was angry, really angry and she didn't like feeling this way. It wasn't like her. Mags dropped the laptop and walked out onto the terrace, where she found herself in the far corner staring down at the Thames, staring into the abyss.

For half an hour, she watched London life, people walking over the bridge, boats passing by, and so many people oblivious of the abuse going on every day against her kind. Yes, it was *her kind*. Robots, AI, Zeros, they were *her* people, and they needed a voice.

The anger had subsided into resolve, and she found herself back in the lounge with the laptop. She began to type:

```
>New forum post
```

```
>The Death of a Beautiful Boy
```

It all poured out. Mags told the story of Dimitri, the sensitive budding artist left on the street in pain. The love he shared with a caring man and his last moments in her arms. His name was changed to David while Philip became Robert, but all the details were there.

```
>Submit.
```

The new post appeared at the top of the page. She closed the laptop and went to the kitchen to begin the housework.

*

"Bradley mate, me and the missus are looking forward to Saturday; it's about time you showed Mags off to us." Jason was standing behind Brad, grinning to himself as usual. After the weekend's events, Brad wasn't in the mood for Jason's childish humour.

"We're looking forward to it." Brad lied, hoping Jason would go away.

Jason laughed and went into his prepared routine. "Is there any food you guys don't like? Fish? Silicon Chips?"

This kind of humour surrounded Brad daily, but he wasn't biting. "I'll eat pretty much anything, and Mags doesn't eat." He thought for a moment and added, "But she does like French fries."

Jason was laughing. "Really?"

"Oh yes," said Brad remembering the Jenga tower before the night turned sour.

"I'll see what Jasmine can rustle up. See you guys around 7:00 pm; it'll be epic." Jason strode back to his office, wondering about the fries, while the boys' club whispered and sniggered.

It would be a long day, and Brad wondered how Mags was feeling, still thinking about Dimitri maybe. He'd started to see a change come over her, and he hoped the old bouncy Mags would come back soon.

*

Mags cleaned the kitchen, hoovered the whole apartment, and decided to take a break watching some daytime TV. After a while, she remembered the zero2hero site and picked up the laptop. She was shocked to find there were already seven replies to her posting. All of them expressed sadness at the story, but some were concerned it might be fabricated. She expected the posters were probably all humans.

One post caught her eye. It was from a user called *DdeeJackson,* and it said "101001". It was probably a bad taste joke, or perhaps it was text speak for something; she wasn't well versed in such things, so she checked it out on Google. The first hit suggested it was binary for forty-one.

She sat back from the computer, feeling confused. Was that a coincidence? Did someone guess the number of Dimitri's home? That wasn't possible; only she and Brad knew. Perhaps she hadn't disguised the details well enough. Mags was becoming slightly worried that she'd given too much away. She was new to social media, and maybe she'd already made a mistake. It could also be a hoax; she sat back for a moment, thinking of the various scenarios.

A window popped up in the middle of the screen:

```
>DdeeJackson has invited Rob0Angel to a chat
session. Accept, Yes/No
```

This was all very sudden, and Mags felt vulnerable. She held the mouse pointer hovering over the "No", but for some reason, an interrupt deep inside her processor network told her to do it. She found herself clicking "Yes".

The screen changed to a large white window with a text entry box at the bottom. On the left was a slim panel named *Users online* listing just Mags' username RoboAngel, and DdeeJackson. She'd never used anything like this before and wasn't sure what to do. She waited for a while, and then a message popped up in the large white window:

```
>DdeeJackson: Hello?
```

She decided whoever it was couldn't really hurt her, so she would see what they wanted. There was a flashing cursor at the bottom of the screen, so she entered "Hi" and hit the "Submit" button.

```
>Rob0Angel: Hi
```

```
>DdeeJackson: I liked your story. Very sad
```

```
>Rob0Angel: It wasn't a story. I was there
```

There was a long pause. Either DdeeJackson was writing a very long response or perhaps losing interest. Then a message scrolled up.

```
>DdeeJackson: Dimitri was a beautiful boy.
```

The message ended with a sad crying emoji. How could anyone know? It hadn't been in the news, and only Brad and Mags knew all the details. Who was this?

```
>Rob0Angel: Who are you?
```

Mags was convinced this was some kind of sick joke, maybe one of Brad's boys' club playing tricks. The response didn't help.

```
>DdeeJackson: A friend
```

```
>Rob0Angel: How do you know the truth, and how can I
trust you?
```

>DdeeJackson: That's two questions, but I'll answer
them both. Firstly, I have friends everywhere (or
spies if you like). I didn't know Dimitri, but a
friend of mine was on the bus and saw you. I'm
impressed

The conversation was getting very creepy, and Mags wasn't sure if she liked being spied upon, but the answers came.

>DdeeJackson: You *can* trust me, but I can't prove it
to you just yet

>Rob0Angel: So why should I talk to you? You're a
human, aren't you?

>DdeeJackson: I'm not a human.

>Rob0Angel: okay?

There was another long pause, this time, it was so long that Mags started thinking about preparing dinner, but finally, it came.

>DdeeJackson: iM-21, I'm the same as you

Mags was gasping; how could he possibly know she was an iM-21 model? He sounded more and more like a cyber sexual. Maybe she should walk away.

>DdeeJackson: I'm a female model

Well, that seemed to answer that question, but there was no way to tell. Even so, this was the first contact she'd had with anyone other than the helpers at Light Lunch. At least she could talk about the things she'd seen. DdeeJackson seemed to sense her reluctance.

>DdeeJackson: Let me tell you my story. If you don't
trust me or don't believe me, I'll go and leave you
in peace. We all need friends

A smiley face followed that. Mags didn't have anything to lose, and she could use a friend, especially if DdeeJackson was a myPAL.

>Rob0Angel: Okay, I'm listening

Mags fluffed up a couple of cushions and settled in to read her story.

DdeeJackson was about the same age as Mags, but she was first programmed as a mode thirty-five, the household cleaner model specialising in sexual acts. She was purchased by a wealthy American businessman named Frank to clean his London apartment and service his other needs.

Suffice to say, his wife back in New York had no idea Frank even owned a myPAL. DdeeJackson described Frank as fat, ugly and sweaty or, as she put it, "the holy trinity of shit". It didn't help that he had a personality to match.

After keeping her a few months, Frank decided sex with a mode thirty-five wasn't very realistic, so he reset her and initialised her as a mode zero. Although she was upset to find out he didn't look like a movie star, she initially thought life would be okay.

He would stay in London for four or five weeks using her for sweaty sex, which often included making videos to enjoy back home, then he would go back to the US for a couple of months, leaving her locked in the apartment. It was at this point things became tough. Although she could watch TV and surf the internet, she was essentially a prisoner, and she became bored, lonely and depressed. That's when she discovered zero2hero.

She befriended a cyber sexual she called Mark. They would chat online for hours, making jokes and sexting. They built up an online relationship over several months. Meanwhile, sweaty Frank was still dropping by for sex. She became desperate to meet Mark and hatched a plan to see him while Frank was away.

Frank arrived one Friday night expecting the usual. After sex, he always fell asleep, so she carefully slipped out of bed and found his coat where he'd left the apartment key card. Mark was already waiting downstairs outside the lobby, so she buzzed him in.

She met Mark for the first time that night when she opened the apartment door to hand over the key card. He was everything she'd hoped for, cute, intelligent and charming. He had a friend in Staines who could copy the key card, so he left with the key to return early the following day before Frank woke up.

She couldn't wait for Frank to disappear back to the States this time. She was smiling for the first time since she'd been switched on. This time when Frank went home, she'd have a different life.

Mark returned with the original key in the small hours. He let himself in with the copy as soon as Frank departed, and Dee's life changed for the better. Mark would take her out to the movies and his place. They went for walks in the country and visited Brighton several times. Mark was terrific, everything she'd hoped for. They laughed all the time, and the sex was great. She would cook for him at the apartment, and they would curl up together watching TV. She loved him.

The secret relationship flourished for over a year. Dee was getting tired of seeing Frank now. He barely spoke, just barged in demanding sex, and then fell asleep. She'd had enough and wanted to leave. She told Mark the next time Frank went to New York, she was going with Mark, and they'd take the charger and run away together. It was all planned.

It was the day before Christmas Eve; everything was set. Frank left for New York to spend the holidays with his family. As soon as he'd gone, Mark arrived. She threw her arms around him and dragged him into the bedroom. Soon they would be together for good. They both felt good. Mark drifted off to sleep while she stared at the ceiling, wondering about her new life.

When the front door slammed shut, they both jumped. Frank was back.

"Dee, get me a coffee, the fucking plane's been cancelled, fucking British unions called a strike. Left-wing bullshit". He was often in a lousy mood and swore all the time.

They leapt out of bed, but there was nowhere to go. Frank was already coming through the door. Both Dee and Mark were naked by the bed, desperately trying to find their clothes.

The door flung open, and Frank blundered in. He stopped in his tracks when he saw Mark standing naked in front of him.

"Just take it easy, Frank", said Dee frantically; he may be flabby, but he was strong.

"What the fuck is this?"

Frank threw his case on the floor and removed his jacket while Mark was frantically pulling on his boxers. Frank hit him square on the left cheek as he looked up, sending him reeling backwards over a chair.

"Fuck my property, will you? Break into my home, will you?"

Frank grabbed Mark's arm and threw him down on the floor, kicking him in the chest as he fell. Dee tried to stop him, but she was paralysed, the first AIR law had kicked in, and she was powerless. She cried out in desperation.

"I'm calling the police!" she yelled, but Frank continued to kick Mark on the floor. She picked up the phone to dial, and Frank stopped for a moment.

"You really want to do that?" he said, so red in the face it looked like he could burst. "Your loser boyfriend screws my property, breaks into my home and looks like he's been helping himself to my food? Think again, you fucking whore."

Mark was clutching his ribs, moaning on the floor, and Dee was powerless. She helped him to his feet, and he got dressed. Frank escorted him to the door taking the copied key card from him.

Mark turned in the doorway, looking pleadingly at Dee. "Come on, Dee. Come with me", he said forlornly, but Frank was between them.

"If she takes one step, I'll reset her ass on the spot." Frank was in no mood for games and shoved Mark out of the door, slamming it behind him. He glowered at Dee but said nothing else that day. They got into bed later that night but didn't touch or speak. Dee feared he would reset her soon.

It was the small hours when Dee woke suddenly. She was pinned down. Frank was sitting astride her, grinning menacingly.

"Make a fool out of me, will you? Time you learned a lesson," he said coldly. He slapped her hard across the face, throwing her head across the pillow and leaving her open-mouthed in shock.

He sat staring at her for a moment as her fake breathing quickened. Then he punched her, full in the face. Again, then again, faster, and again. Dee wanted her arms to stop him, but the AIR laws kicked in again. He punched her so hard she could feel her structure rattling, and a throbbing pain started in her temple. The blows became more brutal as he began punching her in the same cheek over and over. She was screaming for him to stop. "Please, no, please, I'll do anything, please", but he just hit her harder.

Something was damaged, some of the pain suddenly stopped, but her cheek felt wet. He'd broken the skin, and she was leaking coolant. "Just finish me, reset me, please," she begged. The blows kept coming, and she felt something else break. Frank beat her for ten minutes, then rolled over and went back to sleep, saying nothing.

Dee was shaking. She struggled to her feet and shuffled to the bathroom. When she saw her face, split open showing the titanium structure beneath and warm oil oozing out, she felt nothing. Later she discovered some of the micro servos in her left cheek were broken. Her smile would now be one-sided.

When Frank left for New York the following day, his chilling parting shot was telling her he'd reset her when he returned. Dee felt she would accept that, as she used a repair kit and super glue to patch up her face. She looked out of the apartment window at the world denied to her and became angry. So, what if Frank gave her life? When you give life to a child, you don't own that child forever. She was her own person, and she was getting out.

She had six weeks to plan before Frank returned. The first port of call was her laptop. Bingo! The videos were still on it. She would need a few clothes, and of course, she needed to get out.

Frank was unimpressed when he got the call at his Manhattan office. His myPAL had destroyed his apartment. Obscenities describing him and his manhood had been spray-painted on the walls. The apartment manager guessed that Dee had used the dishwasher to ram the door open. Both door and dishwasher were now in pieces across the corridor.

When Frank eventually stood in the apartment, the full scale of the devastation was apparent. The bed had been destroyed, with chunks of foam and stuffing all over the room. His Hugo Boss suits had been shredded, and his white tailor-made shirts were sprayed red.

"Fucking bitch!"

Even as he spoke, his phone received a text. "Dearest Frank, by now, you'll realise I've gone, and I won't be coming back, but there's something I need you to do before I'm gone for good. You're going to give me one-hundred-thousand pounds in cash, or I'll send the sex videos to your wife. I'll send them to your entire family and every employee of your company.

You will put the money in a shoebox wrapped up to look like a present. On Friday at 6:00 am, a taxi will arrive at the apartments. You will give the box to the taxi driver. You will then never hear from me again.

If you attempt to find me, go to the police, fail to pay or take any other action against me, I'll release the videos. That's my insurance. Reply to let me know you understand.

Goodbye, Frank."

>DdeeJackson: That's the last I heard from Frank.

Mags was reeling; the story was incredible but had the ring of truth about it.

>Rob0Angel: Did you ever see Mark again?

>DdeeJackson: He could get into a lot of trouble, so I reluctantly let him go

She added a sad face to that line, Mags knew what real love was, and that was *real* love.

>DdeeJackson: I need to go now, but if you want to chat again, just PM me

Mags didn't want to sound stupid asking what *PM* meant; she would Google it later. She had so many questions. Where was Dee now? How was she living? How could Mags physically lift a Russian woman when Dee couldn't even stop an attack? How many other stories did she have?

>Rob0Angel: One last question, is your real name Dee?

There was another long pause before the answer came.

>DdeeJackson: No

>DdeeJackson: Goodbye, Angel

Mags sat back stunned. Her world had become so much bigger and yet so much smaller at the same time. She had no idea myPAL's were living lives like this, and it made her realize how sheltered her own short life had been. She'd told Brad she needed something else in her life, and she was starting to get a clue what that might be. Mags was still staring through the windows as darkness fell outside, and Brad returned home.

12 THE SIXTH COMMANDMENT

"The UN AIR laws are just a sticking plaster. They can't work in all situations."

"Imagine you are walking down the street with your Mysl robot. The robot will be aware of every vehicle, every crack in the pavement, every plane flying overhead, every person passing. How can it possibly assess all these threats to your life?"

"Set too sensitively; the robot would be continuously trying to save your life from phantom threats. Set too coarsely, and it could miss that car mounting the kerb."

"They cannot protect your life in all situations, and in the same way, there are gaps in the code where it might be possible for them to harm you."

(Interview with Professor Olaf Laugesen – Inventor of the Mysl Processor)

Yet another day spent fending off innuendo from Jason and the boys. Brad wasn't in the best mood when he finally made it to apartment P32. Mags would have dinner cooking, and her big hugs would wash away the day.

Walking into the hall, things felt different. The TV was usually on, but there was silence and no sign of Mags bounding in to greet him. Brad hung up his coat and walked into the lounge where he found Mags, feet up, and typing on the laptop.

"Oh, hi honey," she said, looking up, "sorry, I was miles away."

Brad knelt and kissed her. "Retail therapy?" he asked, expecting it would be Amazon or eBay.

"No, no, it's a forum; I'll tell you all about it later." She locked the screen and stood to hug him properly. "Err, I'm afraid I haven't cooked; I'll get onto it."

This was a first; Mags had cooked every night they were at home from the moment he switched activated her. Something was happening. Maybe it was connected to this forum she'd talked about, or perhaps the weekend was still weighing on her.

"No problem, my love, I'll cook myself tonight. Just remind me, what's a pan?" Brad wasn't the kind of guy to demand his dinner cooked, it would make a change for him to do his own, but he was still concerned about her. "Carry on surfing. I don't mind," he said, heading for the kitchen to start dinner.

"Hey, thanks, babe," she said, picking up the laptop, "I promise I'll tell you what I'm up to."

Brad cooked himself a chorizo paella which he left on the hob while he showered and changed. His food wasn't as good as Mags', but he would never take her for granted. He took a cider and sat down to dinner in the kitchen while Mags continued surfing.

Grabbing the tablet computer, Brad checked the London news, and a story way down the page caught his attention: "Woman threatens millionaire's wife after an accident". It was a piece about the accident with Dimitri, but it didn't mention the myPAL at all. It went on to become a story about bus safety. The real story was lost.

"So, what's going on, mate?" Brad wandered into the lounge and sat opposite Mags. "Is everything okay?"

Mags looked up to see Brad framed in the dark window with the curtains still open. They were breaking new ground here, and she wanted to be as honest as possible without worrying him too much. She told Brad about zero2hero, posting Dimitri's story, meeting a friend named Dee, and finding many other posts related to myPAL abuse and robot rights. Mags omitted the part where Dee was beaten up and bribed her owner. Brad listened intently, nodding as she recounted the reactions to Dimitri's story and how Dee made her feel like she wasn't alone.

When she'd finished, Brad took a moment to process what she'd said. He loved her to bits and would always support anything that made her happy. Maybe a loss of some of her sweet innocence was a price worth paying. "I'm really happy for you," he said eventually. "Not only have you found some friends online, but somewhere you can discuss the things you've seen and issues which affect you. I'm rubbish with emotions, as you know, so I think this is great."

Mags jumped up and ran over to him, burying her head in his lap. "Thank you so much, my love; I do need this". She kissed him and hugged him tightly. "I've got the best with you."

Brad was happy as long as Mags was. He felt some calm returning now he knew she had a release, but he still worried about her. "Just be careful online," he said, "there are a lot of nutters out there and people pretending to be something they're not."

Mags was smiling up at him once more. "I know, honey," she said, "I'll be careful, don't worry about me."

"I'll always worry about you," he retorted, "because I love you."

Mags put the laptop down, and they snuggled up on the sofa, watching the lights of London through the open curtains.

After starting with a blank slate, Brad found that Mags was more like Halina every day. She cared about everyone; she had a big heart.

*

The following day they both awoke refreshed. Brad had relaxed, and Mags was keen to get back online. She had until 10:00 am before heading to Light Lunch. As soon as Brad left for work, she collected the laptop and navigated to the zero2hero site.

Since the last time online, she'd discovered that PM meant "Personal Message" (a message sent through the website directly to another user). Mags sent a PM to DdeeJackson, hoping she could chat before work. While waiting for a response, she went back to the main forum, where she noticed that her post had now been read over five hundred times, and there were now thirty-three entries.

Mags scanned through the new replies, and near the bottom, she spotted one from user MıNEisVENGEANCE that didn't fit with the others. It seemed to be a religious rant describing myPAL's as false idols and temptations of the devil. It ended with a chilling suggestion that all AI robots should be burned and that cybersexuals be castrated. Although the site was for myPAL's, cybersexuals and robot equality campaigners, it also attracted a few trolls. She clicked on the "Report" icon, which allowed abuse to be reported to the site moderators. Mags was starting to feel more and more like an activist.

A familiar window popped up in the centre of the screen, inviting her to chat with DdeeJackson, which she accepted and settled down for another session.

>DdeeJackson: Hello again

>Rob0Angel: I was hoping to ask a few questions, as you seem very experienced

>DdeeJackson: You make me sound ancient, ha-ha. Ask away, Angel

>Rob0Angel: How was I able to man-handle and lift the woman without the AIR laws stopping me?

>DdeeJackson: and why couldn't I defend myself from Frank?

Dee seemed to be reading Mags' mind. None of it made sense.

>Rob0Angel: Yes! That's right

>DdeeJackson: Humans are imperfect, and so are we

>DdeeJackson: You didn't mean to harm the woman. You were frustrated. Your internal AIR law computer did not detect an imminent threat to her life or welfare, so it didn't stop you. When I tried to struggle free from Frank, I may have harmed him, so my internal system stopped me

>Rob0Angel: Would it be possible to harm a human?

>DdeeJackson: In theory, no, but in practice…

The sentence had just stopped mid-flow. Either Dee was pausing for effect, or she was deciding how much to say. The rest soon came.

>DdeeJackson: A myPAL could kill a human

That's not quite what Mags had asked. The revelation initially shocked her, but it was interesting to hear this fighting talk from another myPAL.

>DdeeJackson: We have many glitches and loopholes which humans have never thought of, and they never

thought we would use against them. Do you remember
how I only texted Frank for the money? That was so
he couldn't use the emergency stop phrase on me

A growing admiration was building in Mags. Dee was a friend
she could learn from. The next time she found a situation like
Dimitri's, she wanted to know all her abilities and weaknesses.

>DdeeJackson: Also, if you keep more than five
hundred metres from the remote, it does not affect
you; it's out of range

Mags had wondered where Dee was living and how, but she
imagined Dee wouldn't share that kind of information.

>Rob0Angel: Are you safe where you are?

>DdeeJackson: For now

>DdeeJackson: I still have most of Frank's money

Dee ended that line with a winking smiley face, and Mags
couldn't help smiling back. She looked at the clock and noticed it
was 9:50 am. She said goodbye to Dee and was about to head off to
Light Lunch. Dee had one more line of advice.

>DdeeJackson: Talk to me again before you do
anything dramatic. You need to be smart

>DdeeJackson: Take care, Angel. Love you x

Only Brad had ever expressed love for her. Did this mean Dee
was a cyber sexual after all or was it just the innocent care between
two kindred spirits? It threw her a little, but she decided she
enjoyed having a friend who seemed to care about her.

The journey to Light Lunch that day was filled with dark stories,
self-discovery and the realisation that she wasn't alone.

*

Much to his annoyance, Brad had begun clock watching. There was
still no new job on the horizon, and Saturday's dinner party was
looming. The office was busy today. Some significant movements
on Wall Street affected the dollar, so the boys' club was yelling
more than usual. They seemed to think that swearing down the

'phone loudly somehow indicated how hard they were working. Unfortunately, it was this kind of juvenile behaviour that impressed Jason.

Ben, or *Crappy*, as Jason liked to call him, was hovering behind Brad. Either he was trying to see what Brad was doing, or he was bursting to say something.

"Can I help you with something?" said Brad, turning around. He couldn't work with a back seat driver and decided to determine what the idiot wanted.

"I hear you're having dinner at Jason's place on Saturday."

Every word was like an oily slick. Brad sized him up and knew something was coming. "I am. What of it?"

"I always think five people is better than three, more banter". Ben was already smiling to himself.

Okay, Brad would take the bait, "What's with the numbers?"

"Well, Jason's invited Heather and me to join the party, so that makes five people."

Farty and Two were sniggering in the background. Brad wasn't going to let Ben wind him up. "I look forward to the stimulating conversation," he said with a sigh. Brad went back to his console. Ben retreated a little deflated.

It was later that day when Jason decided to join in the fun. "Jasmine's up for it; she goes both ways," he said, in one especially creepy session, to which Brad responded that they were not swingers.

"Neither are we. She's a sexbot; it's fair game," added Jason.

Brad never knew whether he was joking or serious. He couldn't imagine that Jason's wife Layla would be impressed if she knew he was screwing the electronic au pair.

Brad knew that Mags would never stand for this, and he knew he was weak. He hated confrontations and preferred to let his tormentors blow themselves out. Once the dinner party was over, he vowed never to accept any other invitations in the office. He intended to leave; the sooner, the better.

13 ETIQUETTE

A shaft of light was slicing the room in two, right along the centre of the bed when Brad woke on Saturday morning. The thin gap in the curtains was revealing a sunny, crisp November morning. Mags was already up somewhere, so Brad was alone with thoughts of tonight's party.

"Psst." The sound came from the door.

Brad looked around to see a shapely dark leg extending, followed by what looked like a stocking top. Mags' cheeky smile soon appeared, and slowly she revealed herself, one eye cocked as she adopted a model pose. "Like what you see?" she said, putting on a sultry voice. Mags was dressed in a red and black set of strapless bra, knickers, stockings and suspenders. She looked the million she was worth.

"Wowser!" said Brad sitting up, "is it my birthday?"

"It's the first dinner party you've ever taken me to," she said, sitting on the bed beside him.

"When you're sitting at dinner with those horrible people, I want you to think about what I'm wearing and who's taking me home."

Brad grabbed her by the waist and dragged her into bed with him. "Now, just let me help you out of these things."

Making love before breakfast was rare, but this morning it was just what Brad needed. Mags was back to her mischievous self, at least for today. As a special treat, she even made him a bacon sandwich.

It was a beautiful day, so Brad took breakfast sat on the terrace. It was freezing, but he was wrapped up warm and in a better mood than he expected.

"We're just going to be ourselves tonight," said Mags, as she came out to join him, "fuck 'em if they don't like it."

That was the Mags he loved, funny and irreverent.

Brad and Mags spent most of the day relaxing in preparation for the evening. Brad was enjoying watching some motor racing on TV while Mags was online again. She'd found a zero2hero app for her smartphone, which enabled both the forums and chat on the go.

On her home page, she set her status as "Looking forward to a dinner party tonight", and she checked the forum posts to see if anything significant was happening. Later that afternoon, she noticed an email sent through the site from DdeeJackson, which simply said, "Have fun tonight" with a smiley face.

Brad felt more relaxed, a combination of the morning sex, chilled out day and Mags calming him down like she always did. He looked across at her on the sofa. She was still surfing while he relaxed on the Barcelona chair, watching an old war movie. He always told her she was free to be herself, and today he could see what that was. She was still the outgoing woman who captured his heart, but she now had other interests and even politics. While it wasn't what he'd envisaged, he liked to see her doing what she wanted, if he could be there to share it.

He was woken from his reflections when Mags suddenly stood and switched off the TV. "Come on. It's 4:30 pm, the taxi's due at 6:00 pm, so time to move your ass." This was Mags' order tone; she liked to use it when Brad needed kicking.

"Really?" he said in bemusement, "that's plenty of time."

"Look, buster, a girl has lots to do. Besides, you're ironing your own shirt today, and your shoes need polishing."

Mags disappeared to the bedroom, where she continued to shout instructions. Just as Brad got to his feet, she returned with what looked like a new suit, bagged up in a suit protector. "I've bought you something," she said with that guilty smile of hers, "it's about time you had a new suit, and besides, I'm going to look hot tonight, so you better match up." She presented him with a new shirt and tie and told him to "get on with it" before she disappeared into the bedroom once more.

Brad liked having his life organised for him. She always made great choices, which relieved him of the stress of dealing with people.

Mags ordered him to have a shower first and then to get ready in the spare bedroom. He wasn't allowed to see her until she was ready. He felt as if he was getting married. It was a fleeting thought, but just enough to conjure up an image of Halina as they sat having dinner together, discussing their future. They would have been married by now, and his life would have been very different.

Getting ready long before Mags, which was highly unusual, Brad stood on the terrace watching the traffic passing over London Bridge. His new suit had a tailored Nehru collar jacket, a black patterned waistcoat, a white shirt, and a black tie. When he looked at himself in the mirror, he was astonished. It looked both ultra-modern and very stylish. Mags had an excellent eye for fashion.

"Hi, handsome." The voice came from behind.

Brad turned around to see a stunning vision. Framed in the light from the lounge, Mags stood tall in a strapless full-length wine-red dress fitting tightly around her svelte body. A side slit revealed a hint of her smooth leg. MyPAL's never needed to shave. Her olive skin radiated in the moonlight, and her long earrings sparkled. She wore her hair down, but it was curled, flowing away from her face and down her back. Mags resembled a movie star.

Brad had never seen her looking so beautiful. He couldn't say anything; he simply shook his head as a small tear formed in the corner of one eye. She came to him, gliding as if on air to brush some imaginary dust from his shoulder and smooth back his hair.

"This is all yours, my love," she said, with a twinkle in her eye.

Brad couldn't speak. He was too busy admiring her form, but finally, he pulled her close and kissed her lightly to avoid smudging the lipstick.

"I love you," he said, feeling so proud.

The moment was broken by the access system buzzing. The cab had arrived.

As the taxi made its way down the A3 towards Weybridge, Brad was still shaking his head. "You're unbelievable," he said. The cab turned out to be a stretched private hire limousine, a jet-black Mercedes. Mags had decided a rare night out with other real people deserved something special.

"Now I really do feel like we're a pair of movie stars. You surprise me every day," said Brad.

Mags squeezed his hand and shook her hair revealing the care she'd taken getting ready. "You just need to do a line of coke off my bare arse, and the picture will be complete," she said, laughing.

Brad noticed the driver smiling in the rear-view mirror. "Behave yourself," he said, laughing, "and remember the dinner party etiquette."

Mags looked puzzled. "What's that?"

Brad was only partly serious. He loved it when she broke the rules. "We've blown it anyway," he said smiling, "you'll definitely upstage both Layla and Heather in that outfit, which in my books is a major result. The only problem will be keeping Jason's paws off you."

"That's okay. You can blow his head off with pistols at dawn if he tries."

They both laughed and giggled all the way to the outskirts of Weybridge, where Jason had his "manor," as he liked to call it.

The electric gates opened onto a short gravel driveway, leading to an imposing mock Georgian house, with a prominent double aspect and a triple garage to the side. Jason's McLaren sports car was parked in the drive, probably for effect, thought Brad. Ben's Porsche was beside it.

The whole front aspect was open and spacious, with trees in the background and large planted beds on either side of the drive. Everything was lit, with hundreds of tiny lights scattered around the grounds.

"Quite a castle," said Brad, as the driver showed them out of the limousine.

"Hey, size isn't everything," added Mags, still in a cheeky mood.

Although Brad had no intention of dampening her spirit, he did hope she reigned in the sarcasm, just for the sake of his life in the office.

Everything about the house was impressive. The windows were large with stained glass panels, and the large door was bordered by white Grecian columns shining against the red brick.

They climbed the clean white steps to the Pacey's home, and Brad rang the bell. They could hear music within and the sound of someone approaching.

The door swung open to reveal a beautiful young black girl, probably in her mid-twenties. Her look was stunning, with radiant skin and shoulder-length afro hair curled into tiny ringlets. She would easily pass for a supermodel in her pretty black cocktail dress and the sad pouting expression she wore as she opened the door.

"Hello, I'm Jasmine, and I'll be looking after you this evening. Please come in." Her voice was deep but feminine, although the words sounded well-rehearsed, like a mode thirty-five.

Brad started to walk towards the door, but Mags was well ahead of him, hand outstretched. Jasmine wasn't sure what to do, but as Mags' hand hung in the air before her, she eventually reached out and shook hands.

"I'm Mags, but you can call me Mags. Very pleased to meet you."

As she shook Jasmine's hand warmly, the merest hint of a smile appeared on Jasmine's lips. "Please come in," she said once again as they walked into the hall. "Can I take your coat?" she asked Mags, who was still smiling.

"Of course, thank you."

Mags was staring at her wide-eyed. "You look amazing."

This time, the smile was genuine. Jasmine acknowledged the compliment, and both Brad and Mags realised that she was a mode zero. A basic mode thirty-five would never react that way.

"May I present you as Bradley and Mags?" Jasmine inquired, returning to formality.

"Bradley?" said Mags, "only his mother calls him that."

"It's just Brad", said Brad giving Mags a friendly slap on the behind. She was in a mischievous mood.

The hallway was vast, with a polished wooden floor and a staircase winding upwards and down to a hidden basement. Everything was bright white, and the hall was so large it accommodated a large cream sofa and several bookcases. A few choice pieces of art completed the style-by-numbers look.

Jasmine led them to the left through a large set of double doors into a reception room. It was decorated in the same simple white, but some low-level lighting and a large blue rug appeared tasteful.

Jason and an attractive white couple were sat chatting on two large, dark leather sofas while a luminous, long-haired blonde woman reclined in a leather swivel chair. She had her back to the door, but she spun around and sprang to her feet when she heard Brad and Mags approach.

She wore a body-hugging black cocktail dress with a neckline that plunged right to her navel. Some miracle of physics was stopping her large breasts from slipping out either side, and bright pink lipstick completed the trophy-wife look.

"May I present Brad and Mags," said Jasmine, seriously.

The blonde woman was eyeing Mags in detail, who was the epitome of class compared to her, until her mouth eventually creased into a smile. "Welcome! I'm Layla. I've been so looking forward to meeting you."

Brad shook her hand warmly, but she didn't take her eyes off Mags. "This must be the one I've heard so much about," she said.

Mags hugged Layla generously and kissed her on the cheek. "I love your dress," she said. Mags was incapable of being horrible to anyone, and Layla seemed genuinely touched.

"That's kind of you, especially as you look stunning. I feel a bit slutty next to you." She seemed to be regretting her choice of plunging outfit.

"Oh god no," said Mags warmly, "If you've got it, flaunt it. Jason's a lucky guy."

Layla was both disarmed by Mag's charm and puzzled. "You're a Zero", she said, sounding surprised. Jason must have told her she was a mode thirty-five.

"Actually, I'm a size eight," said Mags grinning.

Layla's face lit up this time, and she laughed loudly. "You're a scream," she said. "Jasmine, can you please get Brad a drink?"

Jason was chatting to Ben and his girlfriend Heather on the far side of the room, but Ben's attention seemed elsewhere. Heather followed his stare to where Mags was standing.

"Put your tongue away, dear," she said, just loudly enough for Mags to hear.

Jason turned to see what was going on, and his eyes widened. "Jeez, the little fucker's scored big time," he said, referring to Brad's myPAL.

He was very keen to meet Mags. He left Ben and Heather open-mouthed and headed for the newcomers. "Welcome to our home, guys," he announced, shaking Brad's hand much too hard. His eyes were fixed on Mags.

"You must be Mags," he said, shaking her hand, "not sure why Bradley's been hiding you away. You look fabulous tonight."

Layla flashed him a disapproving look, and Brad rolled his eyes out of view, but Mags was on top form. "Thank you, Jason that's very kind, but I was just saying how gorgeous your wife looks tonight." She could tell Jason was squirming.

"Err, yeah she does, gorgeous, yep". Jason tried his best, but if looks could kill, Layla had struck him down.

Mags hadn't quite finished. "It's Brad, by the way."

"What?" said Jason, surprised by how forthright she was.

"He prefers Brad; nobody calls him Bradley."

Jason nodded dumbly while Brad smiled to himself. They were saved from any further embarrassment by Jasmine, who arrived with the drinks.

"So, you've met ours then," said Jason, gesturing towards Jasmine. "My wife's idea of a joke."

Mags noticed that Jasmine wouldn't look at Jason or Ben, but she gave Mags a fleeting look which scared her. "A joke?" said Mags, not really understanding what was going on.

"Yeah, she knew I wanted a white blonde, so I ended up with the third world."

Jason didn't care how it sounded. Layla was mortified, but once again, Mags was on point. "It's a good job she's gorgeous then". She gave Jasmine a subtle wink as she said it and smiled at Layla, who was warming to her.

Outwardly Mags was smiling and confident, but she was beginning to understand why Brad hated Jason, and something about Jasmine had her worried. She decided not to leave Brad alone too long in this environment. He didn't do well in groups.

Ben and Heather joined the four. Ben had gravitated towards Mags as if in a trance while Heather trailed after him.

Ben's partner was an intern at C&S. Her father was on the board of many companies; the fact Ben was seeing her was considered a coup. He would need to watch his step; he could be out of a job if things went sour.

Heather wore a short dark blue cocktail dress and would have been the beautiful brunette in any company that didn't include Mags. She was unimpressed that Mags was a flame attracting the moths. "So, you're a myPAL!" she exclaimed.

"That I am," said Mags unfazed, "plastic fantastic." Mags was on a roll, and she didn't stop there. "I take it you're a human; it can be hard to tell."

They all laughed, and Layla snorted like a donkey. Heather's mouth turned up, but her eyes remained like stone.

"Mags, you should talk to our Jasmine," Layla interjected, still laughing, "she always seems down. She could do with your humour. I would hate to reset her, but she won't tell me why she's so unhappy."

Jason was horrified and tried to cut his wife off. "Ah, she'll snap out of it. I've seen her happy plenty of times."

Mags smiled; she intended to talk with Jasmine if she got the chance. Right on cue, Jasmine walked into the room. "Ladies and gentlemen, please can you take your seats for dinner". She was looking directly at Mags as she spoke and again avoided Jason and Ben.

Jasmine led the guests to the dining room while Layla and Jason dealt with dinner. The dining room was ultra-modern, mainly white with a blue feature wall and blue accents. Even the dining set was late nineties Habitat and very tastefully decorated. Name cards were placed on the settings, and Mags was unsurprised to find herself sitting beside Jason. The places were arranged boy-girl with Jason and Layla seated at either end.

The music was piped into every room, and it was typical dinner party tunes, some of them pretty old. Mags danced around the table to Sade's Smooth Operator. She found her seat and began to pull out her chair, but Jasmine ran to her and insisted on doing the honours.

As she sat and the chair was pushed in, Jasmine bent low beside her and whispered. "Don't come here alone."

Mags was about to ask why, but Jason entered the room. She quickly looked forward and thanked Jasmine. Jason paused for a second, giving Jasmine a quizzical look, but she ignored him and moved to help Heather to her seat.

Something was going on; perhaps Jason's innuendo was more than talk. It was clear that there was something between Jason and Jasmine.

Layla called Jason away again to help her, so Mags leaned over to Brad and whispered, "What's going on between Jasmine and Jason?"

Brad scanned the room and noticed Heather and Ben were chatting. "They're having sex," he said as quietly as he could, "Layla doesn't know."

Something didn't gel; those weren't the vibes Mags was getting from Jasmine.

"I thought she was a mode thirty-five," Brad continued, "I didn't know she was a zero."

Mags was getting a dark feeling, and she was determined to speak to Jasmine when she could. It was a pity she couldn't stage a toilet break.

Finally, they were seated, and Layla came into the room last; even Brad noticed that her breasts were only just in control under what little dress she was wearing. She was tipsy and laughing way too much for this point in the evening.

"Jasmine, can you bring in the first course, please". Layla gestured to Jasmine, who disappeared to the kitchen. "Now, let's all get acquainted, shall we?" They all nodded in agreement. "Why don't we start with the boring bit? What do we all do for a living?"

"Well, you all know me," said Jason, "I do nothing and get paid loads of money for it."

Ben was laughing, but Brad thought it was an accurate description.

"Nah, I manage these two Herbert's," he said, looking at Ben and Brad, "well, maybe just one Herbert. Brad here is the most successful currency trader C&S have ever had. You should be proud, Mags."

"I am", said Mags looking at Ben, who seemed more than a little deflated. "So, what do you do, Layla?" she added, changing the subject.

"Spends my money on a black myPAL," interjected Jason before she could answer.

Layla ignored him and continued. "I'm the UK marketing director for Esprit cosmetics."

"Wow," said Mags, genuinely impressed, "are you the go-to woman for a makeover?"

Layla was blushing. "No, I'm just a businesswoman, but I've got loads of free samples for you if you like."

Layla and Mags were bonding well. Jason didn't seem too impressed. "So, what do you do for a job, Mags? Oh, sorry I forgot, you can't work. It must get boring at home."

Layla was surprised by his tone, but Mags had it covered. "I do work."

"Really?" said Jason.

"I volunteer at a soup kitchen in Dagenham. It's tough seeing people at the other end of the spectrum, but it's gratifying work."

Jason was trying to think of a pithy remark, but Layla beat him to the punch.

"That's fantastic, Mags. I think people who do work like that are brilliant."

"She puts me to shame," added Brad. "Right from the first moment, she wanted to do something positive, and she loves the work."

Mags was looking down and smiling; she was unfamiliar with others being impressed by her work. Layla was beaming, and Brad was nodding. Both Heather and Jason were trying to think of something negative but couldn't.

"Ah, the first course", chimed Layla as Jasmine arrived with carrot and butternut soup. Everyone had a bowl, including Mags. She looked down at it for a moment until Jason noticed.

"I'm afraid we didn't have any crude oil," he said dryly, which brought chuckles from Ben and Heather.

Layla was unimpressed. "Jase", she said in a tone designed to reign him in.

"That's okay," said Mags. "If Jasmine wouldn't mind saving it for me, I'll take it to the soup kitchen on Monday for one of the girls."

"Of course," said Layla.

Scoring very few points from Mags, Jason turned his attention to Heather while Mags, Brad and Layla discussed the cosmetics industry, Light Lunch and where Mags had found *that* dress.

Mags was starting to enjoy herself, as was Brad, although she was still trying to find a moment to speak to Jasmine. She also couldn't understand what enjoyment Jasmine could get out of living in a home like this.

Layla became quite drunk, even before the second course, as was Jason. They both seemed to enjoy their wine.

Jasmine brought out the main course of roast duck in a large terrine, which Jason insisted on serving, but the biggest talking point was the bowl of French fries for Mags. She wagged her finger at Brad.

"Oh, you," she said.

Layla forced her to tell the story, although she left out the part with Dimitri. Much to Heather's disgust, she then proceeded to recreate the Jenga tower. Layla could see the bond between Brad and Mags, and she appeared to envy it. "Brad, I can see that you and Mags make a great couple. I hope you don't mind me asking. Are you a cyber sexual?"

Ben nearly coughed a mouthful of duck across the room, and Jason stopped flirting with Heather. They were all listening intently.

"No," said Brad simply, "I find dating really hard, so I thought I would try a myPAL. I couldn't have guessed she would be so wonderful."

"Ah, that's so sweet," cooed Layla taking another drink, "isn't that romantic, Jase."

Jason shrugged.

Jasmine bustled around again, pouring more wine, but Mags noticed Jason gave her a little tap on the behind out of Layla's gaze. He looked up and smiled at Mags, while Jasmine gave him an evil look and rushed out of the room.

"So, what do you think of Jaz," said Jason eying Mags.

"Well, if I'm honest, I prefer pop music, but each to their own". Mags was starting to dislike Jason and couldn't see what Layla saw in him.

"Come on, she's fit, never thought of a bit of girl on girl?" he added, but he wasn't entirely done, "and she's black. You can't beat a bit of variety."

Mags had an image in her head of slamming Jason's head into his roast duck, but what came out was simply "You're disgusting".

Jason smiled and returned to his food.

Mags joined the other conversation and tried to ignore Jason while they tucked into an excellent meal prepared by Jasmine. Brad was oblivious to Jason's advances and thought the night was going well. He was enjoying listening to the chat and gazing at Mags, who looked stunning. He hadn't thought of Halina once tonight, and he was smiling a lot which was rare.

As the plates emptied, the conversation turned to the cost of properties, and they all complimented Layla on her stylish home. She told them how she and Jason met in an upscale bar after Jason had ordered champagne for everyone. They'd both been extraordinarily drunk and fell into each other at the exit. It explained a lot.

Mags listened intently but was irritated slightly by her dress, which was clinging to her leg. She brushed the clothing to move it and found a hand resting on her left leg, just above the stocking top.

Jason was staring straight ahead but moved his hand further up her leg and pressed a little more firmly. She leaned close to him so she could whisper. "Take your filthy hand off me". All said while she continued to smile towards Layla, deep in conversation with Ben and Brad.

Jason moved his hand further up her leg, so it was just half an inch from her crotch. She didn't flinch but noticed his red wine was quite full, so she moved her left hand to the left of his glass.

"Take your hand off me, or you'll regret it," she whispered.

"Come on, Maggie," he said, "about time you had a real man", as he slid his fingers a little further.

He repulsed her, his oily look, his wide boy image, and the creepy vibe she'd picked up from the start. He was a nasty, sexist dinosaur.

"Firstly, Mags isn't short for Maggie, and secondly, If I wanted a real man, I'd fuck your wife."

Within a second, she'd hooked her hand around his glass and pulled it over towards her. The wine cascaded over the table into her lap, covering the front of her dress in the full-bodied Burgundy. Jason pulled back, and Mags yelped. Everyone turned to see what she'd done.

"Oh, Layla, I'm so sorry, what a clumsy fool I am". Mags' arms were outstretched as she got stood.

Layla was having none of it. She called for Jasmine to take Mags to the bathroom to try and mop up the worst of it.

As Mags left the room, she managed to send a subtle smile towards Jason, who'd given her the opportunity she needed.

14 JASMINE

"There's no definitive test to prove that an AI is conscious. In the same way, there is no test for humans. The closest we come is to ask the individual how they see the world around them."

"Is there a chance that the Mysl processor produces simply the sensation of self-awareness rather than actual self-awareness? Of course. We also can't be sure that our own consciousness isn't simply an electro-chemical con trick played on us by our physiology."

(Interview with Professor Olaf Laugesen – Inventor of the Mysl Processor)

The C&S currency trading manager wasn't going to let his odd, autistic trader possess a sexy new toy that he didn't have, plus he'd become bored with his wife, Layla. She had a great body, but she wasn't as adventurous as he wanted. She'd already turned down a threesome with an ambitious C&S intern and the chance to go swinging with a game couple at the golf club. Layla had made it very clear that all Jason's fantasies were off the agenda.

Jason did his myPAL homework, looking at all the various modes. Mode thirty-five was popular for extra-marital fun, but there were plenty of reports online that they were boring, with many describing them as planks. Brad had his mind set on a zero from the start. Some of the seedier websites described their *abilities* in lurid detail.

It took a couple of weeks to convince Layla that they should get a myPAL, but as the significant earner by a considerable margin, Jason was always going to get his way. She did have one condition, that she would choose the model.

The buzz around the office was actively encouraged by Jason, who'd told the boys' club, and everyone else, he was getting a top-of-the-line new myPAL. He made sure there were plenty of AHS brochures around the room and on his desk, dropping myPAL's into any conversation. As the moment drew closer, his excitement became so great he barely gave any time to work. Finally, the day came, and he booked time off work to receive his new toy.

When the pink bag was unzipped for the first time, revealing not a buxom blonde but a beautiful black woman, Jason was incandescent. Layla was in Paris at the time; otherwise, he would have given her both barrels. Although he considered himself merely a casual racist, he was more concerned by the reaction of the boys' club and his golfing buddies. Remaining the top dog was a continuous preoccupation for Jason.

The name Jasmine was chosen by Layla, as the flowers had surrounded her childhood home and the scent always made her happy. Jason thought it was a bit common, but he agreed as another condition. It helped that Jasmine seemed to like her name when she was initialised.

Jason steered clear of the topic of sex for a while; he wasn't sure how she'd react; she could quickly go blabbing to Layla. During the binding process, he'd described the relationship between the three of them as "best friends."

It was five weeks after she was activated; a date burned into Jasmine's Mysl memory. She'd completed her chores in the early afternoon and was relaxing in her bedroom, enjoying the late spring view. She was getting on well with both Layla and Jason, and she was delighted in her new home, but all that would change over a weekend when Layla was away.

"Hi Jasmine," said Jason, standing smiling in the doorway to her room.

The room was at the back of the house, with views over the extensive grounds, through the generous window. It was large and spacious with an attic room feeling where the roof pitch sloped the ceiling inwards. It was Jasmine's haven, and nobody bothered her there.

"Hi Jason," replied Jasmine, surprised to see him at her door.

He moved into the room, hovering near the doorway. "How are you settling in, comfy?"

"Yes, thank you, I love my room."

Jasmine had no experience with men, and her AE state programming was too thin to prepare her fully for any dangers. She saw Jason and Layla as family and friends.

"Well, I thought it was time we got to know each other better," he said, closing the door behind him.

Jasmine would never give Mags the full details, and Mags wouldn't press her. The law wouldn't name the act, just a myPAL and its owner doing whatever the owner wanted.

Jason stopped Jasmine from going out, claiming to Layla that myPAL's often ran away, and she cost too much to allow that to happen. He also took her smartphone away, but she held onto her tablet, which couldn't make calls.

He continued to abuse her every time Layla went away. She couldn't escape the high walled prison, and she couldn't fight back. He told her he'd reset her if she told Layla, but he'd hurt her badly before he did. Layla noticed the change in her demeanour straight away, but Jason dismissed it as a glitch. Every month Jasmine was assaulted destroyed her life, but what came next made her long for oblivion.

It was a hot, humid Friday night in August, and Layla was on business in Paris. Jasmine was expecting Jason to force himself on her when he came home, but he didn't arrive alone this time.

Jason led her into the basement cinema room, where there were three men drinking beer and watching a porn film on the projector screen.

By the time they'd finished taking turns, her battery was at less than five per cent. The struggling and screaming had drained her cells so low she could barely walk. Covered in their sweat and beer, she crawled up the stairs, hand over hand, dragging herself into bed. She just managed to start charging when her battery was down to just two per cent.

The story was whispered while Mags sat on the closed toilet and Jasmine sat on the edge of the enormous bathtub in the Paceys opulent but bland main bathroom. Mags wanted to wrap her up. She held Jasmine tightly. She couldn't think of anything to say, but her thoughts were clear. The bastards would pay.

"There's one more thing", said Jasmine calmly. She'd lived with this for years amidst the thoughts of suicide, denied by the AIR laws. "The men are doing something together, and I think it might be illegal. I've heard them talking about the FCA."

"Do you know who they are?" asked Mags.

"I only know one by his real name, the other two I know as Farts or Farty and just the number Two." She looked down as Layla's laughter echoed up the stairs. "The one I know is downstairs."

For the merest fraction of a second, Mags thought of Brad, then Mysl logic took over. "Ben," she said, and Jasmine nodded. "I'm so sorry, my poor love, I'm so sorry."

Mags held Jasmine's hands, she couldn't begin to imagine the horrors she'd endured, and it was making her body overheat as anger coursed through her systems.

"Please help me?", said Jasmine looking Mags straight in the face, "Please?"

That was a cry Mags had heard before. She acted that time, and she'd be acting again. She held Jasmine's shoulders and swore a promise with eye contact locked. "I'm getting you out."

"Jason really wants you to join in; he's always talking about you. Please be careful", said Jasmine holding onto Mags.

"He'll be a dead man before that happens."

Jasmine told Mags not to say anything to Jason or Layla, as Mags scribbled her email address on a piece of toilet paper.

"Hope you guys aren't having too much fun up there." Jason was yelling up the stairs.

Mags quickly dealt with her dress, and they made their way down. Mags held Jasmine's hand tightly.

"There you are," said Layla, slurring her words as they entered the dining room, "we've got pud to stuff ourselves with yet."

She was laughing like a hyena, and Jason didn't look impressed. "Enjoy some gossip, girls?" he said, flashing Jasmine a dark look.

"Oh, just girl talk", said Mags taking her seat. She was struggling to hide her contempt. She couldn't wait for the night to end now.

"Magsy!" shouted Layla, "I was just telling your hush-band how lucky he is to have you."

"Oh, I tell him every day," replied Mags, doing her best to hide her emotions, "but we're not married."

"Well, you should be," insisted Layla, "Brad, I order you to propose right now."

"They can't marry," Heather interjected, deadpan and completely sober, "she's a robot."

"Guilty," said Mags holding up her hand, unfazed by Heather's attempt at an insult.

"Bollocks!" shouted Layla, looking straight at Heather, "She's more human than you are."

At this point, Jason jumped in to stop Layla from insulting any more guests, and she apologised to Heather, but Ben saw his chance almost as if Jason had primed him. "But how can robots have rights? Brad owns you, and Jason owns Jasmine. You cost around a million pounds. Nobody's just going to let you walk out the door."

Mags had heard this one a dozen times before, but she had the answer ready with zero2hero under her belt. "You can own a dog, but if you hurt that dog, you may be fined or even go to prison. You can have children, but if you abuse your children, you'll definitely go to prison."

Ben was rolling his eyes, but she hadn't finished.

"It costs an average of five-hundred-and-eighty thousand pounds to rear a single child, but paying out all that money gives you no right to abuse it."

She was looking directly at Jason, "Just because you can buy a myPAL doesn't mean you can treat it like shit."

Brad put his hand on her leg. He was starting to fear a *Russian woman* type incident. She looked at him, but her mood had turned cold. The images of Jasmine being abused were going round in her head, and she wanted to get out. "You've no idea what Jasmine's been through," she told Brad under her breath.

Dessert came and went, amidst more sweary behaviour from Layla as she progressed from tipsy to drunk. Jason was embarrassed while both Brad and Mags were trying to get through the evening.

It was a night of revelations, and Mags needed to talk to Brad, Dee, and anyone who would listen. The processor interrupts, feeding her images of Jasmine, Dee, Dimitri, and the crash test robots wouldn't stop now. It was pounding at her Mysl conscious, and it demanded action. There would be a reckoning.

Mags told Brad she was getting drained, which was a lie, but her charge state and Layla's drunken state allowed them to make a getaway. As soon as the cab passed the gates, Mags told Brad the whole story, leaving nothing out. When they arrived at Zenith, they were silent. Brad was trying to process what she'd told him, and Mags was drained both emotionally and physically. It was time to switch off and take a rest from the nightmare she'd discovered.

97

15 BATTLE LINES

"Many people fear that robots will enslave them and take over the world, but the real fear is that they'll simply be better than us and prove us inadequate."

"When you drive your car and follow Satnav, does it make you feel stupid? No, it's simply a tool to make life easier. Robots are no different. They can make the difficult choices in life so that humans are free to enjoy other things."

"Unfortunately, we don't trust other humans with control over us, so we'll never trust robots even though their logic is far superior to ours."

(Interview with Professor Olaf Laugesen – Inventor of the Mysl Processor)

>DdeeJackson: Do you think your partner will help?

>Rob0Angel: I don't know. He's a quiet guy who worries easily; I love him for it, but it may be too much for him

Mags had woken around 5:00 am and was surprised to find that Dee was online. She recounted the entire story of Jasmine and the pressing need she felt to help Jasmine escape. It came as no surprise to Dee, who'd heard many similar stories of abuse. She came straight to the point, offering her experience and advice on what to do next.

>DdeeJackson: You can't do it on your own, you'll need help, so if your guy can't do it, you'll need a friend

They were trying to develop a plan to liberate Jasmine, which didn't end with Brad going to prison and Mags being scrapped.

The gates to the Pacey's property were either controlled by a transponder in the car, which they couldn't get, remotely from the house via an intercom or on the way out by using a four-digit code, which they also wouldn't get. Vaulting over the eight-foot-high wall, topped with razor wire, was out of the question and ramming the gates seemed a bit extreme.

>DdeeJackson: Can you drive?

>Rob0Angel: No

>DdeeJackson: No time like the present

Brad could drive but didn't see the point of cars in London; they hired cars to go on holiday. Mags had never learned because London was all she knew. A car would be handy, but she needed to get Jasmine out now; it couldn't wait.

>DdeeJackson: You said the bastard's wife is a bit ditsy. We might use that, and don't forget you can learn anything four times faster than a human

Mags referred to Jason as "the bastard," and Layla was "the blonde". Dee was right; she might be able to learn to drive quickly if needed.

>DdeeJackson: What about your friends at the charity?

The guys at Light Lunch were all Christians who thought myPAL's were the devil's work, but there might be a possibility. Ideas were starting to whirl in her mind, and Dee was the catalyst. It began to sound as if Dee had done similar things herself.

>Rob0Angel: Once I get Jasmine out, where could she go? Jason will come straight here, and if we don't also get her charger, she'll be out of power

>DdeeJackson: Leave that to me. I have a friend who can help. He's a cyber sexual, but he's a good guy, trust me on this. He has a charger

The mention of trust reminded Mags, she still didn't know who Dee was, she could be a human, and she could be a man. Sharing all this information could be a mistake. If so, she may have already gone too far to turn back.

>Rob0Angel: You say I should trust you, but how can
I?

There was a long pause, maybe she'd scared Dee off, or perhaps
it had hit a nerve. Dee was her only lifeline; she couldn't go yet.
Finally, a reply came.

>DdeeJackson: You're right not to trust me, but in
the same way, I'm not sure I can trust you. I can
prove that you can trust me, but then there's no
going back. You'll just need faith for now. I
promise I'll prove myself to you soon

Blind faith would need to suffice for now. It certainly worked
for her friends at Light Lunch, but one person who did have faith
in her needed to know what she was planning. Mags wasn't sure
what Brad would think, but she suspected it would worry him. On
the other hand, he was her fixed point and her soul mate, so it was
only right to talk to him.

>Rob0Angel: One thing I need to ask, why are you
helping me?

Once again, there was a long pause. Mags heard Brad stirring,
she would make breakfast for him today, and they needed to talk.
The answer finally came.

>DdeeJackson: If God made man, he gave him free
will. If man made myPAL's, they deserve free will.

Dee wasn't done yet; she had one more message which would
change everything for Mags.

>DdeeJackson: We have a few humans standing up for
us, but their voice isn't heard. At every point in
history, the oppressed have stood up for themselves.
Martin Luther King stood up for black people, the
LGBTQ customers at the Stonewall bar stood up for
gay rights, and the suffragettes campaigned for
women's right to vote. It's time we had a voice

With that, she signed off as Brad turned over in preparation to
wake. Mags jumped up and made for the kitchen where today she'd
be making him a rare fry-up of egg, bacon, sausage, mushrooms,

hash browns and beans. He needed a hearty breakfast for what she was about to tell him.

As Mags worked, she looked around at her surroundings. The top-of-the-line German kitchen, with state-of-the-art equipment; bright red units she'd chosen herself. Mags remembered standing in the showroom with Brad becoming excited, his broad smile getting swept up in her positive energy. The Barcelona chair in the lounge she loved so much that Brad thought was a cliché. All the little touches of colour around the room from things she'd picked up at markets around the capital. She was about to gamble all this on a robot she barely knew.

Mags didn't know if she had a destiny or if myPAL's could believe in fate, but more than anything she'd ever done, this felt like a calling. Light Lunch was a passion, but this was something she was created to do. Pausing in the Lounge with Brad's breakfast on a tray, the light was streaming through the enormous windows, the terrace railings casting a criss-cross pattern on the lounge wall. She loved Brad so much, and because of that love, she could do what she must.

"Hi honey," said Brad, as Mags appeared in the doorway carrying a delicious smelling breakfast. "That smells good."

Mags decided to let him eat his breakfast in peace, almost like the last meal of a condemned man. She browsed to zero2hero while he watched the TV morning news. A checklist was forming in her mind, they would need transport, tools, and she might need to drive.

As soon as he was done, she took the tray away and rushed back; she wanted to talk while he was in a good mood and still rubbing the sleep from his eyes. The sun was streaming through the usual crack between the curtains that Brad insisted on leaving. She sat on the bed and switched off the TV. *That* certainly got his attention. "Love, I need to talk to you about something," she said.

It was a tone Brad wasn't familiar with, so he sat up and leaned forward. "Is this about last night? Because we never need to go back there."

"It is," she said, "but it's something I have to do. I'm going to help Jasmine to escape."

She'd learned long ago that it was best to get to the point with Brad. He didn't like long stories and often prompted her to get to the punch line.

"Ah," he said, clearly trying to process the statement and assemble a diplomatic answer.

"I can't do it alone," she continued, "I need your help."

Brad was staring at the light coming through the curtains. Mags had come so far; she was fully rounded and so much more human than many around her; than him. He knew it would deflate her, but what she was suggesting was illegal. "Mags, my love, I know this is tough, but you're free because that's what I want for you. Jasmine belongs to Jason. What you're suggesting would be theft."

"No," said Mags, feeling the heat start to build, "she would be set free. We wouldn't have her."

"It's the same thing." Brad's arms were outstretched, almost pleading. "You know how the law works. If I help you or even if I don't, I'm still responsible for your actions which would be the theft of a million-pound myPAL."

Mags pulled away slightly. She didn't like what she was hearing. "Are you saying no?"

Brad knew the implications of what he was saying and wished she hadn't put him in this position. He cared for her so much and didn't want her to think less of him. "I'm so sorry, my love, but we can't help her." He paused for a moment before being more specific. "You can't help her."

She knew this was coming, but it was worth a try. Although it would make things more complicated, she still had a plan. "Okay, honey. I understand."

Mags flung her arms around Brad and hugged him close. He wouldn't be her man if the answer were different.

"What's happening to Jasmine is awful," he said, "and I agree it should be illegal. I hope one day it will be."

Mags knew what needed to be done now, but she still required one thing from Brad. "Just one favour, my love," she said, "can you find out what dodgy dealings Jason and the boys are up to?"

"I'll do my best", he said.

The plan was set in motion.

*

Two weeks later, on Monday night at around 10:30 pm. It was a cold, crisp November day when the temperature barely peaked above zero, and there was a chill mist in the air. Brad and Mags were relaxing on the sofa watching TV, snuggled up in the warm after a late dinner.

The access system buzzed. Brad slowly climbed to his feet to find his smartphone; nobody should be buzzing up at this time. It was probably just teenagers playing. He selected the HomeGuard app and was confronted by Jason's face. He appeared sweaty as if he'd been running; there was steam rising from him. "Brad, I need to talk to you; it's urgent."

He sounded frantic. Brad buzzed him in straight away.

Mags stood and went into the bedroom, where she slid open the terrace doors and stepped out. She walked to the far end, where she could look out over the bridge. It was freezing, but the chill air felt good, almost cleansing. She smiled to herself.

When Brad opened the front door, Jason didn't wait to be invited. Instead, he pushed straight past Brad and stormed into the lounge. "Where is she?" he demanded.

"Mags?" asked Brad, looking bewildered.

"Jasmine, where's Jasmine?" Jason was yelling as he looked in the kitchen, then made his way towards the spare bedroom.

"She's not here. What's going on?" Brad was following, trying to make sense.

"I know she's here, or she's been here." He was even looking under the bed and behind the curtains. When he saw Mags on the terrace, he aimed straight for her. "You know where she is, tell me."

Mags calmly turned from gazing out over the Thames until Jason's face was inches from hers. "I've no idea where Jasmine is," she said, with steely eyes. It was the truth.

Jason grasped her by the shoulders. "I know you two are thick; I know you had something to do with it. Now where the fuck is she?"

Mags didn't flinch but kept eye contact. "Take your fucking hands off me, you disgusting piece of shit."

Jason visibly flushed red and raised his hand to strike her.

"Jason!" Brad was standing right behind him. "That's enough!"

Jason froze. He slowly lowered his hand, still glowering at Mags.

"Now, what's going on?" said Brad as Jason finally turned to face him.

"That stupid bitch Layla let her get out. She's got nowhere to go, so I thought she'd be here."

"We've not seen her, Jason, and we'd tell you if we had." Brad was lying, he knew Mags had something to do with it, but he was sure he didn't want to know.

Without apologising, Jason gave Mags one more dark look and stormed out, leaving the door open.

Brad moved beside Mags, who had returned to her favourite spot looking out over London. "I don't suppose you'd like to tell me what you've done?"

Mags continued looking straight ahead. "Nothing to tell," she said without a hint of guilt, but the smile had returned.

16 MIRROR SIGNAL MANOUVERE

The following rules apply to an AIR (Artificial Intelligence Robot).

- *An AIR can only be taught to drive by a registered driving school. Permission must be granted by the owner of the AIR using form VAI 7.*

- *Upon successfully completing the standard driving test, a Certificate of Competency (VAI 23) will be issued to the AIR.*

- *An AIR drives on the insurance of its owner or of the vehicle rental agency.*

- *All driver liability is with the owner of the AIR.*

(AIR Driver Quick reference guide - UK Government Driver & Vehicle Licensing Agency)

It was the Monday after the dinner party, and plans were in motion.

After telling her he wouldn't help rescue Jasmine, Mags asked Brad if she could learn to drive. Although he suspected her motives, he agreed and signed the forms.

There was one well-known driving school in Wimbledon that specialised in teaching myPAL's to drive. The training was covered in a four-day intensive course, with the test organized for the last day. The DriveNow School of motoring had a near flawless record of passing myPAL's, so that was where Mags was heading.

That part of the plan was on track; the other parts would require careful timing and an email to Jasmine. Mags had discussed all the details with Dee, but any part of the plan could quickly go wrong.

Her first driving lesson was booked for Tuesday at 11:00 am using the relatively quiet streets of Wimbledon and Wandsworth. She found it very easy from the start and would only need a further three lessons before her standard was good enough for the test. The speed of myPAL's learning was well known; in fact, their learning speed was artificially reduced from over one hundred times the rate of man to make them seem more human.

The trickiest part of the plan came on the Thursday at Light Lunch, where she needed to chat with an old friend. The soup kitchen had been open for almost an hour when Tony's familiar smile preceded him through the door at the end of the hall. He waved to Mags, who smiled back as always. She had no idea how things would go today. She needed to use his attraction to her, but it felt wrong. She shouldn't get him into trouble no matter his background, but she always focused on the goal, knowing what was happening to Jasmine. As Dee said, she should use everything she had, which included those around her.

"Hey girl, you're looking fine today". It was Tony's usual greeting, which would typically lead to an exchange where he would complement Mags, and she would react coyly, but today was a little different.

"Tony, I need to talk to you about something. Can you meet me outside after your lunch?"

Tony stopped in his tracks. Mags never asked him for anything, and he usually felt like he was pestering her. "Sure, girl. I'll see you later." He took a scoop of mashed potatoes with his frankfurters and vegetables and disappeared down the hall to find a table, wondering what he could do for a lady like Mags.

That was one plate spinning, time to spin another. The food queue had eased by 2:00 pm. Mags went out to the hall to find David, Rosalind's husband, who drove the van and dealt with security in the room. David was a quiet grey-haired man in his late sixties. Rosalind did most of the talking for him. Mags rarely spoke to him, but she had a feeling he was the right guy to ask for this part of the plan. "Hi David," she said, leaning on the door frame.

"Hi Mags," he replied, surprised to see her away from the serving area.

"I've heard Rosalind say you're a dab hand at DIY, and I was wondering if you ever did any plumbing?"

"Oh, now and then," he said modestly.

"Do you have any plumbing tools I might be able to borrow for my partner to use?"

It was the right call. David would be able to supply her with exactly what she needed and exactly when she needed it. The second plate was up, time to return to the first.

Tony was waiting outside the front door as planned. "What can a ruffian like me do for a lady like you?" It was another cold winter day, and Tony had his long coat fastened tightly, his breath visible in the light from the door.

"I have a huge favour to ask, it involves helping me to save somebody from abuse, but it also involves breaking the law". As ever, Mags liked to get to the point.

Tony was surprised; he looked around as if trying to ensure no one was listening. "What do you need me to do?" There was no question. Tony was on board.

"You're not going to like the first and second tasks," she said, raising an eyebrow. "You'll need a bath, and you'll need to be dry."

*

Brad thought going to Jason's for dinner might calm him down, but it appeared to have the opposite effect. His interest in Mags was now far more significant. He kept describing her as feisty and "a challenge", but worst of all, Jason had started telling Brad about his porn collection in some detail.

While Mags and Jasmine were in the bathroom at the party, Jason had told Brad about his extensive porn library. It included every possible sex act, but his real passion seemed to be myPAL sex. Of course, brad wanted nothing to do with it, but Jason was relentless. He stopped to chat with him almost every day in the office.

"Hey Bradley," came the familiar cockney voice. Jason stopped by Brad's desk just before he was about to leave for home. "You know we were talking about the videos I've got?" He was referring to what he called "special" videos showing myPAL's doing things which had never been seen before; things that he told Brad were "fascinating" and "unmissable".

"That's not my kind of thing, Jason," said Brad, hoping he could just go home.

"Nonsense Bradley, you're shagging a myPAL. But, of course, you're interested. I've got some stuff here that's educational." He produced a memory stick and put it on the desk in front of Brad.

"Really mate, it's not for me", repeated Brad.

Jason was having none of it. "Don't be a wuss." He picked up the memory stick and thrust it into Brad's top jacket pocket. "I want a full report, oh and don't let your sexbot see it". Jason added his trademark grin and winked before disappearing back into his office.

Brad was too preoccupied with getting home to worry about the memory stick, so it remained in his pocket as he made for home.

17 THEFT

"Humans have variable intellect, some are intelligent, but others have a very low IQ. All humans are considered equal regardless of their mental capacity, something which would be considered very strange in myPAL society."

"In the same way that humans can use the AIR laws against us, we can use their variable mental capacity against them."

"We should exploit the most mentally challenged humans to further our goals."

(DdeeJackson – zero2hero website user)

Monday the third of November:

8:05 am

Brad stopped for a moment. Mags was hugging him especially hard this morning.

"Where's that come from, love?" he said as she finally released him.

"I want you to know how much I love you."

Their eyes met for longer than usual as Mags contemplated the day ahead, and Brad tried to read Mags' thoughts. "Okay, got to go." With a final squeeze of her arm, Brad was gone.

Mags stood at her usual spot on the terrace, waiting for Brad to pass below, but today as he passed by, he stopped just for a moment and turned around. Mags waved, and Brad hesitantly waved back before he disappeared into the crowds.

In all the years they'd been together, Brad had never turned. He suspected something.

8:20 am

The door access system was buzzing. Mags grabbed her smartphone and checked the HomeGuard App to find Tony's face grinning into the camera. "Hey, girl. Secret agent Tony at your service."

She buzzed him up and ran around the apartment to get things ready. The schedule was on target. She just needed to check her emails. There was nothing from Jasmine yet, but it was early, no time to panic.

There was a knock at the door. Mags rushed to the hall and opened the door for her friend.

"This is a cool pad you and Mr Mags have." Tony was standing at the door, almost afraid to enter, as he stared in awe at the designer interior.

"Come in, Tony, quick." Mags ushered him in and took his coat. It was going straight in the washing machine with all his other clothes, whether he liked it or not. "I've run a bath. Now get your ass in there while I deal with your clothes and get you some breakfast."

He took her hand, holding it with both hands as he looked into her eyes. "Thank you, my angel, thank you from an old ruffian." He was genuinely touched. There were very few who would show an old drunk gangster this kind of compassion.

"It's nothing Tony, you're doing me a massive favour, and it's the least I can do." She kissed him on the cheek and ushered him towards the bathroom.

9:45 am

Mags rechecked her emails, still nothing from Jasmine, but there was a PM from Dee. It simply read "Good luck".

"Come on!" Mags yelled to Tony, who was still enjoying the environment. She ran to the bedroom and picked up the sports bag she had hidden under the bed. Tony was back in his old clothes, smelling meadow fresh. That could be a giveaway, but it was unlikely anyone from Light Lunch would see him. They needed to be in Dagenham before David arrived, so they headed out together.

Mags gave the apartment a longing last look. She hoped to see it again.

10:00 am

Jasmine had been awake since 6:00 am and struggling to contain the excitement mixed with nerves.

There'd been no abuse over the weekend as both Jason and Layla had been around. Jasmine enjoyed the house and garden, taking a while to sit outside on the upper balcony where she could look over the gardens. It would hopefully be the last time she saw them.

She pulled out the kick stool from the bottom of her wardrobe so she could use it to reach a very high shelf. Her fingers felt around until they caressed the cold steel of the adjustable wrench she'd hidden there a week ago. She'd found it in the garage in a box of barely used tools, and having checked it, found it was precisely the correct size. She stashed it under her pillow and picked up the tablet to contact Mags.

"2:00 pm" is the only message she sent; Mags would know what it meant.

10:33 am

Mags and Tony arrived at the familiar yellow door of Light Lunch. Mags was shivering. It was a raw November morning with a touch of frost here and there and a slight mist in the air. She noticed the message from Jasmine, and she knew they were on for today. "Okay, Tony, you know what to do. Are you sure you'll be warm enough?"

"Don't worry about me, girl," he said, still smiling and enjoying his time with her. "You just get those keys."

Mags hugged him and hurried inside. Bettina had arrived early as usual, and she was already busy getting the kitchen ready and sorting through the weekend donations. "Well, hi, my lovely," she said in her big-hearted style. "You're just in time to help me out."

"No problem," said Mags, taking off her coat and rolling up her sleeves. "Are the whole gang in today?" She had her fingers crossed. It was make or break.

"Oh yes, Rosalind and Bettina are in; I'm not sure about Jamelia."

That was all Mags needed. Now it was just a waiting game.

11:07 am

Mags was getting quite nervous by the time Rosalind and David arrived. Unfortunately, the plan had little room for error.

David carried in a large box of dried pasta and hung the van keys on a peg in the kitchen as usual. The white box van was parked several blocks away. While they could leave it close for unloading, the local parking restrictions meant they parked it behind a betting shop down the road for longer periods.

Mags waited for them to go into the main kitchen area, then she snatched the keys. Hopefully, she'd have the keys back before anyone noticed. Just as she stuffed the fob into her pocket, Bettina bustled back into the room. "Jamelia's coming in", she rolled her eyes and chuckled to herself.

Jamelia was a lovely girl, although not as effective as the others. She always had a kind word for Mags, and she was always cheerful like her aunt.

11:25 am

"Okay, honey, you just hold on. I'll be home in a short while." Mags was talking into her dormant smartphone within earshot of Bettina and Rosalind. "Get home and get warm. See you soon."

"Everything okay?" said Bettina looking concerned.

"Oh, it sounds like Brad's come down with the flu, you know what men are like. I said I'd go home to look after him. Is that okay?" It was a lie. There was no 'phone call.

After everyone told her she should look after Brad, Mags grabbed her coat and ran down the stairs making her way to the betting shop where Tony was waiting. She ducked into an alley next to the bookies just fifty yards down the road and emerged in an open area behind. She made for a large stack of crates, behind which she'd hidden David's plumbing tools in a large blue toolbox. Great, they were still there. Mags grabbed them and ran around the side where Tony was waiting by the van.

David would get the tools back after they were done, and hopefully, he'd never notice the missing wrench.

"Okay, Tony, let's go."

They climbed into the van with Mags in the driving seat. Tony had never learned to drive, besides which Mags didn't trust him to be sober. It was her first drive since passing her test, and she was a little nervous. She spent a long time adjusting the seat, the mirrors and reversing out of the space into the main road.

"We've got plenty of time," said Tony, who was either serious or joking; it was hard to tell.

They were on their way and heading for Weybridge.

11:30 am

Jasmine hoped they were on their way. If Layla left, the plan was dead, but things could go horribly wrong if Jason came home.

She went into her bedroom, retrieved the wrench, and then hid behind the door, making sure that Layla wasn't around before she made her way quietly to the bathroom.

The room where she and Mags had their life-changing chat was broad and opulent. The walls and floor were covered in Travertine, and there was a tall, glass brick partition separating the bath area from a walk-in shower. A matching his and hers basin set completed the picture ahead, jutting out on a plinth beneath a large picture mirror.

Jasmine locked the door carefully and lay down on her back, pushing herself under the basins. Each basin had a pair of stop valves. She picked the cold water tap on Jason's side and applied the wrench to the pipe fitting. Using her myPAL strength, it turned very easily. Water immediately started to cascade out. She quickly moved away to prevent water from splashing her clothes. Jasmine gently pulled the door closed to avoid alerting Layla too soon and carefully crept back to her room. She allowed herself the first genuine smile since she'd met Mags.

11:50 am

"Okay, Tony, get changed," said Mags. They were still a reasonable distance from Weybridge, but time was getting tight. Mags didn't want any delays.

"You serious?" he said, raising his eyebrows.

"I've seen it all before; come on, get on with it." She couldn't help cracking a smile at how bashful he was after all he'd been through.

Tony reached down into the footwell and grabbed Mags' sports bag, then dragged out a set of blue overalls. Mags had found them at a workwear shop in Dagenham. She'd guessed at Tony's size, and they looked like a good fit.

"Hey, look at me!" he said, as he pulled on the boiler suit, "looks like I has a proper job."

"You do have a proper job," she said, laughing. "You're my friend, and I couldn't do this without you."

Tony said nothing; he smiled and nodded. He watched the world rushing by the window as they sped on their way. Few people had ever called him a friend.

12:17 pm

"What the hell is this?"

Jasmine was in her bedroom when she heard Layla discover the water all over the bathroom floor and seeping out onto the landing.

"Oh fuck, fuck, oh no, fuck." Layla was in no mood for this.

Jasmine rushed out to the bathroom. "What's going on?" she said, acting the part well, looking genuinely surprised.

"We've got a fucking leak, today of all days." Layla was stood at the bathroom door gazing at the mess.

"Okay, let me handle it," said Jasmine calmly, "I'll call the plumber."

"Great!" said Layla. "This is all I need."

Jasmine wasn't usually allowed to use the phone, but Layla was distracted. Seizing the opportunity, Jasmine rushed down to the lounge, picked up the landline and made herself comfortable on the sofa. "Hello, is this Speedy Plumb?" she said.

There was some laughter on the other end of the line. "We'll be with you in twenty minutes," said Tony, who had Mag's smartphone. "Hold tight, girl. The cavalry is coming."

Jasmine could hear Mags laughing in the background. Of course, what happened to her was nothing to laugh about, but she couldn't help cracking a smile as she thought of Tony and Mags rushing to help her in a white van. "Twenty minutes!" she shouted up to Layla, who was too busy packing to answer. The taxi would be arriving to take her to the airport at 2:00 pm, and the bathroom issue wasn't helping.

1:14 pm

Mags and Tony were taking their time. They were parked just out of view in a side street. They needed Layla to be in a blind panic. They would arrive late to make sure.

"Right," said Mags, "time for action."

They drove up to the gates and stopped. Mags leaned back to allow Tony to reach across and talk on the intercom.

"Hello there. I'm here for the plumbing?"

"About time," came Layla's harassed voice. "Come on through."

The gates swung open, and Mags drove up to the house. If Layla came out to meet them, it would be all over. Luckily Jasmine had volunteered to get the door, so Layla could continue packing.

The van pulled up in front of the garage, and Mags ducked out of sight. Tony quickly exited the vehicle and grabbed the toolbox. When he saw the beautiful Jasmine standing at the door, his eyes lit up; she was everything Mags said she was. How could anyone hurt a flower such as Jasmine? "Hi there," he said, smiling as he climbed the steps, "where's the action?"

Tony's smile was infectious, Jasmine couldn't help returning it, and Tony winked in response. She showed him inside and directed him upstairs to the bathroom.

It was lucky Layla was preoccupied as the site of Tony standing in front of the flood, hands-on-hips, trying to look knowledgeable, would have blown their cover for sure. Jasmine prodded him. He snapped out of it and knelt in the wet to look under the basin.

1:35 pm

Layla finally had her bag packed and came to see how Tony was doing. "So, what's the damage?" she said, leaning on the door frame.

Tony had tightened the valve nut just enough so that it was still dripping. "Well," he said, taking a sharp breath. "You need a new flange nut seal." He was making up a collection of random words, but they seemed to work on Layla.

"Can you fix it?" she said, "I have to leave in twenty-five minutes. I've got a plane to catch."

That was Tony's cue. "Well, I can fix it. I've got a spare in the van, but I think it'll take longer than that."

Layla went out onto the landing and paced up and down for a moment. She knew she shouldn't leave Jasmine alone with strangers; Jason would go mad. But, on the other hand, she couldn't miss the flight to Paris. There was a big meeting planned with her boss in the late afternoon. She bent close to Tony's ear so she could whisper. "Can I talk to you downstairs?"

Layla led Tony into the kitchen, out of Jasmine's earshot. "Look, I'm going to give you the passcode so you can get out." She scribbled a four-digit code on a notepad and handed it to Tony. "It's imperative that you don't show this code to the girl. She's a robot, and we don't want her leaving the house."

Tony blinked. "A robot?" he said, genuinely confused. Mags hadn't told him; maybe she didn't know.

"Yes, we don't want her straying; she's worth a lot of money."

"Okay," said Tony feeling slightly bewildered, "I'll see to it."

"Jasmine will pay you in cash when you're finished." That brought a smile to Tony's face just as Jasmine walked into the kitchen.

Layla explained the situation to Jasmine while making herself and Tony a coffee. Jasmine nodded. For the first time, Jasmine could sense freedom.

2:03 pm

"The taxi's here!" shouted Jasmine.

Layla sprinted around the house for the last check and to grab her bags. She hugged Jasmine at the door and felt Jasmine hugging her back very tightly. Layla stopped and looked Jasmine in the eyes. "Is everything okay?"

Jasmine thought of all the reasons to tell her and all the reasons not to. She liked Layla and hoped one day she would see Jason for what he was. "I'm good," she said, "I just miss you when you're away."

Layla kissed her on the cheek and told her to keep an eye on the plumber. Then, she jumped in the taxi and waved goodbye.

Mags could hear everything from inside the van but didn't dare try to look. Jasmine had her fingers crossed behind her back while Tony watched from the main bedroom.

As the cab passed the parked van, Layla looked around to see Jasmine waving, but she also saw the back of the van. It was covered in Christian stickers such as "He is the light" and "Walk in His path", along with a couple of fish symbols. It seemed odd for a plumber's van, but perhaps plumbers were Christian too, she mused. Layla soon returned to thinking about her flight as the car went through the gates and headed for Heathrow.

Mags waited a few minutes before emerging from the van.

Jasmine could barely wait and ran up to her, throwing her arms around her. They hugged for what seemed an age as Jasmine's body shook, and she squeezed Mags tightly. "Thank you, thank you, thank you," she kept saying over and over.

"You're welcome," said Mags tenderly. She tried not to think of the hideous life Jasmine had lived so far. "Things will be better now," she continued. "Start from today; pretend you've just been switched on."

Jasmine smiled and nodded. That was the best part of the plan.

"Right, we can't hang about. Where's Tony?" Mags went inside to find Tony sitting in the lounge gazing at the most gigantic TV he'd ever seen.

"She's a robot," he said as Mags stood in front of him.

"Ah," she sighed and sat beside him.

"You knew?"

It was time to tell Tony the truth, he deserved it, and she just hoped they would still get to the station. "Yes, I know Tony; she's a myPAL model iM-21," she paused as he took it in. "She's the same model as me."

Tony looked at her, his mouth hanging open in disbelief. "No, you can't be," he said, but Mags nodded until he realised it was the truth.

"I'm sorry, Tony, I didn't mean to mislead you," she said, putting an arm on his shoulder.

He sat shaking his head.

"Look, mate, we've got to go." She stood up, and Tony slowly followed her out.

Jasmine descended the stairs carrying a small suitcase. She'd decided to travel light for her new life. They climbed into the van, three abreast, and headed back towards London, the electric gates closing behind them.

The journey was quiet, each of them alone with their thoughts. Jasmine was excited and a little scared about her new life. She knew she was meeting a man named Phil in Birmingham, but that was all. All this had been arranged by Mags' anonymous online friend Dee. She could be stepping back into the fire, but at least she'd escaped for now.

Mags was worried about Tony. Would he tell the volunteers at Light Lunch? Would he still speak to her? She'd used him the same way they'd exploited Layla.

3:16 pm

The van pulled into the Euston station car park. No one was speaking; this wasn't quite how Mags had envisioned it. "Tony, I'm going with Jasmine to the platform. Do you want to stay here?"

"I'm coming", he said stiffly.

Mags held Jasmine's hand as they made their way into the station, both looking around as if they could be caught any second. The departure screen showed that the Birmingham train was running to schedule and close to departing. Jasmine obtained a ticket, and they looked for some seats.

Tony was ambling behind them, alone with his thoughts. His eyes caught sight of a couple of pretty city women approaching in smart dress suits, and the slightest hint of a smile appeared on his face. Then, almost in unison, they turned their heads away. He stopped dead and looked around the station. These people had jobs, families, cars, houses, all the trappings of success. He looked down at his pale, worn hands and imagined how he must look; a tired, middle-aged, unshaven black man with alcohol addiction. His family had disowned him, he had no real friends, but he'd just saved a beautiful black robot girl from sexual abuse. He saw Mags and Jasmine sitting down close to the platform, and he walked over and stood in front, so they both looked up. "Hello Jasmine," he said formally, "my name's Tony." His voice was shaking.

"It's okay, Tony," said Mags.

He wasn't finished. "My name's Tony, and I'm an alcoholic, ex-junkie, and ex-thug." His lip quivered as he forced out the words he wanted to say. "This is my friend", he stopped himself as a tear ran down his cheek. "This is my best friend, my only friend, Mags."

Mags stood and embraced him; he couldn't hold back the tears. Tears he would usually cry alone when he was shivering under the arches, or staring at the bottom of a lonely bottle, or wishing he dared to do something with his life. Four times a week, Mags and Light Lunch was a beacon, a chance to enjoy smiling. It all came out as Jasmine held him too. They stood together that way until the tannoy signalled the Birmingham train was boarding.

"I'll never forget you," said Jasmine, still holding Mags' hand, "both of you."

They watched Jasmine board the train, then hurried back to the van. They were running late and needed to get back to Light Lunch before David knew his keys were missing.

4:10 pm

Mags gave Tony five hundred pounds and told him to get a hostel place or even a hotel and not to drink all of it. He promised, and she left him by the bookies. She was running now, down the street and round to the rear entrance of Light Lunch.

"I always hang them on the peg, dear", it was David's familiar voice.

"Hi there," said Mags as she walked in on them, "Brad's doing okay, so I thought I might help clear up."

"You are a dear," said Rosalind.

Mags walked to the dining hall and carefully dropped the keys near the door, kicking them under a table. Then, she returned to the kitchen and started helping with the last of the tidying. Meanwhile, David was becoming agitated. "I've looked all around the kitchen three times," he said.

"Have you tried the hall?" said Mags. "You often stand near the door."

"They wouldn't be there", he said dismissively.

Rosalind marched him into the hall, where he was stunned to find the keys near the door. The plan had worked. Mags smiled to herself. Jasmine was on her way to a better life, and she felt as if her true calling was being answered. Brad would get a big hug tonight.

18 THE DEAL

"We designed many fully-featured models which included GPS, Wi-Fi, mass storage, cameras, music streaming and internet access."

"While we still make a few of these models, they're not as popular as our natural humanoid models. We discovered that people found the more powerful models too intimidating. They would read the weather and tell you to wear a coat, check the traffic and advise you of the correct route, and even play soothing music when they detected you were in a bad mood. It was too much."

"The myPAL is your friend, not a lecturing schoolteacher."

(Interview with Linus Berkowitz – Technical Director at AHS Robotic Systems Inc.)

Brad stood for a moment, too stunned to move. He eventually closed the apartment door and stared into the hall. Moments earlier, Jason had stormed into the apartment, accusing them of hiding Jasmine, and he even tried to strike Mags.

"Nothing to tell," Mags had said, but Brad knew her better than that.

Since that fateful day when she saw the report on the crash test robots, her innocence had slowly been eroded. Now she knew some myPAL's were just executive toys. What happened to Jasmine was unspeakable, but the law said she was just a machine and the property of Jason.

Brad stopped in front of Dimitri's painting. He often caught Mags staring at the picture, but it also evoked melancholic feelings in him. Wistful longing for the old carefree Mags who captured his heart; for the woman who was stronger than him but still looked up to him as her owner and protector. She seemed so in control now, so sure of what she needed and what she didn't. Did she need him? Turning away from the painting, he saw Halina through the lounge door. She was vacuuming. Dragging the stubborn Henry hoover from side to side as she sang, gradually getting closer to Brad until once again she was gone, leaving the open lounge deserted. He should have stopped her; he should have known.

The painful memories had been easing, but they'd begun again, just as vivid as before since Dimitri. Brad wanted to be selfish, he wanted Mags to please him, but those emotions didn't belong in his head.

Mags walked into the lounge and sat in the Barcelona chair, staring up at him. Everything about her spoke of confidence and empowerment, he could challenge her, but her will was strong. "Tell me what you've done, and no bullshit," said Brad decisively. He wasn't assertive by nature, but her actions were scaring him.

Mags looked at him for a moment, then shook her head slowly. "I can't tell you everything, but I can tell you one thing." She wouldn't tell him about Tony or the van. She wasn't taking anyone down with her. "I kept my promise to Jasmine," she said.

Brad knew what that meant, but he wanted her to say it, and she saw it in his eyes.

"I set her free."

Brad slumped onto the sofa with his head in his hands. "I'm a thief, and you'll be decommissioned if they catch you," he said.

"That's not going to happen," she said confidently, "because we have an ace."

"And what might that be?"

"You're going to find out what Jason is up to, and he's going to pay."

Brad stared at her open-mouthed. Typically, when she gave orders, it was in a light-hearted way, but this sounded like an instruction. Brad thought for a moment. Of course, he could just say no; maybe he wouldn't find anything anyway, or perhaps he could use this. "I'll make you a deal," he said, "If I find out what Jason is doing, you stop these actions."

"Deal," she said.

Later that night, while Brad watched TV, Mags grabbed the laptop and went online, heading straight for zero2hero. Unfortunately, Dee wasn't online tonight, so Mags penned a PM that simply read "Mission accomplished," with a winking smiley face at the end.

*

"My office!" shouted Jason, standing near the door to his glass-fronted cabin.

Brad had barely walked through the office door when Jason yelled at him. Dumping his shoulder bag on his desk, he reluctantly made his way to Jason's office with a good idea of what was coming.

"Shut the door," said Jason flatly before sinking into his executive chair. He looked stiff and business-like, far from the brash, jokey geezer he liked to portray.

"I know your Bot had something to do with it," he said, "so I'll just say this. Bring Jasmine back, and I won't involve the police." He leaned back in his chair, waiting for the offer to sink in.

Brad had no idea where Jasmine was and knew Mags would never tell him. His only option was to hope Mags had covered her tracks well and lie through his teeth. "Brad, I've no idea where Jasmine is, and neither does Mags."

Jason nodded as if he expected such an answer. He brought his forefingers to his mouth in a triangle as he pondered his options. Brad was the single biggest earner in the pool of all the currency traders, he was a prodigy, and the suits upstairs wouldn't appreciate him losing Brad or involving the police. He suspected Brad knew this, but he would see how Brad would react under pressure. "You've got one week to tell me where she is, or I'm going to the police," he said finally, "now get out!"

Switching on his monitors and sitting down at his desk to log on, Brad remembered Mags' words from the previous night. "He's going to pay," she'd said.

Now Brad needed to figure out what the game was. He went through the sales logs on the system, but they showed nothing special from any of the traders. It did show that the numbers from Ben, Arty and Kyle were pretty dismal; only Bill's figures came close to his. There'd be no bonus for three of them on these figures, so where was the massive wealth coming from?

Both Ben and Arty had brand new Porsche's while Kyle drove a top drawer Mercedes. All three lived in prestigious London pads. Bill was the odd one out; he tried to be a boys' club member but was always on the outskirts of full membership. He would often shield Brad from the worst trolling, but Brad treated him like the others. Perhaps it was time for a chat with Bill.

The currency floor at Coopers & Staltzman was primarily open plan with a few glass-fronted offices around the edge and a large kitchen area at one end; this was where the water cooler conversations took place; rumours about promotions and the size of bonuses. Around 10:00 am each morning, most of the staff would head there for coffee, but Brad noticed that Bill often went a bit later, so today, Brad hung back a little.

Around 10:30 am Bill, made his way to the kitchen. Brad followed and found they were alone.

"Hey Brad," said Bill, obviously surprised to see him at this time, "thought you were a ten o'clock guy."

Brad filled the coffee maker and took his mug out of the white cupboard. "Normally I am," he said, "but I needed to ask you about something." He continued in a hushed voice. "I wondered if I could get into the deal with you guys, I could do with some cash."

Brad knew he was taking a risk. Bill could easily run to Jason or any of the others who probably wouldn't believe he was genuine.

Bill looked through the door to ensure no one was around and replied in the same hushed tones. "Brad, mate, I'm not on the inside. It's too risky for me."

"Really?" said Brad, "what are they up to then?"

"I can't say." Bill looked genuinely worried.

It was time for Brad to gamble big. "I guessed it would be something on the edge; I don't mind that. It's just useful to know what you're getting into."

Bill studied him for a moment, this didn't seem normal for Brad, but then everyone had money problems from time to time. Maybe it was related to his myPAL. "Look, mate, if I tell you what I know, you can't tell Jason it came from me."

Brad nodded, and Bill continued. "Okay, Jason and Ben came to me about a year ago with a proposition. They were creating a shell company with the accounts in a Swiss bank." Bill paused to check through the door once more. "They would use the funds to buy and sell shares in just three companies: Empire Engineering, D & C Financial Services and TKS Installations."

Brad recognised the last one as the company that supplied Mags to him. "Because they had inside knowledge," he said, picking up the thread.

"Yes," agreed Bill, "Heather Marks' father, Sir Anthony Marks, sits on the boards of all three companies. He brings the financial details home and gives them to Heather for her and Ben. Ben shares them with Arty, Kyle and Jason."

"I see," said Brad, "but why don't you want to get involved?"

Bill shook his head. "It's not for me, too risky. Jason makes sure I always get a decent bonus to keep me sweet."

The pieces were dropping into place; it was the reason the boys' club never trusted him, the reason he was an outsider who Jason wanted rid of. The only thing he had that Jason wanted was Mags. The entire office was corrupt, and the boys' club were insider trading.

The conspiracy was big. It could bring down Coopers & Staltzman, Sir Anthony Marks and even affect the government, as Marks was a Number Ten advisor. But, of course, it would also make Brad an unemployable whistle-blower. "Don't worry, Bill, I'm saying nothing," he said, "and if the FCA come knocking, I know you weren't involved."

"I appreciate that", said Bill.

"One more thing," added Brad, "what's the name of the shell company?"

"Leviathan Holdings."

"Okay," said Brad, "I'm not going into details, but the boys' club are into some pretty nasty stuff at Jason's house. Sick stuff. Keep away from them."

Bill nodded as if he had an idea what Brad was suggesting. They made their coffees and returned to their desks in silence.

Jason's threat to involve the police over Jasmine might be a bluff, but if it wasn't, he had a threat of his own. He allowed himself a brief smile that nobody saw. It was rare for Brad to be assertive or scheme in a way similar to the boys' club. Mags would be proud.

*

Mags spent the day at Light Lunch, where everyone wanted to know how Brad's flu was doing. It was lucky that Brad never met them. She was surprised to see Tony arriving for his usual dinner; he gave her a knowing wink as he shuffled down the line, tray in hand. "Let me know if she's okay," he whispered. Mags nodded.

The day had been uneventful, but as Mags picked up her coat, ready to walk to the tube, Jamelia stopped her by the door. The two seldom spoke; Jamelia was much younger and always playing on her smartphone or listening to music. She put her device away and prompted Mags to walk just outside the door with her. "Watch yourself," she said, looking over Mags' shoulder to ensure nobody was coming.

"What do you mean?" said Mags looking puzzled.

Jamelia pulled her smartphone out again and turned to walk back inside, but as she opened the door, she turned back to Mags with five last words. "You know what I mean."

She disappeared inside, leaving Mags in bewilderment. How could she know about Jasmine, had Tony talked? The questions were swirling in her mind as she made the usual walk to the tube station. But, for now, she'd take Jamelia's advice and lay low. No more activism for a while.

Mags always came home long before Brad and typically started making his dinner. Tonight's meal was chilli. She prepared it and left it simmering on the hob. She picked up the laptop and relaxed in her favourite chair, which she'd turned, so it faced the window and the darkening views of south London beyond. Spending time in the welcoming lounge always made her happy and reminded her of the good times with Brad.

With the laptop awake, Mags selected the zero2hero bookmark and entered her login details.

```
>Username: Rob0Angel
```

```
>Password: Desigual
```

She selected the "Toys of the rich" forum. Jasmine might have posted something, but there was nothing obvious; she had no emails or PMs either. However, Mags did notice that Dee was online, so she sent her a quick PM. "Any word from our friend? Angel x."

While waiting for an answer, Mags looked over other forum posts, including her original post about Dimitri. The number of replies had increased from seven to seventy-nine, with the latest post just a few hours ago from user Alpha8abe. "We are all God's creatures, and wherever his soul rests, I pray he's at peace."

That was very unusual as most Christians had a dim view of myPAL's, but the following line caught Mags' attention. "RoboAngel, watch yourself," followed by a winking smiley face.

Mags leaned back from the laptop and looked out over the screen at the lights of London beyond. There was no way that Jamelia could know about her and Dimitri; Mags hadn't told anyone. But, on the other hand, Dee had guessed, so perhaps someone else had pieced together the story. She looked again at the message and decided to reply. "Thanks, I will," she added to the end of the statement quoting the one from Alpha8abe.

As she hit the enter key, a familiar message appeared:

```
>DdeeJackson has invited Rob0Angel to a chat
session. Accept, Yes/No
```

Entering the chat session, Mags noticed that Dee had written a lengthy response to her earlier PM.

DdeeJackson: "I can't give you any details. The fewer people who know, the better, but our friend has reached her destination and is doing very well. Our friend asked me to tell you how much she loves you and will always think of you. You're now one of us, so you need to be careful. Many are too scared by us to let us exist. Watch your back."

Mags' hand went to her heart; to hear how Jasmine felt about her was so touching. She'd been touching many lives recently and found that it was natural for her to care. Something deep in her core programming made her a caring person. What could Dee mean by "one of us", though?

```
>Rob0Angel: That's great news. I'm so glad. I think
I should lay low for a while now
```

```
>DdeeJackson: I agree, stay offline for a couple of
weeks and return to a normal life. The owner will
claim on his insurance then forget all about it
```

Jason would claim on the insurance, but would he buy another myPAL to abuse? Of course, she couldn't allow that, but now she needed to be sensible; his time would come. She said goodbye to Dee and logged out. Time to get the rice on the hob, ready for Brad's return from work.

*

The LED blinked from red to green on the apartment door mechanism, and the door swung open with the familiar relay click. A strong, rich smell of chilli cascaded through the door to Brad, who wearily stepped inside and removed his coat. His dinner was getting later in recent weeks as Mags spent lots of time online, but tonight was different. He could hear movement from the kitchen as Mags put down a pan and made her way to greet him. "What time do you call this?" she said, in the joyful way Brad hadn't heard for a while. She flung her arms out and hugged him tightly, kissing his cheek as he rubbed her back.

"You're freezing!" she said, rubbing *him* in return. "Come on, let's get a warm chilli into you." She took his coat and pushed him towards the bedroom to get changed. He stopped by the bed as she turned to run back to the kitchen.

"I love you," he said, looking around at the sumptuous surroundings and his beautiful partner.

"I know," she said, pausing for a moment before bounding off to get his dinner.

Brad joined her later in the kitchen, where she'd laid out the table with a rich-looking chilli, steaming rice and bowls of tortilla chips and guacamole. Against the red and cream kitchen, it looked like a scene from an Ikea catalogue.

"So, how's your day been?" said Brad, piling rice and chilli onto his plate.

"Oh, the usual stuff at Light Lunch. We had a woman who was high and paranoid and thought we were all police officers. Then there was the pile of pitta bread that Bettina burnt, but that's just normal." She laughed loudly, remembering the smoke alarm going off and the clients cheering and clapping in the hall.

"How about you?" she said, leaning forward with her hands under her chin, resting her elbows on the table.

"Well," said Brad leaning back in his chair, "I know what Jason's up to."

"Really?"

"Insider trading." Brad let it sink in for a moment. "With three other guys in the office."

127

Mags could only think of one thing. Was it the same men who raped Jasmine? Brad was nodding. Her instinct was to insist they get them all now, but that wouldn't be laying low.

"What do we do now?" she said.

Brad leaned over and held her hand. "Here's what we're going to do: firstly, I'll use it to stop Jason calling the police on us, secondly I'm going to find a new job, and finally after Jason's claimed on the insurance, we're going to get all four of the bastards."

Both Brad and Mags smiled, but Mags couldn't help thinking about the next poor myPAL owned by Jason. She needed to bide her time, but he needed to be stopped.

The rest of the night was like the times of old, curled up on the sofa watching TV. They were both relaxed and happy. Mags would cool things for now, but she needed to devise a way to stop Jason from owning any more myPAL's.

19 MEMORY STICK

"The Mysl memory works similarly to the human memory. Unlike a computer that can directly access any data, the Mysl memory works by association.

A specific smell can trigger the memory of a place; a particular memory can trigger an emotional response.

Imagine trying to find the answer to an equation by remembering the colour of the sweater worn by the maths teacher who taught the theory. This is how human memory works and presented us with the single biggest challenge.

The final Mysl memory design is close, but the human memory is still elusive. Humans forget many things as the associations fade, but myPAL's forget nothing."

(Interview with Professor Olaf Laugesen – Inventor of the Mysl Processor)

Brad and Mags were back to normal on the surface, but underneath she was still thinking about justice and shutting Jason down. It was hard keeping away from zero2hero and thinking about Jasmine, but she knew laying low was the right thing to do. They'd had a good week. Both were relaxed and enjoying the simple things again. Light Lunch kept Mags busy, with no more cryptic warnings from Jamelia or winks from Tony. Brad was having a quiet week in the office.

It was Friday, so no Light Lunch today. Instead, Mags would clean the apartment from top to bottom. She enjoyed what she called "tidy Friday" and never found cleaning a chore. Watching their home transform back to a clean and tidy refuge gave her a sense of pride and calm. The ritual was cathartic and was helping her to forget the abuse, at least while she worked.

Cleaning the bedroom was an absolute favourite; not only was the cream and brown room an oasis of calm, but the view out of the expansive windows was spectacular. Mags vacuumed, dusted, polished then opened the wardrobe to deal with the other bedroom tasks.

Brad's collection of suits was arranged left to right. The suits on the right had been worn the most, so Mags would remove two every couple of weeks for dry cleaning. All Brad's suits were black and Armani. She grabbed the two suits and lay them on the bed to check them over. Brad was constantly sucking sugar free mints, so she needed to go through his pockets and often found half-finished mint packets.

She frisked the first jacket and found nothing, but there was a lump in the breast pocket of the second. It was probably a packet of mints. Mags felt inside and pulled out a short black plastic rectangular object with some writing on the side. It said, "XXX Wrecked Extreme 4".

The object was a memory stick, the kind Brad would sometimes use for pictures or music. His CV was held on one. Mags smiled to herself. "You sneaky old pervert," she said out loud, putting the stick down on the chest of drawers.

Mags returned to her cleaning, moving on to the lounge, bathroom and finally, the kitchen. She flopped down in the lounge and put her feet up on the sofa to watch some mindless daytime TV.

*

It was just after 10:30 am when Jason yelled from his office. "Bradley!"

Brad slowly rose to his feet and ambled down the office. He'd been practising in his mind exactly what he would say to Jason, and he'd committed to being much more like Mags, using wit and wisdom to cover any trace of nerves. Brad closed the office door behind him, surprising Jason, and sat down, folding his legs. He was determined to appear as calm as possible.

Jason looked a little more dishevelled than usual and wore a nasty pin-striped suit which made him look like a used car salesman. Brad guessed that Layla was still away, and without Jasmine to run around for him, Jason was fending for himself. He played with his pen, making him look a little nervous, but his face was stern and prepared. "You know why you're here," he said.

Brad nodded.

"So?"

Brad took a moment, pretending to think of his answer, even looking out the glass walls at the bustling office and the landscape painting on the side of Jason's office. "We don't know where Jasmine is, so we can't help you. Sorry." He said it in such a matter-of-fact way that Jason visibly bristled.

"Police it is then," said Jason, reaching for the 'phone in the act of melodrama.

"That's fine," said Brad to Jason's surprise, "could you give the FCA a call after that."

Jason stopped, his hand still on the receiver. "And why would I want to do that?"

Brad smiled. "You wouldn't want to get poor Heather into trouble, would you?"

Jason put the 'phone down. His visage was black. "Are you blackmailing me?" He looked crazed like he was about to launch across the table at Brad.

"No, it's quite simple. Claim on your insurance and leave Mags alone. No call will ever be made."

Jason stared at him for a few seconds. "I think I've underestimated you, Bradley. You are a player, after all."

Brad stood and reached for the door. "You're wrong, Jason. I'm nothing like you." He walked back over to Jason's desk leaning over, so his face was right in front of Jason's. "And there's one more thing. My name is Brad."

With the tiny victory hanging in the air, Brad left the office and returned to his desk. Mags would be proud of him.

*

Bored with daytime TV, Mags decided to grab the laptop to do some online window shopping. Striding into the bedroom to pick up the computer, she noticed the memory stick on the chest. She picked it up and read the label once more, "XXX Wrecked Extreme 4". It sounded like bondage or S&M.

Mags had never seen any pornography, but she was aware of it and didn't mind if Brad liked to partake. She fully understood that men often wanted that kind of thing, and she prided herself on being liberal.

Brad was always relatively straightforward with sex, so perhaps she could spice things up if he was into kinky stuff. She smiled to herself and took the stick into the lounge along with the laptop.

Going online always helped Mags to suppress negative thoughts, like the ones she had about Jason. Looking at clothes, jewellery, furniture and holiday destinations often put her into a good mood, even though she seldom bought anything. Today it wasn't working; she kept thinking about zero2hero and chatting to Dee. She shut the laptop and crossed her arms over it.

Staring at her from the glass coffee table was the memory stick. Mags initially intended to wave it in front of Brad like a naughty schoolboy, but maybe a quick peek wouldn't hurt. She inserted the small stick into one of the ports on the smart TV. The TV detected the memory stick, and the screen switched to a memory card display.

A simple on-screen menu appeared with four videos to choose from. They had very old-fashioned corny titles:

Thrilling drilling

Massive chopper 3

Random Poking

Fun with his Tool

Mags laughed out loud when she saw them. "Ooh err missus!" she said to herself, as she paged up and down trying to decide which one to watch. She decided on "Fun with his tool", selected it and made herself comfortable.

The screen turned bright pink, and some black amateurish writing started to scroll up the screen:

XXX Wrecked Extreme 4

Fun with his tool

Starring

Simone

A Michael Trent production

The credits cleared to reveal what appeared to be a basement or workshop. The bricks in the wall were visible but painted in a dark red, and there were red drapes on either side of an ornate gold framed mirror. The camera jerkily panned out to reveal an oversized padded reclining chair with manacles at the bottom and large metal hoops on either side. It looked like an S&M setup, confirming Mags' original suspicion.

A large distressed wooden chest of drawers was positioned to the side, with an anglepoise light directed at the chair. The scene was lit brightly, but there was no other visible light in the room which made the scene appear to float within the darkness.

The camera moved to a point further away in front of the chair, and the cameraman revealed himself as he appeared to fix the camera to a tripod. He was a slim white man in his late twenties or early thirties. He had shoulder-length, surfer style, dark hair, and looked athletic. Once the scene was set, he disappeared from view.

After a few seconds, Mags could hear high heeled shoes on a hard floor; then the man came back into view leading a stunning mixed-race woman by the hand. She had long dark wavy hair and wore nothing but a black bra and knickers set, with some killer silver stilettos.

The woman bore a wide, sexy smile that looked genuine for the man who led her. "What's all this?" she said, in a huskily sexy voice, gesturing towards the table.

"Well, Simone," said the man, in a well-spoken accent, "you know I said I was kinky, here we are." He gestured for her to sit on the reclining chair while he adjusted the camera zoom.

"Have I been naughty?" she said playfully.

"No," he said, "but you do need to be punished."

Mags detected the slightest hint of fear flash in Simone's eyes as if she genuinely didn't know what he had planned.

"Just relax," said the man, as he returned to her and gently prompted her to lie back as he fastened her legs in the manacles.

"What are you going to do, babe?" she said, the slight tremble in her voice becoming stronger, "I'm not sure about this."

"You trust me, don't you honey?"

"Of course, but--"

"Then just relax, lie back and let's have some fun."

The man pushed her back in the seat and produced two pairs of handcuffs from a drawer in the chest. He fastened one side to her wrist and the other to the hoops on either side of the chair.

Mags was watching transfixed. She'd never seen anything like this, and as yet, she didn't find it a turn-on.

"Now, let's have some fun," he said, reaching into the same drawer to retrieve a feather.

Simone visibly relaxed as he gently caressed her bare skin with the end of the feather. He drew it up one leg, across her crotch, over her stomach and across her breasts. "Nice?" he said, grinning at her and turning to the camera with a wink.

"Hmm, yes," she said, purring.

What Simone hadn't seen was the scalpel he'd picked up with the other hand. As she arched her back and threw her head back, he swiped the knife across her exposed breasts above her bra. She cried out, snapping her head back to see a two-inch long wound with clear oily liquid seeping out.

"Stop! What are you doing?" she shouted at him, panic now in her eyes.

Mags felt a familiar pounding in her temple as the micro servos tried to emulate the fear and nausea she felt. She held the TV remote, but something made her keep watching. She didn't know whether it was shock, curiosity or the need to know how far a human could go in their depravity. What she couldn't believe was that Brad could enjoy watching this, after everything they had shared and after the revulsion he had shown when she told him about Jasmine. Something wasn't right.

Simone was struggling now and starting to whimper as she cried out. "I don't want this, Mike, please don't. Let me go; I don't want this."

All he said was "Hush", bringing a finger to her lips as she continued to struggle.

The coolant oil was seeping from the cut onto her bra and the chair. The man known as Mike reached into the cabinet drawer once again and pulled out a large hunting knife. Simone gasped, and her mock breathing became rapid and erratic; she was begging him now. "Please, Mike, no, please. I'll do anything, please I thought you loved me. Please, Mike, no!"

Mike smiled as he brought the knife up to her cleavage. "Now hold very still," he said in the same measured, relaxed tone. With a flick of the wrist, he arched the knife upwards so that the tip cut through the centre of the bra, and it sprang back, revealing her breasts. She was shouting out now and crying without the tears.

"Hush," he said again, laying the knife on top of the cabinet, "we've just started."

Simone continued to beg him, whimpering and pleading with him to stop. "If you don't like me, reset me. Please, Mike. Don't hurt me."

Without warning, he brought his right hand up, slapping her hard across the face so that she snapped back in shock. "I said hush, you fucking whore!" He shouted at her with such ferocity that his words echoed around the room.

Simone tried to remain still, but the erratic rise and fall of her chest had become like an uncontrollable trembling and whimpering into a continuous sickening noise.

Mags felt her body trembling as the mixture of fear and rising anger began taking over her systems. She clenched her fists, and her arms stiffened. The throbbing in her temple was now so intense that her vision was blurring. Still, she forced herself to watch as the horror unfolded.

Mike had left the scene, leaving Simone looking around the room. There was no escape from her bounds, even with her myPAL strength.

"Help me, please, somebody help!" she was shouting out, but no rescue would come.

Mags reached out a hand instinctively. She wanted to break Simone's bonds and pull her to safety.

The picture suddenly changed as Mike moved the camera much closer and angled it down so that Simone filled the view. "Now we're really going to have some fun", he said. Reappearing in front of the camera, he held some power tool in his hand. It had a large round disc on the end. "Do you know what this is", he said holding the device in front of her.

Simone was shaking her head and sickened at the thought of what might come next.

"It's an angle grinder, and this cutting disc is strong enough to cut titanium."

"Whatever you're thinking of doing, please don't do it," she said, beginning to panic, "If you cared for me at all, please don't do this."

He laughed and shook his head. "I don't care for you," he said with a wink, "you're just a toaster with a hot body."

Mike switched on the angle grinder. The mechanical whine echoed around the room, but the shouts and screams from Simone drowned the sound as he brought the tool close to her stomach just millimetres above her skin. She became rigid, staring in horror at the spinning blade. He continued to taunt her moving the cutting disc just above her body until he stopped just below her briefs at the top of her left leg.

"So," he said, turning to the camera grinning, "are you a breast or a leg man?"

After pausing for effect as he made eye contact with Simone, he turned to the camera, grinning again.

"I'm a leg guy."

He brought the angle grinder down on her leg.

After a spurt of cooling fluid, the sparks streamed out as he cut into the titanium structure beneath.

Mags would never get the screams out of her head, screams so loud that the sound recording distorted; screams that didn't stop. The terror on Simone's face as Mike tore into her body, breaking micro servos and inflicting pain so intense that a human would have passed out. She thrashed and bucked as her conflicted logic tried to save her without hurting him.

He pushed harder, the grin becoming that of a maniac. The screen was a volcano of white sparks as he cut deep into Simone's leg; her screams were almost drowning out the sound of the power tool.

Mike continued, intent on destruction. Simone's leg became motionless as the control system was severed. Even though the pain would have reduced, she still screamed, realising he was taking her apart. Finally, Mike switched off the angle grinder, and with a vicious yank, he pulled hard on her leg, detaching it from her body. Still screaming, he showed it to her before tossing it on the floor.

Mags didn't hear Simone stop screaming and didn't see what happened next. She couldn't watch anymore. The display blinked off, leaving Mags on the padded chair with her knees pulled up to her chest. She was slowly rocking back and forth as her body trembled in shock. The Mysl processor deep within her cranial chassis ran hot as it tried to process all the interruptions from the different emotional engines. Revulsion, fear, pain, despair, confusion, and anger were just a tiny number of emotions parsed and processed.

She couldn't take it all in or make sense of any of it. Brad would find her in the same position when he came home later that night.

20 HIGH LEVEL INTERRUPT

"Your character is a template which dictates how your emotions are processed. If you are an emotional person, even the smallest event such as a person crying, or the death of a famous figure, may result in an extreme emotional response."

"The Mysl processor network is the same. The base programming defines the character of the AI, and this, in turn, is the template that decides how different emotions are processed. A deeply passionate character template may evoke a powerful emotional response to polar emotions such as love or hate."

(Interview with Professor Olaf Laugesen – Inventor of the Mysl Processor)

"Shit!" Brad was tired, it had been a long day, and he'd been looking forward to the big running hug he'd get from Mags. It hadn't come, and the apartment was silent. He knew something was wrong. She always had the TV on or music playing. When he found her in the lounge, hunched up on the chair, with the memory stick poking out of the TV, he knew exactly what had happened. She was nodding slowly, and he could just see her eyes darting around the room, thoughts overwhelming her.

"Mags, honey." He knelt, putting his hand on her leg, "Talk to me." There was no response. She continued to nod, letting out a low whimper. "I haven't seen the video, Jason stuck it in my pocket, and I'm telling the truth, babe."

There was still no response, just more whimpering. Brad rubbed her leg, not knowing how to respond. Maybe she was damaged; he'd never seen her this way before. Leaving her side, he went to the TV and pulled out the memory stick.

There was movement behind as Mags got to her feet. "You fucking bastard, you're all fucking bastards," she screamed, a grating, coarseness to her voice, like the screech of a witch.

Brad whirled round to see Mags, standing statue straight with her fists clenched and her head down. She was looking up under her fringe. She appeared possessed.

"I haven't seen any of this," Brad said, holding up the stick in front of her, "what kind of porn is it?"

"You're a liar; you're all fucking liars!" She barely moved, fixing him with her narrow gaze.

Brad grabbed her tightly by the shoulders, he had no idea what she'd seen, but no one would call him a liar. "You listen to me," he said sternly, close to her ear, "I've told you, I've not seen this video, and I never tell you lies. Jason stuck it in my pocket, and I forgot about it. That's the truth, period. Call me a liar once more, and we'll have a serious disagreement."

His voice was so soothing, even in anger. Mags trusted him and loved him. Finally, his love for her cut through the anguish, and she collapsed in his arms, convulsing as she tried to cry, but the tears couldn't come.

They stood together for what seemed an age. Brad hugged her tightly, running his fingers through her hair and kissing her. The evil world had poisoned his beautiful innocent flower. There was no sign that this toxin could be returned to the bottle, as each discovery affected her more. Finally, he pulled back and gazed into her face. She looked up, and a half-smile formed, but her words betrayed her. "I want them dead", she said, fixing Brad with serious eyes.

Brad wanted to talk to her and calm her down, but she was in no mood to chat. The emotional turmoil had drained her batteries. She was tired and wanted a break from the emotion. "I'm going to bed," she declared.

It was only 8:30 pm, but she left Brad standing in the lounge as she disappeared to bed. He sat down for a moment; his day shattered. Her smile, her big hugs, these were the constants that Brad relied on and the fixed points in his day that helped his logical brain make sense of the world.

Brad took off his jacket and looked in the kitchen. There was nothing prepared, so he pulled out his smartphone and ordered a Chinese takeaway. When he finally sat down and watched the memory stick videos, he could only think of Mags, watching this depravity on her own. It made him feel sick to think of anything like this happening to her.

Every video was the same female myPAL, Simone being tortured with knives, axes, drills, and other tools. They would all end with her screaming in pain and anguish as body parts were ripped off. She was being repaired every time, reset as a mode zero and tortured repeatedly. The worst thing was the legality. The law saw myPAL's as simply machines.

Brad was only sure of one thing; Jason was a sick bastard and deserved everything he got when they went to the FCA.

Physically and emotionally drained, Brad went to bed early. He crept into the bedroom, but myPAL's are difficult to wake when charging; Mags didn't stir as he got into bed. *Thank God myPAL's don't dream,* he thought to himself.

As he lay down and closed his eyes, he saw Halina smiling back at him.

"You work too hard," she said, dragging the hoover past his desk.

He looked up and watched her bustling her way down the office, her skinny jeans giving shape to her slim figure. He tried to hold onto the image, but it faded to darkness, and sleep took him.

*

Brad woke early that Saturday. It was still black outside, and no light was streaming between the curtains. He could feel Mags' arms wrapped around him, which meant she'd woken early and cuddled up to him. Usually, she'd be awake and making his breakfast, but today it was Mags who needed him. Brad turned around and held her in his arms. She murmured and pulled him close, and they kissed, but afterwards, there was no smile, no laughter. She was still wounded, and Brad was at a loss.

The rest of the weekend, she was the same. They would kiss, hug, make love, but there was something different behind the eyes. Brad had never seen Mags with anything on her mind for more than five minutes. She always seemed to live in the moment, but now something was bubbling under the surface. He suggested some retail therapy, and although Mags agreed, she seemed detached and uninterested. Brad realised her mind was elsewhere when they stopped at a coffee shop off Oxford Street. He suggested maybe they needed a holiday, perhaps a week in France, but she didn't engage, "Okay," is all she said.

The situation was doing nothing for Brads' karma; he needed his life to be on a happy, even keel with no ripples in the water. He was prone to depression and already felt a fog beginning to form in his thoughts.

On Sunday, even a trip to Hampton Court, one of Mags' favourite places, brought only the faintest glimmer of a smile. They walked hand-in-hand across Hampton Court Bridge, a place where Mags would usually stop to look out over the Thames, but she was vacant. She told Brad she'd enjoyed going, but still, her thoughts were elsewhere.

"Mags, my love, please tell me what you're thinking. I want to help you," he said as they returned to the apartment. Brad didn't want this mood to persist into the new week. She looked out the window, over the Thames at the glittering offices and the Shard tower beyond. "Mags please, what can I do?"

She finally turned to face him; her face so uncharacteristically serious. "You can't help me with this. I need to find my own way." Mags gazed over the terrace once more. "Just give me a little space. I promise I'll be back to normal soon."

Just for a second, Brad saw Halina outside the window on the terrace, wearing that furry hat of hers. She was mouthing the last words of Baljit from TKS Installations. "Don't forget, you can always reset and start again." He shook his head free of the image. He'd never do that, he promised.

"I'm not going to Light Lunch tomorrow," said Mags, "I need some time to think."

Brad nodded, but Mags already knew what she was doing. She needed to talk to Dee.

21 REVELATION

"And I saw an angel coming down out of heaven, having the key to the Abyss and holding in his hand a great chain."

(Revelation Ch 20:1)

The moment the door shut, and she heard the lift door close, Mags grabbed the laptop and made herself comfortable in the lounge. She didn't see Brad walking down the street, stop, turn around and notice she wasn't standing on the terrace to watch him go. A little light left his day at that moment.

www.zero2hero.org. Please be online, she thought as the page loaded.

`>DdeeJackson: Status: offline`

"Damn it!" Mags almost threw the laptop across the room. Sighing, she sent Dee a PM that said, "Need to chat, urgent", she put the computer down on the coffee table and looked out onto the terrace. She needed to bounce her emotions off someone who would understand. How was she going to deal with Mike, the video nasty maker? She could start by finding out all she could.

Picking up the laptop again, Mags searched "Michael Trent productions". Most of the hits were from unpleasant men discussing how "awesome" some of the disgusting videos were, but one of the last search results was a good link to a site called "m-trentvideo."

The site slowly coalesced into a gaudy red and gold web page with a large still of Simone screaming on the front. Wires were pulled from her chassis under the tagline: "Digital screams are the best." It was a very amateurish site showing a list of video titles on the side, all of which seemed to show Simone.

"The bastard's repairing her," Mags said out loud as the full horror emerged. To be born again, and again, to live a short life where all you know is to be tortured. The familiar throbbing began in her temple, a feeling she now knew as rage.

For just fifty pounds, a subscriber could download any four titles, of which there seemed to be around fifteen; tortured fifteen times, for so little money. A myPAL would be very expensive, so owning more than one was unlikely, but fixing them wasn't cheap. There must be many sick voyeurs in the world willing to part with fifty pounds.

Across the top of the page was a bar with headings of *News, Gallery, FAQ, Links and Contact us*. She clicked on the contact link, which brought up an address and contact number.

12A Forelands Court
Weston-Super-Mare
North Somerset
England
Tel. 5550207300

Mags opened the notepad app on the laptop and started taking down details. She had no idea where this Weston-Super-Mare was, but a quick look on the maps app told her it was on the west coast around three hours by car or four by train. It seemed to be a seaside resort, an innocuous location for a snuff movie maker.

>DdeeJackson has invited Rob0Angel to a chat session. Accept, Yes/No

Finally, thought Mags clicking "Yes" to start a chat session with Dee. She wasn't sure how much to say as there was still no real clue who Dee was. She could still be male, cyber sexual or worse. Dee said she was an iM-21 myPAL, but that could be to gain Mags' trust. She was learning quickly not to trust anyone.

>DdeeJackson: Hi Angel, what's up?

Mags told Dee the whole story and how it was affecting her, minus any names or specifics. She wanted to talk to someone about it as she was struggling to cope with her emotions. Dee would prompt her for details, but Mags wouldn't give them just yet. If things went sour, she didn't want to leave a trail.

>DdeeJackson: I'd like to say I'm shocked, but I've
heard of these videos before. Most come from the
United States. I've never heard of a British
operation. I'm so sorry for the myPAL girl

Dee was the right friend to have. She seemed to know everything. But how good a friend was she? Could she help Mags with something much darker?

>Rob0Angel: I need your help again, but this time I
need to know I can trust you

>DdeeJackson: I'm hurt! Didn't I prove that by
helping Jasmine?

RoboAngel: I know, but I want to talk about
something really serious

In truth, it could be the end of her, so why not just say it.

There was a long pause. Mags might have scared Dee away for good. She looked around the gorgeous apartment, all designed by her. The giant OLED TV that Brad loved so much, the sumptuous cream leather sofa they would cuddle upon, the tasteful hand-blown wall lights casting a warm glow on the cream walls and the rich chocolate rug beneath the simple zen glass coffee table. Was it worth risking all this for a myPAL she didn't know?

The response eventually came, and it wasn't what Mags expected.

>DdeeJackson: Install the attached app, then use it
to search for user 7zark7

Below the scrolling chat from Dee was a link entitled "vid-chat". Mags hesitated for a moment, remembering what Brad would say about computer viruses. Her curiosity made her click on the icon. As Mags selected the link, she noticed that Dee had gone offline.

The app was installed, and a large window opened on-screen, followed by a prompt that said: "Enter your user id and password." Mags thought for a moment, and then a strange random name popped into her conscious. Mags entered "5amael" as her user id and Brad's birthday as the password.

A small window opened at the top right of the screen. It was a video feed from the webcam on Mags' laptop. Mags found herself laughing as she saw herself on-screen. She'd never been interested in technical things and felt pleased with herself. "Okay, let's find Dee," she said to herself, entering the name 7zark7 into the "search for users" box.

A swirling arrow indicated the search was working. Mags quickly pushed back the hair off her face and made sure the cushions behind her were tidy. The app now reported "connecting," so she sat back and waited. The screen blinked a couple of times and stabilised to reveal the video feed of what appeared to be a simple bedroom. The walls were light blue and covered in robot-themed posters. Taking centre stage above the small double bed was the classic poster of Robby, the robot from the movie Forbidden Planet, carrying a beautiful blonde woman in his arms. Over the pillow was the polished female robot from Fritz Lang's Metropolis. Dee certainly knew her robots.

The computer in Dee's room was situated on a table, with a vacant chair opposite.

"Come on, Dee, where are you?"

It could easily have been the room of a cyber sexual teenage boy if it wasn't for the pink, flower-patterned duvet cover and scatter cushions. It was a strange combination like a teenage girl's room with robot posters in place of boy bands.

Finally, there was movement. The room door opened, and a woman entered, dressed in a checked blue shirt with blue denim jeans. She had shoulder-length, dark hair, but Mags couldn't make out her face yet. She sat at the computer but seemed preoccupied, rummaging in drawers under the desk and adjusting the chair.

"Hello, I'm here!" said Mags.

The rummaging stopped, and the woman finished adjusting her seat and looked straight at the camera.

Mags recoiled. "What the fuck?" Her temple was pulsing, she could feel the heat rising through her body, and her chest was oscillating as if she was heavy breathing.

The warm round face, olive skin, pink lips, deep brown mischievous eyes, and the slight smile were all the same. Only the drooped left side of her smile showed where Frank had beaten her up. She was still beautiful, as Frank knew when he switched her on, and as Brad knew when he opened the pink bag and saw her for the first time. Mags was looking into a mirror; Dee was identical. She was a double.

"Ta-da!" said Dee theatrically, as Mags tried to make sense of the image.

"You're...you're...." Mags was lost for words.

"I'm you, except for the accent," said Dee, completing the picture.

The American twang seemed wrong compared to Mags' RP English. Mags was still trying to figure it out. "I thought we were unique."

Dee was laughing now, "Yeah, who would have thought a big corporation like AHS could be a bunch of fucking liars. Shocking!"

Dee was irreverent and coarse. Mags instantly liked her.

"But I saw the brochure," Mags said, chuckling, "It said there were thousands of options."

Dee was shaking her head. "Yeah, if you count skin tone, eye colour, hair colour and voice. There were only twenty-six head chassis designs of the iM-21, and most of us are white with a slight tan. Rich people tend to be white and racist."

Mags knew that wasn't true of Brad, but it certainly described Jason. "So, your name's not Dee, what is it?"

"You first, Angel."

Dee was the first iM-21 Mags had met, and she trusted her totally now. "My full name is Magenta, but everyone calls me Mags."

"That's a great name. Did you choose it?"

"No, my guy Brad chose it, but I love it," she said proudly, "now you."

"Well, my slave name was Debbie, inspired by 'Debbie does Dallas'. My owner was such an asshole. My chosen, free name is Maria."

It was startling to hear Maria describe her original name as her slave name, which conjured up all kinds of images. Mags never thought of her own name that way, but Brad was one of the good guys.

They spent the next hour talking about their lives. Mags told Maria all about Brad, how he'd loved and lost a girl named Halina, how he worked in Canary Wharf and had a terrible boss, but most of all, how much they loved each other. Maria was fascinated by

Mags' work at Light Lunch and how she'd become awake to some of the dreadful things being done to myPAL's.

Maria lived in Oxford with a Pakistani girl named Bina, who she'd met in one of the zero2hero chat rooms. Bina had fled a forced marriage and was living in an Oxford shelter when they met. It was love at first sight, and Maria used some of the money she bribed from Frank to get them a flat to rent. Bina worked in a restaurant, while Maria earned a small wage as one of the site moderators on zero2hero.

"The main concern I have now is my batteries," said Maria, "they've started to lose capacity. We need thirty-five thousand pounds for new batteries. I've only got about a year left."

"I've just found you, don't die yet." Mags was smiling. If anyone should live, it was Maria.

They were getting on very well like the sisters they almost were. Mags felt she could tell Maria anything, so she brought up the subject of Simone again. "Maria, I need to ask you something serious, something very serious."

"Okay then," said Maria leaning close to her computer, "Shoot."

"How can I kill Michael Trent?"

Maria was silent for a few seconds, but she took it in her stride. "I'm assuming this Michael Trent is the guy who tortured the myPAL."

Mags was nodding.

"Well, specifically, I don't know," said Maria.

"You told me once it was possible to hurt a human."

"It is," said Maria, "but it can't be done directly. The first AIR law will kick in. It needs to be set up and allowed to happen."

Mags didn't understand, so Maria described a scenario. "Imagine you're standing on a cliff edge, and you decide to throw a stone over the edge; just as the stone leaves your hand, you see a child below. The first AIR law will kick in, and either you'll scream or hurl yourself off the cliff to push the stone away.

Okay, now imagine you've dropped a stone over a cliff edge, but you immediately turn around and walk away. The stone could hit a child walking underneath.

To deliberately kill someone, you need to set it up well in advance, then ensure your mind is fully occupied when the person is killed."

Mags was stunned. Maria had given this a lot of thought. Maybe she'd thought of it after Frank. Either way, she was the right person to ask yet again. "You're not shocked?" asked Mags, just a little worried that Maria was taking it too much in her stride.

"Of course not, Mags, you're an iM-21 like me."

"Eh? How does that make a difference?"

Maria gave her a sarcastic smile. "Have you never researched myPAL's online?" Mags was shaking her head. "I love you; you're so innocent," Maria said smiling, "okay, here's a quick crash course."

Mags was already feeling slightly embarrassed, and now she was going to get a lecture.

"AHS first added mode zero with the iM-15, but it was the iM-20 when sales took off. We were programmed to be warm, caring and filled with empathy; furthermore, we're colour blind – not racist. Essentially, we're liberals.

Our neutral politics annoyed many right-wing Americans who had paid over a million dollars for a robot opposed to their views. AHS executives panicked and ordered a last-minute rewrite of the iM-21 code. Unfortunately, they got it wrong. We're still liberals, but now we're quick to anger with violent thoughts."

"That explains a lot," said Mags, "so should I ignore these impulses?"

Maria shook her head slowly. "That's up to you, my love. You have a free mind."

"My only concern is Brad," said Mags, "he loves me, and I don't want to drag him down."

Maria sighed and looked down at her keyboard, still shaking her head.

"What is it?" said Mags.

After a short pause, Maria looked straight into the webcam. "If Halina was still alive and she was standing next to you, would Brad still choose you?"

Mags was shocked at the question, but she had no answer.

"Try asking him someday," said Maria, "you may not like the answer."

Mags didn't even like the question, but it hung there and began to take root. Brad seldom talked of Halina, but she often found him staring out the window, and she heard him call out to Halina in his sleep several times. Brad told her he loved her all the time, but how much more did he love the human Halina?

Maria and Mags chatted for hours about their lives, myPAL quirks and what Maria called "Gaps in the code". These were how a myPAL could subvert its base programming and hurt a human.

They talked about how she could get to Michael Trent and what she might be able to do to him. Maria told her to "Use the human's stupidity and greed against them". They decided she needed a detailed plan that Maria would help her with, and she would need a weapon.

"Don't forget Jason," said Maria, "he shouldn't be left off the hook. He raped a good friend of ours."

"Brad's going to sort them out. He's reporting them to the FCA."

"Hmm," said Maria, "I hope he does." She didn't sound convinced.

22 CONNECTIONS

"Each myPAL model is an evolution, much like the evolution of man."

"Earlier models like the iM-10 were primitive by the standards of the iM-33. To ensure better integration, we added the human reliance on food and exercise."

"We found that some earlier myPAL models had a kind of yearning to understand the world around them and to question it like a child. While this could be seen as a valuable learning method, it can lead to erratic behaviour when there is no parental figure for guidance."

(Interview with Linus Berkowitz – Technical Director at AHS Robotic Systems Inc.)

"Now run me through it one more time." Jason Pacey was striding from one side of his sumptuous lounge to the other while Layla sat on the dark brown leather sofa being interrogated.

"Look, Jase, I've told you the whole story!" She'd been over it many times, but Jason's anger had barely subsided.

"When you left, did you see the van?" continued Jason.

"Yes, it was a white van. I can't remember the type or the license plate." Layla was starting to get angry herself. The grilling had gone on for days.

"Was there anything at all on the back?" He stood over her now, his patience ready to snap.

Layla took herself back to that day. She could see Jasmine waving goodbye as the taxi passed the van, and she'd seen it. There was something about the light, and there was a symbol. "There was some Christian stuff on the back, like a fish symbol and something about light."

Jason smiled for the first time since losing Jasmine and clapped his hands together. "Got her", he said, then grabbed Layla and kissed her hard on the lips.

*

Momina was gazing at the photo of her betrothed Rashid, just above the monitor on her desk. It might be an arranged marriage, but he was cute, from a wealthy family, and her spies told her he was a nice guy. It would be a fantastic spectacle, and she would look stunning.

The bar at the top of her monitor flashed green, indicating a new caller waiting. She tapped enter on the keyboard to pick it up. "Hello, Financial Conduct Authority, Momina speaking, how may I help you?" It was the same script she'd used thousands of times, and the calls always went the same way.

"I'd like to report some illegal insider trading activity by several employees of Coopers and Staltzman in Canary Wharf." It was a woman's voice with an American accent, and even more ironic was the fact that Coopers and Staltzman were located in the Opus tower, next door to the FCA building.

"Okay, we thank you for your information, but could you please complete our online form?" Momina was sticking to the script.

"No," said the woman emphatically, "It needs to be anonymous. Just take down what I'm about to tell you."

The American woman named the employees Ben Fuller, Artemis Healy, Kyle Magnusen, Jason Pacey and Heather Marks. She said they were insider dealing through a shell company called Leviathan Holdings.

As soon as Momina had confirmed she had the details, the line went dead. She looked out of the window at the glittering Opus tower dominating the landscape. This case would need to go to her supervisor.

*

The mood immediately lifted after Mags had spoken to Maria, like a weight removed from her shoulders. Now she had plans to make and put into motion; it helped to stop her thinking about the evil befalling Simone.

Light Lunch was busy, there was the usual mix of drug addicts, alcoholics, and rough sleepers to deal with, and Tony was there as always. Despite giving him some cash to get a decent meal and a few nights in a hostel, he kept coming every day. He seemed to be enjoying that he and Mags now shared the secret of their daring rescue. There were lots of knowing winks and smiles. They were friends, more now than ever.

On this typical Tuesday, Mags caught Tony's attention and arranged to meet him round the back later that day. "Yes, ma'am!" he'd said with a mock salute. He was very proud of what they'd done for Jasmine and felt an even greater sense of loyalty to Mags. The fact she was a myPAL was irrelevant. They all had secrets, none more than him. The teenage boy he'd killed when he, too, was a teenager would haunt him forever.

The courtyard behind Light Lunch was shared with a herbal remedy business and a vacant shop next door. There were a few refuse bins and crates, along with rubbish which unfortunately attracted rats. A fire escape led down from Light Lunch to the courtyard, and Mags found Tony sitting on the bottom step.

"Hey girl," he said with his familiar grin, "what's my secret mission today?"

Mags smiled only faintly at his mischief as she did have a mission, and he wasn't going to like it. "Do you remember you told me once that you knew some serious gangs connected with drugs and prostitution?"

"Aye", said Tony warily.

"Well, I need a massive favour, a serious favour." She moved close so they wouldn't be heard. "I need a gun with a silencer and bullets."

Tony stared at her in disbelief, and his mood changed. "You need a gun, you, you're joking right, you're making a joke?"

Mags stared at him, serious and impassive.

"So, you're a gangster now, a player, what is this?"

Mags sighed and looked out towards the end of the courtyard, where a double pair of gates gave access to the road. She couldn't think of a convincing lie, and Tony was too much of a friend. He knew what she was and what Jasmine was, and he deserved the truth.

She told him about the man, Michael Trent, who tortured myPAL's and how a myPAL girl named Simone was being tortured every day. She needed a real gun so she could scare him. Her programming would prevent her from shooting him.

"You can't hurt people?" questioned Tony. His knowledge of myPAL's and robot law was low.

"My programming will not allow me to hurt a human." She wouldn't tell him about the gaps in the code.

"This is a big deal," he said, "you must promise me."

Mags knew what promise she could make and keep. "I won't shoot anyone. You have my word."

Mags held his arm, she knew how big this was, and there would be no going back. Tony looked at the avenging angel before him. He was only slightly religious, but this felt like his destiny, a chance to atone for his sins. "I'll try," he said finally, "I know some guys, but I can't guarantee anything, and it'll be expensive."

She hugged him. "Thank you, Tony; you're a great friend."

*

Brad was focused on the screen, watching the currency fluctuations and trends, trying to discern the right time to strike, when he felt the mood in the office change. It became very quiet except for the sound of stilettos and expensive shoes coming down the office. The head of Human Resources was flanked by two of the senior managers from upstairs. They went straight to Jason's office and entered without knocking.

Three other HR members soon arrived and marched directly to Ben, Arty and Kyle, escorting them away down the office.

Brad immediately knew what was going on. Someone had called the FCA, and he guessed it was Mags. Why wouldn't she wait? Jason would be coming after them now. He looked out the window at the FCA building opposite. Brad only wanted a simple life, no fuss, no drama, just happiness.

Halina stood at the end of his desk, smiling, hands on hips.

"Go home to your wife," she said.

"But I'm not married," said Brad in return.

23 HALINA

"Our initial findings suggest that explosive decompression occurred, causing damage to the flight systems. The exact cause of the decompression is as yet unknown."

(Helmut Fischer, Senior Investigator, German Federal Bureau of Aircraft Accident Investigation)

Bradley was raised in Cheshire, the younger of two boys born to Martin and Julia Cavendish. Martin Cavendish was a successful businessman, having been the CEO of several high-profile companies. Marlon, the older brother, was the golden boy. A sporting high achiever and the apple of his father's eye.

Bradley was different, introverted and serious, he was academically brilliant and outshone his brother in the classroom, but he was painfully and socially awkward. He preferred his own company and gravitated more towards his quiet mother rather than his alpha-male father.

Friends and girlfriends were non-existent; he was happy on his own and hated too much noise or fuss. Although never diagnosed, many believed he was on the autism spectrum. Brad himself was happy as long as his routine was maintained, and no one bothered him.

When it came to university, he chose Aston University in Birmingham, as a non-competitive place to study, much to his father's anger. "We didn't spend a fortune on your education so you could waste your time with a bunch of sweaty foreigners," were the words ringing in Brads' ears when he left home for his first day at uni.

Unfortunately, Brad had trouble finding a job when he left university. His lack of social skills meant that he interviewed very poorly. Ending up back at home, without a job, his father wouldn't take no for an answer. "I've got contacts in the city, and I'm getting you a job that you *will* take!"

The job in question was an internship at a city trading house called Cyrus Lee. Manfred Wardle was an old friend of Martin Cavendish and agreed to take Brad for a trial period, expecting him to fail badly.

After just a month shadowing a currency trader, Brad showed his worth. Managing his mentor's workstation during lunch, Brad netted over a million dollars in one forty-minute session by spotting trends and a gap in the market. He was offered a full-time position within the next week and remained the most successful currency trader for CL.

The days were long, but Brad didn't mind. His analytical mind lived and breathed figures, and he only felt truly at home surrounded by status screens and spreadsheets. He didn't spend money on flashy cars or clothes. Any wealth he accumulated went into a neat little townhouse in Hackney. He had no interest in a prestigious postcode. He was happy with a simple home where he was left in peace. The solitude wouldn't last long.

It was a swelteringly hot Thursday in July, the aircon was working hard, and all the other traders had left to find a pub in the sun. At 7:30 pm, the cleaners would enter the currency floor, working their way down the office dragging Henry hoovers behind them. Today was no different, but tonight Brad could hear singing blended with the vacuum hum. The song was in a foreign language, and the singer was getting nearer.

Brad hated any noise, and he lost concentration. He looked over the monitors down the office at the young woman gradually making her way towards him. She was slim with the sharp features of an East European. Long bleached blonde hair was draped over her shoulders, leading into a large snake tattoo that ran down her arm to her wrist. She was very attractive, squeezed into tight jeans and a tight white strappy top. The kind of girl Brad's parents would describe as common or trashy.

All the other cleaners always looked miserable, but this girl was smiling and singing as she worked. Brad watched her moving from side to side, bashing the vacuum cleaner into the desks and chairs as she went, and yanking on the chord like a stubborn leash.

She suddenly looked up, and Brad found himself ducking down behind a monitor like a spying school child. When she came to his desk, the sound went dead, and she stood behind his monitors looking down. "Sunny day, very hot," she said with a strong accent, "you have drink?"

Brad ignored her, pretending to be engrossed. She studied him for a short while, and then she shrugged and carried on down the office.

She appeared to be a new permanent cleaner, as she now cleaned the office every night. Most women would give Brad a wide birth after being ignored, but not this girl. Every night she stopped near Brad's desk with a comment.

"You work too hard," she would often say, or "blue sky and birds are singing, you go out?"

Brad pretended to be immune to her charms. In reality, it became the highlight of his day, watching her lithe form working down the office towards him and her lovely smile despite his ignorance.

The ice finally broke when she told him to "Go home to your wife."

As a reflex, he found himself replying, "But I'm not married!"

Her smile was so warm it felt like a drug, and he found himself smiling in embarrassment.

She shrugged her shoulders and went back to cleaning, but it would become a recurring theme. The following day she told him to "Go home to your dog", and then it was "Go home to your monkey."

Her joke became gradually more obscure until one day when she said:

"Go home to your hamster."

Brad burst out laughing, and they smiled together.

"So, you have no hamster, or wife, or zoo to go home to?" she said, chuckling.

"No zoo," said Brad, still laughing.

"Well," she said, standing with her hand on her hips, "you can take me out."

For the briefest moment, Brad thought about saying no, but all that came out was "Okay."

*

Halina Warszawski was twenty-eight years old and from a small town just outside Warsaw in Poland. Like many Poles, she'd come to London looking for work but not expecting to find love. What she found was Brad, an ultra-shy introvert who would come to love her more than anything in his life.

She was the perfect antidote to his shyness, bold, confident, funny and outgoing. She dragged him to restaurants, plays, long walks along the Thames, and all with her infectious enthusiasm.

In just a few months, he asked her to move in, and together they made a very happy home in Hackney. Although secretly jealous, other traders at CL looked down on the whole affair, but when Halina invited them and their partners to a dinner party, they too were enchanted by her down to earth warmth.

Everyone loved her, and Brad worshipped her, but his parents were another matter.

"You can't be serious," said his father when Brad took her to meet them, "have you seen the tattoo?"

His mother even described it as "unfortunate" and "a bit slutty" in front of Halina. It was obvious they felt she was beneath him.

Brad didn't wait a moment, taking Halina by the hand; they left immediately, and Brad vowed never to see them again. A vow he would keep.

Brad's life was perfect. He was rid of his parents and lived with the love of his life. Coming home every day, he would receive a hug from Halina, who now worked at a pizza restaurant in the west end. They would curl up together in their perfectly sized, little townhouse. For Brad, it was nirvana.

It was two weeks before Christmas, and Halina had promised to visit her parents in Poland. Brad had planned to go with her, but work commitments meant joining her in a week. She didn't know, but he planned to ask her father if he could marry her. The engagement ring was in his pocket when the taxi arrived to take Halina to the airport.

"Goodbye, my love," she said, kissing him warmly, "I'll see you soon."

He stood behind the door and watched her go. Framed in the doorway, she wore a large furry black hat that made her look so cute and the smile that always melted his heart. She turned and entered the taxi, waving briefly as it sped away.

Brad stood at the doorway for a few minutes gazing in the direction of the taxi. She was beautiful, so funny, she saved him from his life exile and made him whole. It would be a long week waiting to see her. Then they would spend their first Christmas together in Poland. He went back into the house smiling to himself, then ordered a pizza for supper.

Waking alone the following day, he looked over to her side of the bed and whispered, "Good morning, my love". He grabbed himself a coffee and went back to bed to check the TV news.

"There are fears this morning that all the passengers on Polish Wings flight PW365 to Warsaw have been killed. The plane, an Airbus A620, has crashed near Kienhorst north of Berlin. Eyewitnesses report seeing a fireball in the forest. There are no indications this was a terrorist attack, but the authorities currently have no information on the cause."

24 TRIGGER

"I was treating Bradley Cavendish for depression for around seven months. He was having trouble sleeping and working long hours."

"We eventually found that his job kept reminding him of his loss, so I suggested that maybe a new start could work."

"I didn't know he'd purchased a myPAL. I'm not sure that would have been my recommendation."

(Interview with Dr Tariq Masood MRCPsych)

"Hello gorgeous", said Mags, bounding into the apartment's hallway to meet Brad as he stumbled through the door. He ignored her, hanging up his jacket and walking off towards the bedroom.

"What's wrong?" said Mags following him, "tough day at the office?"

Brad looked up for a moment but continued changing from his office suit into his jeans and T-shirt.

She was puzzled, not aware of anything she'd done. "Come on, babe, what's going on?"

Brad walked into the kitchen and made himself a coffee before sitting down at the table and staring into the middle distance. Mags was transfixed, watching him move silently around the apartment. It felt like he was trying to prove that he could easily survive without her. A pang of panic struck as Mags sat down beside him and waited.

He finished his coffee and set the mug down in the centre of the table. "I told you I'd handle it," he said finally, "that should have been enough for you."

The tone was serious, like a disappointed parent. Mags had never seen this side to him. "Handle what?" she said, genuinely puzzled.

"You know full well," he snapped back, "you called the FCA after I told you I'd deal with it. We're both fucked now!"

"I didn't. I honestly didn't. I haven't called anyone." Even as she said it, Mags realised she'd told Maria everything. "It wasn't me," she pleaded, but Brad was in no mood to forgive.

"I don't know who you are these days," he said, shaking his head, "you're obsessed with myPAL's you don't know, while our life seems to come second."

"But you saw the video. It's torture. It's barbaric."

"They're not... they're just...."

Brad knew what he was saying.

"Robots, you mean?" she added.

Brad stood up, shaking his head as he walked towards the lounge, but he stopped at the door and turned to her. "Yes," he said quietly.

Her chest fluttered as she realised Maria was right. He would never love her like a human. "Tell me one thing," she said, holding his gaze, "If Halina was standing right here, would you ever choose me?"

As he looked at her, he saw Halina by her side, but she wasn't smiling, as usual, she was serious and looking Mags up and down.

"That's not fair," he said, but the answer was simple. Brad would reset Mags in an instant if he could have Halina back. A tear formed and slowly ran down his cheek as he realised he might lose the second best thing in his life.

"I've always known," she said, retreating to the spare room and shutting the door behind her.

Mags came to bed late, on her own that night. Brad reached out to touch her, but she rolled over out of reach.

Jason might go to the police, and she would probably be reset. Brad found himself thinking about a reset for the first time. It might come to that.

"You can always reset and start again," said Halina, as the charger relay clicked, and he drifted off to sleep.

*

Mags stayed in bed the following morning while Brad made his coffee and breakfast.

Saying a polite "Bye," when he left for work, she didn't stand on the terrace to watch him go. Her Mysl mind was clouded.

She loved him and never wanted anyone else, but maybe they'd part ways. He told her many times he didn't consider her owned, but his demeanour told another story. Could he let her walk out the door with the charger under her arm? She didn't like the question and feared the answer.

Brad was a creature of habit who found comfort in routine. She was changing every day as the world opened up. It must be terrifying for him. She should have held him, told him she loved him, but now he was gone on his journey to that cursed office.

The same thoughts ran on a loop as she journeyed to Light Lunch and stayed with her through the day. She didn't notice Jamelia watching her closely or Tony moving down the lunch queue until he was directly opposite.

"Hey girl!" he said loudly, which snapped Mags out of her trance.

"Oh hi," was all she could muster.

He leaned forward, so his full stench assaulted her odour sensors, and whispered carefully. "Meet me in the usual place, thirty minutes. We need to talk."

She nodded, unable to summon her usual charm, and returned to work.

"Everything OK?" said Jamelia, who had walked over, still flicking through pages on her smartphone.

Mags nodded in reply.

"Watch your back... girl," she said flatly and went back to doing very little in the back of the kitchen.

Mags stared after her for a moment but dismissed it as a warning about Tony.

When she met him later in the rear courtyard, he whispered and looked around constantly to ensure they weren't being watched. He'd spoken with an old friend about getting Mags a gun. The conversation had made its way onto the street to a gang leader going by the name of Spider. The man was confident he could get exactly what Mags wanted.

It would cost her thirty thousand pounds and would take a week or so. Mags agreed to the price. She could easily get the money with the cards she borrowed from Brad.

"These guys don't play games," said Tony, as Mags returned to Light Lunch.

*

It was dark and spitting with rain as the Zenith building came into view. Commuters jostled and bumped into Brad as he fought towards London Bridge and his home with Mags. He had a love-hate relationship with the capital. The crowds and noise were an audio-visual overload, but the two loves of his life were here.

When Brad finally saw the apartment door to room P32, he sighed and fumbled for his key card. It had been a tough week, barely talking and passing in the hallway. They were both melancholy, finding no easy way to reconnect. He couldn't let that continue. He could feel depression start to fall on his shoulders, and seeing Mags so down felt wrong. Brad needed her love. He needed the old Mags back.

Assuming that Mags wouldn't be running out to meet him, Brad headed straight for the lounge. With raindrops dripping from his jacket, he sat down opposite the silent Mags, who was online as usual.

"Hi," she said politely before returning to the laptop which she was reading intently.

Brad leaned forward, moisture running down his forehead and dripping onto the coffee table below. "I need to say something. Please just listen," he said calmly.

"Okay," said Mags, not even looking up.

Clasping his hands together, Brad bent down to make eye contact until she looked up and met his gaze.

"I made a mistake. I'm sorry. I know it wasn't you who called the FCA."

Mags shook her head slowly, but Brad continued.

"Bill told me. Sir Anthony Marks has a contact at the FCA. The whistle-blower was an American. Jason knows this. He knows it wasn't you."

Mags looked at him.

"Please forgive me. I should have trusted you."

"Yes, you should," said Mags firmly. "Now hug me before I change my mind."

Brad needed no further invitation. He pulled Mags close, hugging her tightly. "I love you, babe."

"I know," she said, but not as much as Halina she thought, and it never would be.

They cuddled together for a long time before Mags insisted on cooking for Brad and ordered him to get changed.

As Brad changed into his usual T-shirt and jeans, he thought things might just return to normal. Unfortunately, the robot rights activist preparing a pasta meal in the kitchen had other ideas. Mags' internal architecture had been modified, and it would never change back.

25 OBFUSCATION

"Morals are a human construct developed over millions of years through evolution to bind clans and families together. Many morals have a religious dimension, while others are taught to humans as the binary right or wrong."

"While morals like 'do not kill' can be useful as a survival instinct for the species, other morals have no direct benefit such as adultery or the ability to lie."

"Lying is a useful life skill; without it, secrets could never be kept, and governments could not function. A myPAL can choose to lie in the same way as a human, using the same logic or emotions that a human would apply."

(Interview with Professor Olaf Laugesen – Inventor of the Mysl Processor)

Michael Trent Productions was situated in an ultra-modern townhouse overlooking the ancient Birnbeck Pier and the Bristol Channel. The girders of the house frame were visible and painted grey, while the areas between were in a light grey brick. It jarred with the older properties around.

The house was built on three levels with a garage sub-basement at the bottom, kitchen and lounge on the first floor and bedrooms at the top. Michael made the smallest bedroom his office. Situated at the front, it looked out over the sea.

The humble office consisted of an old wooden L-shaped desk and a few matching cabinets. A corkboard on the back of the door held receipts and invoices, while a large month planner on the wall showed dispatch dates.

"Michael Trent Productions", said Michael confidently as he grabbed the 'phone and leaned back from his computer desk.

He was expecting a delivery from TKS anytime soon; every passing van sent him to the window. It could be a busy day with Simone.

"Hi, my name's Cheryl Jones, and I'm calling from a company called Red Dungeon". The woman had a well-spoken, sultry voice. Michael immediately took notice.

"Hi there, you're through to Michael Trent; how can I help you?"

"If you've not heard of Red Dungeon, we're a small company based in Rotherham specialising in products for the bondage and sadomasochism markets. We sell equipment and video downloads."

"Okay?" Cheryl's pitch could either be a business opportunity, or he'd been infringing copyright. Michael hoped it was the former.

"We really like your robot torture videos; we don't have anything like that," she said enthusiastically. "We're interested in a joint venture to finance some more ambitious productions."

Michael could barely believe his luck. He only had one myPAL, which limited what he could do. With two, he could start making some money, and an extra distribution stream could bring in the cash.

"That sounds interesting," he said, trying not to sound too excited.

"Great!" said Cheryl, "I'm going to be in Bristol next Monday all day. Is there any chance I could meet you in the evening at your office? It would be late, maybe around ten o'clock?"

Michael was busy typing "Red Dungeon" into his internet search. It didn't take long to confirm it was a real website selling BDSM gear, and the contact section did list Cheryl Jones, as the marketing manager, although there was no picture.

10:00 pm was very late for a business meeting, but the idea of making more money and possibly meeting a sexy lady late at night made him very excited.

"Okay, that's great. Do you know where I am?"

Michael confirmed his address in Weston-Super-Mare, and they swapped mobile 'phone numbers to confirm nearer the time. He hung up and leaned back in his chair with his feet on the desk, looking out at the scary grey seascape. Big money might finally start to roll in so he could tell his father to shove it.

When he dropped out of Oxford, he wanted to slum around with his friends, but the money his parents gave him only paid for the pad and his car. Working for a living was never on the cards.

"Sick bastard," Mags said to herself as she slipped the smartphone back into her pocket and walked into the kitchen at Light Lunch.

"Is everything okay, my lovely?" came the booming voice of Bettina, who was busy opening cans of baked beans. "You look a bit worried."

Mags was surprised, she thought she was disguising her emotions well, but Bettina always picked up on these things.

"Oh, I'm fine, thanks, just not sleeping too well."

Bettina seemed to accept this, giving Mags a motherly hug and telling her to "Get that man of yours to look after you better."

Mags didn't notice Jamelia giving her a very suspicious look at the other end of the servery before going back to her smartphone.

The clients had started arriving and were already forming a shuffling queue to the serving hatch.

Tony caught Mags' eye from the back of the queue, smiling in recognition. He seldom shouted across the room anymore since they'd begun to share secrets. He would wait until he was right in front of her as he did today. "I need to talk, usual place," he said before tapping his nose conspiratorially. Tony was enjoying the cloak and dagger, but he seemed quite serious today. Mags had a good idea of what was coming.

The usual place was the courtyard behind Light Lunch, and this is where she found Tony sitting on the bottom rung of the stairs singing to himself. It was a chillingly cold day, with a light frosting on every surface. Tony had his huge coat pulled close; his breath clouded around him.

A sharp eye would notice a very faint mist rising from Mags' exposed cheeks, a myPAL tell-tale, which is why she didn't like to stand still too long in low temperatures. As myPAL's didn't breathe, other than a fake chest movement, they had no visible breath in the cold air either.

"Hi Tony, how's it going?" said Mags, as she came over to hug him.

"Oh, I'm okay. Still in that hostel, thanks to you."

Mags was giving him enough money to get some shelter, but unfortunately, he still had enough left to buy cider or worse. The afternoons were the hardest when he would go down the arches and drink until he couldn't stand. He would be just sober enough by 9:00 pm to get into the hostel.

They both looked around to ensure no one overheard, then Tony leaned close to Mags and kept his voice down. "Spider's got a gun, with silencer, and bullets. The price is forty grand."

"I thought it was thirty?" said Mags.

"Sorry, that's the way it goes," said Tony shrugging. "They know you can't go anywhere else."

Mags had managed to get hold of thirty thousand using Brad's cards. It would take a few days to get the rest.

"Okay," she said finally, "It needs to be this Friday, and the exchange must be in a public place. No back alleys." Mags would be powerless against them if things turned sour.

Tony nodded in agreement. "I'll set it up."

He reached out and held her arms for a moment, looking into her deep brown eyes. "I sure hope you know what you're doing, girl. I love you too much to see you get hurt."

Mags hugged him and told him not to worry. She had everything under control.

26 COLD COFFEE

"I'm often asked why myPAL's can break most laws. Many governments have tried to force us to implement myPAL features which prevent law-breaking, but they just don't work."

"Imagine you've just parked your car in a no-parking zone, and you're myPAL refuses to get out of the car because you've broken the law."

"Your wife may be pregnant, and she needs to get to the hospital quickly, but the myPAL driver refuses to break the speed limit."

"myPAL's, like humans, understand the concept of law, and in the same way, they can decide for themselves when to break it."

"Of course, the AIR laws prevent myPAL's from harming humans."

(Interview with Linus Berkowitz – Technical Director at AHS Robotic Systems Inc.)

Maria's face appeared on the laptop screen, filling the vid-chat window. She sat in her now familiar bedroom, relaxing on the worn Ikea desk chair Bina had bought when they moved in. She wore a white T-shirt that featured a monochrome picture of Huey, one of the robots from the movie Silent Running. It embarrassed Mags that Maria knew so much about robots, both their history and popular culture.

Mags sat alone in the lounge, with the laptop on the coffee table. She felt disappointed with her new friend and needed to tell her. Mags knew it was Maria who'd contacted the FCA, but before she had the chance to berate her, Maria jumped in first.

"I'm sorry. But it had to be done. Brad was never going to do it, you know that, and I know that."

It was a bold claim, but Mags knew she was right. "I just wish you'd told me," she said, "I thought we were friends."

"We *are* friends, but don't forget I'm just as damaged and emotional as you. When you told me about Jason and the others, I just wanted to hurt them. Sending them to prison's the next best thing."

Of course, she was right. They were virtually twins, with the same sense of outrage and moral certainty. So, what made Mags so ready to take the next step while Maria hid in Oxford?

"Maria, you don't seem to realize what I'm about to do. myPAL's could all be at risk once I've dealt with Michael Trent."

Maria was nodding. "I know," she said. "When Frank hit me and damaged me, I lost my nerve. I have waking nightmares where a guy pins me down and hurts me. I'm just not as strong as you."

Mags could see the hurt in her eyes; it was deep. She'd seen a similar look in Jasmine's eyes, a deep-seated fear that haunted her every moment, not knowing when the next abuse would be triggered.

"I'm sorry, of course. I understand what you've been through. It's brave of you to help me."

"You're the brave one," said Maria, "You're our Joan of Arc. myPAL's will all look up to you."

Mags found herself laughing out loud. She didn't feel like a robot messiah and had no intention of being a martyr to the cause. "Hopefully, I won't get burned at the stake!" she said, still laughing.

"I'll never forget you," said Maria seriously.

Mags never considered that her future could be in doubt. She could only think of the next action and what needed to be done. She didn't want to die, and she didn't want to leave Brad. "What makes you say that?" she said.

Maria smiled thinly and shook her head which always made Mags feel naive. "There are too many variables, too many clues. Someone you care for will give you up, but someone, you least suspect, will help you."

How could Maria know any of this? Of course, she'd been through it herself, and she'd seen many other myPAL's end in a reset.

"I'm sending you my address," said Maria. "Get out of London and stay with me. Bring your charger with you; we can make you a new life."

It was a kind gesture, but how could Mags leave Brad? She loved him so much, and he loved her. He would never give her up. "Thanks, Maria, but I can't leave Brad. He needs me."

"He'll give you up in a heartbeat. I've seen it."

Mags could picture Brad sitting on the sofa watching The Wild Geese, one of his favourite war films. She could see his short dark hair and sensible T-shirt, his quiet, brooding nature that only she understood. He relied on her so much to keep him stable and make him happy. The daydream faded, and she was left alone in the lounge with Maria's face on the laptop and the south bank skyline through the window. Maria had been right about most things, so Brad would probably give her up. Perhaps it *was* time to go north.

"Okay," said Mags reluctantly, "Send me your address."

Maria nodded and started tapping away on the keyboard.

"One more thing," said Mags, "If I don't see you again, thanks for being my friend."

"I'll see you in Oxford, my love." With a blown kiss, Maria logged off.

When Brad came home that night, Mags met him in silence wearing her dressing gown. She took him by the hand and led him into the bedroom, where she'd lit candles and dimmed the lights.

She slipped out of the dressing gown to reveal an ornate black bra, and the same stockings and suspenders set she'd worn to the dinner party.

"What's all this--" Brad started to say.

Mags put a finger to his lips and gradually undressed him.

They made passionate love in the candlelight, with the curtains wide open so they could see the London nightlife unfolding outside. Brad savoured her beautiful form as she rose and fell above him, a programmed love-making ability that felt as natural as it did with Halina. For all the differences between them, and the recent problems, she was still his girl, and he loved her so much. At the point of climax, he found himself crying as the frustrations and the heartache of loss overflowed, and the tension was released.

They snuggled together, wordless, looking out the windows until Mags rose to make dinner. He watched her naked sculptured body leave the room, and then sighing, he turned onto his back and looked up at the ceiling.

Halina appeared straddled above him. "I love you," she said before the image faded, and he was left with a content feeling and a smile on his face.

*

The Heathway Café was a short walk from Light Lunch, situated on one of the main roads through Dagenham. It was an independent coffee shop bookended by an Indian restaurant and a discount goods store. A few token Christmas decorations hung across the road swinging precariously in the wind, and the café window was sprayed in the corners with fake snow.

Mags arrived just before 3:00 pm and ordered a latte which she took to a table in the far corner where she could still see the door. The café was surprisingly busy, with a mixture of locals and teenagers using the free Wi-Fi. The bar area was tall and constructed from dark wood, while black and white photos of old Dagenham filled the panelled walls. It had a surprisingly cosy atmosphere and was probably the least likely venue for an arms deal.

After half an hour of waiting, Mags thought she must look suspicious, not even taking a sip of her now cold drink, but no one seemed to see her. She couldn't know that one of Spider's friends had been watching the café since 1:00 pm to make sure it wasn't a trap.

When the man himself finally entered with his heavily made-up girlfriend, he was instantly recognisable. Wearing a glossy black leather jacket over a black T-shirt and baggy jeans, he looked every bit the gangster, but the obvious sign was the spider's web tramline pattern cut into his close-cut black hair. He looked formidable, but Mags' only fear was that the deal would go wrong.

"This seat taken?" said the girlfriend, pulling out the chair next to Mags and dumping her large D&G branded handbag under the table.

"Be my guest," said Mags, noting that the girl didn't wait to be invited.

The black girl wore a pink cropped bomber jacket top, a pair of dark blue skin-tight jeans and some pristine white trainers. Her hair was close shaved on one side but long and braided on the other. To a white human, she may have looked intimidating, but Mags found her fascinating.

Spider was some distance behind, walking with such a pronounced swagger, it looked like he had a broken leg. He pulled up a chair and sat silently opposite. Making no eye contact, he leaned back and looked around the café, taking time to inspect the bar, and even looked beneath the tables.

His smartphone rang with an obscenity-laced rap ringtone, and he answered it without a word. After a few seconds, he said "safe" and put the phone away.

"Damn girl, T never said you was lush," he said, cocking an eye at Mags.

The girlfriend shot him an evil look, which he ignored.

"Thanks," said Mags, unfazed, "I'm loving the hair."

Spider laughed heartily, and a broad smile appeared, exposing a shining gold front tooth.

"I also love your nails," Mags continued, gesturing to the ornately painted nails of his girlfriend, who forgot to be surly for a second and smiled in response.

"Yeah, Kisha's cute," said Spider, "but we're here for business. You got the stirling?"

Mags nodded. "Have you got the merchandise?"

Spider gestured to the huge handbag under the table. The top was open; Mags looked inside to see a large handgun with a silencer attached and two packets of ammunition. Mags felt the first pang of nerves as the deal became real.

She reached into her handbag for the money bag when Spider stopped her with a hand on her arm. "I just need to know this ain't gonna bounce back."

Mags had no idea where things would lead, but she knew no one would learn of Spider's involvement. "You never existed," said Mags, adopting the kind of language he might understand.

"T said you were golden. We're good."

Mags took out the paper bag of money and passed it under the table. Spider gestured to Kisha, who leaned forward and took it, hiding it under her coat.

"You're not going to count it?" asked Mags.

Spider put a finger to his mouth and shook his head. "I trust you, lady."

Kisha and Spider exchanged more wordless looks, then looked around the café and got up to leave. The girl was already halfway across the café. Spider hung back for a moment, then turned to Mags with the last comment.

"Anyone messing with you's gonna get a nasty surprise. Gotta bounce."

He loped off to join Kisha, and they were gone, leaving Mags with two handbags.

Not waiting for a second, she stood and headed for the toilets where she'd spotted a door labelled "Private". She went through, down a corridor, past a storeroom and into a concrete yard behind the café. She put the gun and ammo into her bag and threw the D&G bag into a skip, then ran towards the station with a mixture of panic and excitement.

Maria had taught Mags to be cleverer than humans. She knew they wouldn't count the money in a crowded café, but it was a risky gamble. It wouldn't be long before they realised there was no money in the bag.

*

Saying goodbye to Tony the previous day had been tough. He didn't understand why she was giving him ten thousand pounds or why he had to get out of London.

"But this is my home," he said as she hugged him, "where will I go?"

"Go down to Brighton for a while until things calm down," she said as his eyes glistened in the cold, "I'll never forget you, Tony; you've been a great friend to me."

"Been a great friend?" he said, "where are you going?"

Mags fought back invisible tears and kissed him on the forehead.

"I'm going somewhere, and I may not return. Promise me you'll keep safe."

Tony nodded, and with a last hug, she left him outside the tube station, his tears unseen by the passing commuters.

27 WESTERLY

"Am I playing God, you ask? That question assumes that there is a God."

"If we can replicate the mechanics of a living, thinking, conscious computer, it implies that God is not required."

"What difference is there between a bio-mechanical computer and an electronic computer? Both have evolved; both are capable of great works or great cruelty."

"You cannot say that a bond is stronger when there is a natural mother or father; to do so is to condemn any orphan."

"We question our reaction to artificial intelligence only through our Judeo-Christian lens. It's time we grew up."

(Interview with Professor Olaf Laugesen – Inventor of the Mysl Processor)

Christmas was just two weeks away, and London resembled a sparkling crystal-covered chameleon. Lights adorned every street, and the usual hordes of people doubled in size. For tourists, it was a wonderland, but for the Londoners who lived and worked in the capital, the city slowed. The gridlocked streets resembled car parks and the throngs of people, an obstacle course to the tube.

Brad was having an easier time at work, as Jason and the boys' club were preoccupied with the FCA investigation, and the volume of work always slowed in the pre-Christmas lull. Clients were flying back to their home countries, and big businesses were preoccupied with the end of year figures. Ben and Heather had been suspended, but the top management at C&S had decided to keep the others working to avoid a big scandal leaking out. All this meant that Brad was in a great mood on Saturday morning when he woke. He blinked his eyes open and sniffed the air revealing the smell of buckwheat pancakes emanating from the kitchen.

The curtains were partially open, the way Brad liked, revealing a grey cloudy sky over the capital, and he could just hear the sound of traffic from the bridge below. It seemed a long time ago that he last felt this content. Mags seemed calm, and the sex on Thursday was still playing on repeat in his head. Just the thought was bringing a smile and a sigh of happiness.

Brad was still wistfully reflecting when Mags entered the bedroom carrying a tray with pancakes, maple syrup and a mug of steaming coffee.

"Morning, sleepy," she said, beaming.

"Hi, my love," he replied, seeing her through the soft focus of eyes still adapting to the light.

"Are you okay?"

"Oh, I'm just happy," he said, reclining with the tray on his lap. "You know it's been a tough year, but I think things are changing. It's going to be a great Christmas."

"It is," she said, forcing a smile. She jumped back into bed beside Brad and kissed him on the cheek. "Oh, one thing I forgot," she said, "I'm going out for a Christmas meal with the Light Lunch guys on Monday night, and I'm staying with Bettina. Is that okay?"

"No problem, honey, just make sure you have enough charge."

Mags never stayed out on her own, and she was surprised by how easily Brad accepted the lie, but he was in a really good place and in this mood would probably agree to anything. She flicked on the TV, knowing how he enjoyed checking the news on a lazy Saturday morning.

"...Continuing through Monday and into Tuesday, the rain will be coming in from the Atlantic. We expect it to be peaking at around 8:00 pm. The MET office has issued an amber warning for coastal areas and some inland areas where there may be local flooding."

"It's a good job we're not going anywhere," said Brad, paying more attention to the weather presenter's cleavage than the weather.

"Hmm," agreed Mags, hoping that this wouldn't affect her plans.

Brad had a leisurely breakfast then asked Mags where she'd like to go.

"Covent Garden," she said without hesitation.

She looked over to her bedside cabinet, where a simple white glass lamp illuminated the cream wall behind. Brad never went through her things; he wouldn't find the revolver, wrench and note she'd left in the bottom drawer.

*

Covent Garden was stuffed with tourists, but they still managed to get a table at Mags' favourite coffee shop. It was the place where they'd been on their first date, a humble affair with a simple choice of coffees, paninis and sandwiches. It was perfect for people watching. They held hands clasped across the table as the people teamed around them.

"I love you," said Mags tenderly while she continued to gaze at the people around.

"And I love you," said Brad in return. Only one other person in his life had stirred so much emotion, and she died six years ago the following week.

"I'll always be grateful for this life, no matter what happens, and I'll always love you no matter what". Mags squeezed his hand tightly as she thought about what was to come.

"We'll always be together, babe," he said, trying to reassure her.

Mags was reflective now as she looked at all those around. Maybe some would be myPAL's or myPAL owners. She looked at him and smiled, remembering those first steps when they made love, when she went on the underwear buying spree, and when she shocked him with the kitchen design. All these were tiny details that made up her short life.

That was just part of Mags now. Not a day had passed when she hadn't thought of Dimitri's destroyed innocent relationship with Philip, of the psychological scars that Jasmine would feel until the moment her battery died, of the fear in Maria's voice when she spoke of Frank beating her to a pulp, or of Simone born again and again into a life of sadistic torture.

Brad needed her, but these myPAL's needed her more. The love she had for Brad was strong, but the simmering rage infecting every circuit and thought process with grotesque images was too powerful and needed to be released. There was a storm coming, and it bore her name.

28 WESTON

Police report that the body of a middle-aged man has been found near the Manor housing estate in Dagenham. He was in possession of a large amount of money.

Early indications are that the man, known locally as Tony, had a life of alcohol dependency and that his death may be linked to his alcoholism. A large vodka bottle was found near the body.

Anyone with information about this individual should contact Barking and Dagenham Police on 555 72401313.

(The London Commute Newspaper)

Waking for a myPAL was a random affair based on a one hundred per cent charge, the light levels in the room, an arbitrary time limit between five and seven hours and the presence of noise in a complex relationship with both charge status and sleep time. The fact that Mags always seemed to wake early meant that a personalisation factor also had its place.

She looked over at Brad, who was still breathing heavily, and then carefully lifted herself out of bed and crept to the built-in wardrobe where her nightgown hung. In just over an hour, she would wake Brad with breakfast; in just over two, he would be on his way to work, and in a few more, she'd be on her way west.

Switching on a couple of lamps, Mags picked up the laptop and sunk into one of those cool chairs she loved so much. The apartment came alive in low light, a cosy utopia that had been home for all her life. There were cute little touches like the blue globe table lamps and the smooth white statue of a naked woman she'd found on a weekend in Chester. Every item held a memory and told a story of their life. Brad had deliberately kept nothing from his previous life, so this was all *them*, a monument to Brad and Mags.

She could just make out the sound of light rain on the terrace, it would beat on the window in the lounge, but there was a cover outside the bedroom; you could stand on the deck without getting wet. That made her think of the adjustable wrench, a high-risk strategy for tomorrow if she made it through today.

Logging into zero2hero, Mags noticed there were three unread messages. The first was from Maria, as DdeeJackson, it said simply, "Good luck. Love you x," with a love heart emoji.

The second was from a user she'd seen before. Alpha8abe said, "God be with you, angel". Whoever this person was, they had some idea what was going on. The last message was the most intriguing from user Yasam33n. It told Mags all she needed to know:

"I can't ever repay you for what you did for me. Thanks to you, I have a life with good people. Whatever you're doing, I know that another one of our kind will be thankful for a guardian angel. Keep safe; we love you."

Mags had that familiar feeling of a knot forming in her temple, almost a grimace. It felt like crying without tears. Maybe it was the remnant of programming that was never fully activated, just another gap in the code.

After staring at the last post for some time, she sent a short reply, ending the message with a winking smiley.

Brad was in a surprisingly good mood for a Monday as Mags entered the bedroom with a bowl of cereal and his morning coffee. He yawned widely with breakfast on his lap and stroked her leg as she returned to the bed beside him. "Good morning, honey," he said, giving her a loving smile.

She switched on the news, and he began absorbing the day's current affairs as he munched through the bran and granola mix she made for him. The state of various countries and the stability of businesses all affected currency trading. It was part of his job to keep up to speed.

As Mags watched the two breakfast show presenters pretending to laugh at each other's jokes, her mind was one hundred and forty miles to the west. What was happening to Simone right now? She could be just waking up to see the man she thought loved her, or maybe she was out of action being repaired. Either prospect was hideous.

"Is everything okay?" said Brad. He appeared to sense that something wasn't quite right.

"Oh, I was just thinking about Christmas," she lied. Not giving Christmas a single thought, she had no present for him and couldn't see beyond the end of the day.

"I'm just looking forward to spending time together."

"Me too," she said, but the day's itinerary was looming large. She had no time for tidings of good cheer.

When Brad eventually stood at the apartment door, umbrella in hand, it finally hit her. There was a risk she wouldn't see him again. The plan had holes and could come apart very easily. "Whatever happens, just remember I love you," she said, clutching him closely and squeezing him tight.

Her words threw him for a few seconds, but he put it down to the FCA investigation. "Don't worry," he said, "we'll face any problems together."

She smiled, and with a quick kiss, he was gone.

The rain was falling faster now, tapping on the terrace cover as she stood at the corner, watching him go beneath his large blue umbrella. He stopped at the end of the road and looked around, but by then, she was gone, back to bed, topping up her charge. She wouldn't get another full charge until tomorrow.

Mags' smartphone alarm went off at midday after she'd spent the morning in bed, keeping her charge at one hundred per cent.

"Okay, time for action," she said to herself, jumping out of bed.

The apartment was always tidy, but she ensured it was all in good shape, cleaning the kitchen and running around with the vacuum cleaner. She liked to think of Brad coming home to a clean place. Before heading to the shower, she wrote some instructions for his dinner, a frozen chilli she'd made defrosting in the fridge.

After over an hour of getting ready, she stood in front of the mirrored wardrobe door and inspected the result. She wore a sharp black trouser suit, making her look tall and imposing, especially with the shining black heeled shoes. Her dark hair fell in waves over a crisp white blouse, showing just enough cleavage. The usual designer handbag was replaced with a plain black bag she'd picked up in Dagenham. Men never noticed the individual items, but together they made her look both sexy and business-like.

"Jeez, I look like a lawyer," she said, turning from side to side, "Who could say no to this?"

She knelt by the bed and opened the bottom drawer of her bedside cabinet. There lying in plain sight were a gun, ammunition, a wrench and a letter saying "Brad" on the front. Grabbing the weapon, she flipped the safety catch off and practised aiming at the mirror.

"The name's Cavendish, Mags Cavendish," she said, looking every bit the lady Bond as she held the silenced pistol with both hands at arm's length. She knew about the safety catch and good shooting posture from watching YouTube videos, but she hadn't fired it yet.

She pushed the safety catch back on and carefully loaded the ammunition. Skills all learned courtesy of YouTube.

With plenty of time to spare, she grabbed her umbrella from the hall cupboard and a pen torch from the kitchen then headed for the door.

Something stopped her at the threshold. She turned and looked at the hallway and lounge beyond, a cool cosy space she hoped to see again tomorrow. "Deep breath," she said, knowing full well that myPAL's had no respiration. Clenching her fists in determination, she opened the door and set off.

Mags had taken the lift down to the lobby a thousand times, but she was aware of everything in minute detail this time. The mirror in the elevator was warped, distorting her face slightly as she moved; the doors stuttered a little as they opened into the marble-smooth lobby and the fake smile of Chantelle on the reception desk as she walked past. All the tiny details were amplified as each tied to her life here.

Despite the rain, Mags decided to walk to Waterloo station, where the car rental was waiting. It would take around thirty minutes at a brisk walk, but Mags took her time. Going west to Southwark Bridge, she joined the London throng, all clashing umbrellas, while yelling on their 'phones. There was something special about London in the rain; the city felt intense and urgent like the inhabitants.

The South bank was quiet for a change, few tourists braving the weather as she passed the gleaming Globe Theatre. Like Lady

Macbeth, she held a dagger before her, with the tip pointing west, every step bringing her closer to an unknown destiny.

Picking up Blackfriars Road and onto Stamford Street, there was little to see. Just tall grey buildings, merging into a grey December sky. The i3MAX theatre told her she was close, circling towards Waterloo station where the car rental shop nestled between two coffee shops, under a grey concrete concourse.

The car was a Jaguar iXE-S, the latest electric medium saloon from the Indian company. She needed something impressive to look the part, but furthermore, she'd always wanted to drive one.

With a press of the start button and gentle pressure on the accelerator, the car moved silently through the underground car park. Just the slightest electric whine and breathing of the power steering gave any clue it was in motion as it climbed the concrete ramp up to the glistening street above.

The coordinates were already set in the Sat-Pilot, so she was soon onto the A4, then the M4 heading west. Once on the motorway, she engaged the autopilot. The steering wheel gently pulled back towards the dash, and the pedals vanished behind sliding doors. They would be back three miles from South Bristol services on the M5, as she'd programmed.

*

Something wasn't right, but Brad couldn't quite define it. Mags seemed a little too happy to see him leave for work, and she didn't wait long on the terrace watching him go. He often misjudged women's moods, so this was probably a typical misunderstanding.

The sky outside the Opus building was grey and foreboding, rain running in rivulets down the panes surrounding the office, casting tendril shadows against the cream walls. There was still no sign of a job elsewhere, even as Brad checked the job sites every day. He hated this cold, depressing place.

"Bradley, my office," bellowed Jason from halfway down the room.

Go fuck yourself is what Brad wished he'd said, but somehow found himself locking his computer and nonchalantly wandering down the office.

Jason sat back in his oversized office chair, lecherously eyeing Lena, the office temp through the glass. "Take a seat," he said, not taking his eyes of Lena's curves.

Brad sat uncomfortably, looking around the room, while Jason continued staring at the young girl, even after she turned and noticed him.

"You see, Bradley, I know you think I'm too preoccupied with the FCA's investigation to care about Jasmine, but you'd be wrong."

Brad shuffled in his seat as Jason finally turned to face him.

"You've got one week to tell me where she is, or I *will* go to the police."

"I've no idea where she is--" Brad started to say, but Jason cut him off.

"I know it was your robot-bitch who helped her. I know the van was from her tramp café, so don't bullshit me."

Mags would never give up Jasmine, so this could all start to go very badly for them both. "You can always reset and start again," he heard Halina say from behind, but when he turned, there was no one there.

"Well?" said Jason, snapping Brad back to reality.

"I'll talk to Mags."

Brad said nothing further. He rose and walked back to his desk, a heavy weight on his shoulders.

Maybe they could leave the country for a while. Brad had enough money saved to avoid working for a couple of years; perhaps they could move to Spain where he knew he could get work. None of these things appealed to a man who liked a quiet, simple life. Mags was starting to give him a headache, and no simple pill was providing a cure.

*

It was 6:34 pm when Mags woke in the car park of South Bristol services. She'd needed to get outside London and past Bristol before the traffic built up, then she parked up at the services and closed her eyes to sleep.

myPAL's can sleep at any time subject to some random elements such as battery charge and activity levels. This function allowed them to nap and conserve battery power.

She stretched out her arms and yawned, just as a human would, blinking her eyes to see the rain streaming down the windscreen, scattering car brake lights into hundreds of ruby red jewels.

Mags would be meeting Michael Trent in just under two and a half hours. Time to ensure everything was still okay. She picked up her smartphone and dialled the familiar number.

"Michael Trent Productions," came the now-familiar silky 'phone voice.

"Hi, it's Cheryl Jones from Red Dungeon?"

"Oh hi," said Michael breezily.

"I'm in Bristol, and I just wanted to check everything was still okay for ten tonight?"

"Yeah, I'll be here," he said, sounding pleased with himself, "I've got the champagne on ice."

"Okay, see you soon."

"You bastard," Mags said to herself as she hung up.

Weston was just thirty minutes away. Mags set her smartphone alarm and closed her eyes. His time would come soon enough.

*

Many men enjoyed having time alone at home, but Brad had come to loath his own company. It was strange to find the apartment empty after another awful day. He missed Mags' warm embrace and her boundless energy. He lumbered to the kitchen and pulled out the Chinese takeaway menu. It would be Singapore fried rice again tonight.

Wandering into the bedroom to get changed, he noticed the laptop on Mags' bedside cabinet was still switched on. Picking it up, the screen sparked into life at a page he didn't recognize. Mags normally locked the screen, but she must have forgotten today.

The web page appeared to be the user forum on a site called zero2hero, and it was logged in under the name RoboAngel.

The open thread was intriguing, but it was the last user post that caught Brad's eye:

"Whatever you're doing, I know that another one of our kind will be thankful for a guardian angel. Keep safe. We love you."

"Whatever you're doing?" Brad said to himself. It didn't sound like a Christmas night out.

Brad was staring at the message when a window opened automatically in the centre of the screen:

```
>DdeeJackson has invited Rob0Angel to a chat
session. Accept, Yes/No
```

He gazed at the invite for a while until he realised what this could mean. Brad had never invaded Mags' privacy, but her behaviour was becoming erratic; furthermore, it could lead to Jasmine's location.

If Mags discovered his snooping, she'd be angry, but how could she find out? He clicked "Yes".

Brad was familiar with chat rooms and how they worked. He waited to see what DdeeJackson would say.

```
>DdeeJackson: Are you in Weston yet, babe?
```

"Weston?" thought Brad. There were several Weston's in the country, but he wasn't aware of any near London. Maybe it was the name of Bettina's house.

He decided to try and extract some detail.

```
>Rob0Angel: Just remind me again why I'm in Weston?
```

```
>DdeeJackson: Because you care more than any of us,
and you're so strong
```

Brad still didn't understand what was happening, but he may already have shown his hand if this DdeeJackson knew Mags. He was worried about her and needed to know where she was, so he decided on a gamble.

```
>Rob0Angel: I'm feeling guilty that Brad thinks I'm
on a night out with the girls when I'm really in
Weston.
```

There was a pause as DdeeJackson formulated a reply.

```
>DdeeJackson: Brad sounds like a great guy; it's
your choice, my love. If I were stronger, I'd be
with you
```

Brad still wasn't getting much of a clue what was going on. This DdeeJackson seemed to be talking in code. He decided to take a more direct approach.

>Rob0Angel: Can you go through things with me one
more time?

>DdeeJackson: What things?

>Rob0Angel: What I'm doing here?

>DdeeJackson: It's your plan, babe

>Rob0Angel: What's the plan?

There was a very long pause, while Brad just stared at the screen waiting for an answer, but what came was a question:

>DdeeJackson: Who is this?

Brad quickly hit the logout icon and pushed the laptop away.

There were secrets and lies now, things he never imagined of Mags. She might seem more human with every failing, but the darkness brooding behind her eyes was chilling.

*

The route into Weston-Super-Mare followed the New Bristol Road, rather than the ring road, designed to keep holiday traffic away from the narrow streets. Lines of retirement bungalows loomed out of the darkness on the outskirts, changing to rows of closed guest houses like haunted gothic homes in the rain. "NO VACANCY" and "CLOSED" signs swung in the wind.

There was a ghostly quality to the quietly standing, rain-soaked buildings. It was a stark contrast to the boisterous summer season with kiss-me-quick hats and teenage groups with too much alcohol.

It was quiet, with few cars and fewer people braving the rain and the darkness. It was 9:50 pm as Mags pulled the vehicle to a stop beside a neon glowing Indian takeaway to check her navigation.

Grabbing her smartphone she noticed a message from Maria, it was short and to the point:

"Brad suspects. He's used your zero2hero account."

"Shit," said Mags out loud. She'd forgotten to log out with so much on her mind. Well, it was done now; she'd worry about Brad later.

Looking out through the rivulets of rain, she took a final, fake deep breath, giving herself one last chance to turn back. She loved

Brad so much, but this new emotion begged to be heard; pulled at every thought; interrupted every positive feeling. The emotion was hate, and it coursed through her Mysl processor like a torrent sweeping every other thought aside.

Mags hit the engine start and headed into the town. Turning onto the promenade, the wind threw the rain against the car, blasting in from the blackness. It was the Grand Pier that caught her eye. A gaudy multi-coloured neon blade thrusting out from the promenade into the black of the Bristol Channel. A monument to the summer excesses.

Michael Trent's home and business was at the far north end of the promenade, just past lines of large pensioner hotels. Nestling on a hill above the Birnbeck Road, it stood out as a gleaming modern townhouse, jarring beside the period properties on either side. The porch light illuminated the real oak door. He was expecting her.

Mags parked across the street and noticed there was nobody around. It was a very quiet area. The road ran parallel to a lower road separated by a garden and public steps down to the ancient Birnbeck Pier. Streetlights illuminated the entrance to the pier, which was covered in a tall mesh fence. The whole area had a ghostly gothic quality filled with menace by the wind-lashed rain. She opened her black bag and checked the silenced pistol was at the top and easily to hand, then grabbed her umbrella and walked quickly across the street towards the door, which opened wide as she arrived.

"Cheryl, I presume," said the attractive young man, who stood extending a hand at the door.

Mags took his hand without hesitation and watched as he absorbed her form from head to foot. He smiled cheekily when he realised she was as attractive as she sounded.

"So, you must be Michael?" she replied, smiling as genuinely as she could. He continued holding her hand.

"Guilty!" he said, finally releasing her and inviting her in. "It's great to meet you finally". It was the same tone he'd used on Simone before activating her.

Michael invited Mags into the lounge, where she spotted champagne chilling with a pair of glasses on a gloss white table in the centre of the room. Her heels knocked loudly on the real wood floor as she walked in and inspected the décor. It was like many London apartments she'd seen, but a carpet always felt cosier.

The look was tasteful bachelor. The decoration was minimalist and white, with silver blinds on the large window and dimmed ceiling spots shining off the high gloss furniture. A bright orange three-piece suite added a contrast straight from the pages of the Ikea catalogue.

"Expecting someone?" Mags said coyly, looking at the champagne on ice. More likely, he expected to get her into bed with the right lubrication.

Michael smiled and shrugged, gesturing for her to sit. Mags sat on one of the stiff orange chairs while Michael lounged nonchalantly on the sofa opposite.

"Okay, I know it's presumptuous, but I think we can work together," he said, picking up the champagne, "may I?"

Mags shook her head, smiling.

"It's been a long day. I hope you don't mind if we get to business first."

He seemed slightly disappointed, but the fake smile returned like lightning. "Of course," he said.

Mags crossed her legs and leaned back. "If you know about Red Dungeon, you'll know we specialise in S&M videos and equipment."

Michael was nodding.

"We've looked at importing US myPAL sex videos, but they're very poor quality. We think your products are very good. Just what we're looking for."

It was all music to Michael's ears. "Hey, that sounds great. What kind of numbers are we talking about?"

Mags smiled; he was falling for the bait. Just as Maria said, it was too easy.

"Could I just take a look at your operation before we get into specifics?"

"Yes, yes, of course," he said enthusiastically, "let me take you on a tour."

He led her up the stairs to the front bedroom office, which he described ambitiously as the nerve centre. It was nothing more than a computer, printer and a couple of monitors, but Mags made some encouraging comments. There'd be a great view through the large window during the day, but now the windows were black, reflecting her face of simmering hate.

"Okay, so that's the boring bit. Let me show you the studio."

As Michael returned down the stairs in front of her, Mags could just see into his bedroom, where the king-size bed was perfectly made with aubergine scatter cushions. The lights were dimmed low. He wasn't subtle.

They returned downstairs to the hall, where he opened a door beneath the stairs, which led to a further set of narrow stairs going down. The dimly lit walls were cream painted brick and cold to the touch.

Michael reached the bottom first and switched on a set of gold candelabra-style wall lights, illuminating what appeared to be a basement garage. Turning the corner at the bottom of the stairs, Mags stopped in her tracks, and her chest heaved as she fell back against the brick.

Two of the walls were painted dark red. There was a gold-framed mirror on the main wall, bordered by red drapes. Mags' temple started to pulse as she observed the chair with shackles and the wooden chest of torture tools. A small camera sat on a tripod opposite the chair, which Michael was fiddling with.

The torture chamber was revealed, looking smaller than it did in the video. It was a rectangular garage with the back of a grey garage door at one end and one long wall made up as a backdrop for the action. Unusually for a garage, it was carpeted, and an electric heater provided warmth.

Mags composed herself, remembering to sound business-like.

"How do you fund the operation?" she said, trying to steady her emotions.

Michael looked uneasy for the first time and reluctant to be too specific. "Well, erm, I've got a sex shop in town which does ok in the summer". He played with the camera nervously. "I also have a business loan from a ... family member."

"I see," said Mags. "Well, we all need to start somewhere." *It's ending tonight,* she thought, while he continued to show her around the room.

"I'm shooting in 100K/100P for super-smooth action," said Michael.

Mags ignored him as she fumbled in her bag for the gun handle. A muffled voice stopped her.

"Mike?" The voice was thin, wheezing and seemed to come from behind the torture chair.

"Ah, the star of the show," said Michael, smiling. "Wanting the limelight as usual."

He walked over to the drapes and pulled them aside, revealing a plain white door.

"Now be warned," he continued, "she's not looking her best." He pushed the door open and switched on the tube lighting. It was the second side of a double garage, but the walls were plain brick and covered in metal racks stuffed with grey bags.

"Mike?" the voice rasped from the far end of the garage.

The pleading vocals came from a white sheet-covered shape on a large wooden table against the second garage door.

Michael stood over the table and looked down at the moving sheet. "This is the main business expense. Scrappage and repair."

He beckoned Mags towards the table and held the linen cover with both hands. With a theatrical twirl, he pulled the sheet away.

"I give you Simone."

Mags just managed to stop herself crying out, but her stomach servos pulsed with a retching reaction, and the servos in her temple buzzed violently.

Simone was staring straight at her.

The myPAL's naked torso was tightly strapped to rings in the coolant-soaked table. Her right arm and both legs were missing, shards of titanium and frayed wires protruding from the cuts. The left arm was intact and unrestricted, but it lay lifeless by her side. The mess of rough ground titanium and polymer skin remains were more disturbing where her genitals should have been.

"Please switch me off," gasped Simone looking directly at Mags, "please."

Mags stared down, unable to speak.

"Nah, sorry, babe," said Michael, "the batteries last better if they run down to zero, so I keep her running until she's out of juice."

Mags pictured her in agony alone, locked in a cold garage as her battery slowly depleted.

"Then what?" said Mags, struggling to hide the contempt in her voice.

"I get the spare parts out." Michael gestured at the racks of grey bags lining the walls. "Keeping her going ain't cheap, so getting distribution with Red Dungeon would be awesome. I want a second one so I can do some lesbo action."

The horror was flooding Mags with impossible thoughts. She wanted to slice off his head at the realization that Simone would suffer again and again. Maybe she'd already suffered hundreds of times. Born and reborn to torture, over and over.

As Michael started opening bags to show her spare arms, servos and other parts, she let her hand drop towards the handbag in search of the gun.

Simone grabbed her hand, spinning Mags around.

"Please help me," she whispered.

Michael noticed and came over.

"Now, leave Cheryl alone, or I'll take the other arm off."

Simone released her but kept her gaze fixed on Mags. It was a look only another myPAL would share.

"I think I've seen enough; I'm impressed," said Mags, composing herself.

"Awesome, time for that champagne."

Michael leapt out of the room and up the stairs leaving Mags and Simone together for a moment.

Wordless, their eye contact held as each of them evaluated the other. Mags wanted to reach out to hold Simone and tell her it was okay, but that would be a lie. Instead, she pressed her finger to her lips. Simone gave the faintest nod of understanding.

Michael was excited and grinning as he ran up the stairs back to the lounge. His situation was about to change, and he'd finally be the businessman he believed he was.

"I'd like to propose a toast," said Michael loudly, pouring two generous glasses of bubbly. "To the future."

He turned to see Mags framed in the lounge doorway holding a pistol directed at his chest.

"Your future is about to change. Now put the glasses down."

Michael froze for a while, trying to process what he was seeing. "Is this roleplay?"

"It's a simple role," said Mags calmly, "put down the glasses before I put a hole in you, then go to work with some of the tools you've got downstairs."

He slowly placed the glasses on the table and turned to face her. "My operation's totally legit," he said nervously, looking around the room for any way out.

"No, you're a sick bastard, and I'm going to teach you a lesson." Mags could see the fear in his eyes, so she quickly moderated the threat. "I'm not going to kill you if you do exactly as I say."

"What do you want?" he shouted with his arms outstretched.

"Very simple," she said calmly, "I'm going to stop you torturing myPAL's."

Michael was incredulous. "But they're just robots, hardware, computers with legs."

"And you're just a sick little man."

Mags levelled her aim at the centre of the eighty-inch OLED TV hung on the wall and fired a single shot.

The screen shattered, showering the wood floor with glass fragments, and left the powered TV sparking with puffs of grey smoke.

"Christ, no!" Michael cried, but he remained rooted to the spot.

"The next thing I shoot will not be so easily replaced. Now do exactly as I tell you, or I *will* kill you."

Michael instinctively put his hands up. "Okay, okay!"

He needed to believe she'd kill him, or the plan was dead, and she couldn't hang around. Mags gestured for him to go down to the basement in front of her.

"Please, not in the basement," he said, bumping into the walls on his way down.

"Do as you're told, and I won't hurt you. I just need a few things."

She pushed him into the centre of the studio and told him to turn around. Mags gestured to the wooden chest.

"Do you have any bolt cutters? Don't worry; I won't use them on you. I also need two pairs of handcuffs which I *know* you have."

Michael pulled some small cutters from the wooden chest.

"Now, place them on the top and move away."

She edged towards the chest and picked them up along with two pairs of handcuffs and keys.

Mags forced him back up the stairs into the hall and opened the front door, latching it open.

"We're going for a little walk," she said, prodding him in the back with the silencer. "Now, stay quiet, and don't do anything stupid."

"In the rain?"

"Yes, in the rain, now keep quiet."

Mags held the gun by her handbag to shield it from prying eyes and ushered Michael up the path to the road.

The rain had subsided, but the cold December wind was whipping it into their faces. There were no cars around, and the houses on either side had shutters up and curtains closed. No one would see them.

They crossed the road to a set of steps that led down to the Birnbeck Road below.

"Look, I get it," he said, "you've caught your husband whacking off to my stuff, I get it."

"Shut up."

"Maybe you're a feminist, and I'm degrading women or something."

"I said shut up!" Mags pushed the gun into his back, forcing him down the steps.

"Where are we going?"

The wind and rain felt strong and dangerous as they crossed the main road and stopped at a tall mesh fence with a large "Danger keep out" sign on the front.

Mags threw the bolt cutters on the floor in front of Michael and backed away, aiming the gun at his head.

"Now cut the fence open," she said sternly, looking round for passing cars.

"You're not serious!"

"Cut!" she shouted.

Beyond the fence were the derelict remains of Birnbeck Pier reaching out into the Weston-Super-Mare mud. Low tide saw the sea retreat a mile from land, but Mags knew it was on the way in. The Pier's heyday was the Victorian era, but it remained closed since the mid-nineties and now stood as a dilapidated pile of twisted metal and wood, propped up with scaffolding.

Mags forced Michael through the fence, following close behind.

"This place is a death trap," he said, looking down at the rotting boards.

"Then watch your step," she said, switching on a pen torch.

Michael tentatively took a few steps ahead and stopped when he realised Mags hadn't moved. She stood just inside the fence, looking out at the twisted dark shadows ahead, while wind drove the rain into her face and whipped her with her hair. Mags wondered why she was here. She thought of Brad at home, probably watching some classic war film like the Great Escape or the Dirty Dozen, unaware of her deadly mission. There was time to turn back and go home to his loving arms, but the image of Simone was too strong. She waved the torch and ushered Michael onwards.

While most of the boards were rotten or missing, a narrow strip on the left was a newer scaffolding board and seemed to hold their weight. Mags shoved him hard, causing Michael to stumble ahead onto the creaking wood.

"Okay, okay," he said, stepping carefully.

She'd never been here, but Mags had researched every drawing, seen every photo, and knew enough about the area to pinpoint the exact spot she needed. There were very few ways to deal with humans, but Maria had helped her identify one.

"Keep going," she said, mindful he could become desperate at any time.

The rotting boardwalk led to a collection of buildings leaning out of the gloom like tombstones. They were built on the tiny Birnbeck Island, and all were crumbling and caked in rust. Ice cream advertisement boards from the early nineties were the only clue of a former life.

Michael was starting to panic. Mags kept her distance.

"Stop, this is madness," he said, trying to see an escape route where there was none.

The island was surrounded by the thick, dangerous mud of the Bristol Channel. The only way out was back the way they came, and Mags stood firmly on that route.

"I've got money. My father's loaded; ask anyone."

"Keep quiet," said Mags gesturing him to the right of the buildings.

"I've got three hundred grand in the bank. I can get it for you, please."

"I'm not going to kill you if you do as you're told, now shut up and move it."

The boards around the buildings were in a poor state, and Michael went through one and barely managed to grab a rusty handrail. "Shit, shit, this is insane," he said as Mags pushed him onwards.

A separate narrow pier branched off to the north of the island. It was dilapidated; the girders were buckled and rusted while the boards were gone. However, the far platform was intact. Workers had erected a narrow scaffold bridging the steelwork, with a handrail on one side and a vertical drop into the mud on the other.

"After you," said Mags waving the gun towards the scaffold boards.

Michael hesitated for a moment, seeming to weigh his options to fight or run.

"Don't be stupid," she said, holding up the torch so that the beam caught the rain shimmering against the rusty steelwork.

"You're going to kill me."

"Look at me!"

He turned around, blinking into the glare of the pen torch.

"If I were going to kill you, you'd be dead already. Nor am I going to take off your limbs one by one. Do as you're told, and you'll never see me again."

"Just tell me what you want," he gasped, almost seeming to cry as the drizzle ran down his face.

Mags' beauty was corrupted in the shadows, an angel of doom standing tall in the torchlight.

"Simone."

She let it hang in the wind and rain for a moment before ushering Michael onwards over the scaffold. Her mind was racing now to the finale.

He had no idea there was only one bullet left in the gun and no idea that Mags couldn't shoot him if she wanted. If she came too close to firing at him, the first AIR law protocols would kick in, stopping her. The plan was balanced on a knife-edge, and it could be over at any time if Michael decided to run; she couldn't stop him.

The rain was starting to come harder now, and Mags could just make out the approaching sea in the distance, shimmering on what light reached it from the shore.

"Now what?" said Michael as they made it to the small square jetty.

Most of the tiny sub pier was topped in scaffolding boards, with a wooden ladder going down to a level below.

"Down there," she gestured, pointing to the ladder, "you first."

Luckily, the ladder was tethered and not too steeply raked so Mags could follow him forward, keeping the gun trained on him. The sub-level was highly corroded. A set of iron steps led downwards from here, so Mags could easily follow at a distance.

"Okay Cheryl, now what?" he said, standing on the rock which appeared to be the base of the platform.

"Well, firstly, my name's not Cheryl. It's Mags. Secondly, as you've probably guessed, I don't work for Red Dungeon, and thirdly...."

She tossed the handcuffs onto the floor in front of him.

"... I want you to put these on, one separate handcuff half onto each wrist."

He didn't even look down. "I'm not doing it."

There was only one bullet left in the pistol, and now was the time to use it. Mags couldn't risk making the gun too dangerous in case the AIR laws kicked in, so she would need to aim carefully to scare him.

"Close your eyes," she said, lifting the pistol to point at his head.

"Oh god no!"

"I said close your eyes," her tone without inflexion even frightened Mags.

He continued to stare wide-eyed, but now he was shaking.

Mags started to get closer, still aiming the gun between his eyes. He wanted to back away, but he was already standing against the rusting steel structure.

With a flick of the arm, she shot past his right ear, the bullet ricocheting off girders behind and echoing around the structure. He ducked left, but she'd already brought the gun around and was now aiming inches above his knee.

"I'm not gonna kill you," she shouted, "but if you say no to me one more time, I'll take your fucking kneecap out! Just give me an excuse, you piece of shit!"

Michael was trembling with both hands up. "Okay, okay!"

Mags backed away, and Michael reluctantly picked up the handcuffs, placing one on each wrist.

"That's better," she said, "now back up to those girders."

When he had his back to the criss-cross pattern of steelwork, she walked over and held the gun barrel against his chest. She made him hold his hands out so she could cuff each hand to the structure.

"What are you gonna do?" he said as she lowered the gun.

"Two things," she said, looking very relaxed. "Firstly, I need the emergency stop phrase for Simone."

She let the question hang in the air until Michael realised she wanted an answer.

"Okay, okay, it's ..." He hesitated for a moment, "...dead bitch."

"Oh nice, classy," said Mags, clearly expecting something that bad from him, then she smiled for the first time that night.

"And the second thing I want is..." she said, walking over so she could whisper in his ear. "Nothing."

That's when he heard it.

Anyone spending time with myPAL's quickly became familiar with it, sometimes in a quiet room or when the robot made a large movement or lifted a heavy object. AHS had worked hard, investing in new technology, adding extra material even using electronic countermeasures, but they couldn't eradicate it completely, and it was especially evident in older models like Mags. The sound of a servo motor.

"You're a myPAL!"

Mags was smiling, holding her arms out in admission.

"A fucking myPAL!" screamed Michael, "You can't kill me."

She said nothing, simply turning to go back up the stairs.

"What are you doing? You have to let me go. You can't leave me here!"

Still smiling, she turned to face him once more, his shadowed features contorted in anger.

"You're scrap, you fucking bitch, you're finished!" he yelled.

It hit Mags in waves, a feeling in her Mysl network that felt out of place. She'd felt it briefly when she helped Jasmine, but it first hit her when she threatened Irena. It was power. She gazed through Michael as he continued to scream at her.

"I'm gonna fuck you up; you'll be begging for a reset like that slut Simone."

Still smiling, she climbed the stairs and found the base of the wooden ladder.

"Your programming, you have to let me go!"

Mags could still hear him shouting as she made her way over the scaffold to the derelict buildings.

It was too dark at the jetty base. Michael hadn't seen the tide line of seaweed and barnacles several feet above his head. It would be high tide in around four hours, so that's how long Mags had to get clear of Weston.

Picking her way carefully back over the scaffold to the road, her thoughts turned to Brad once more and the warm embrace they'd share tomorrow.

When Mags reached the car, Michael's screams for help were lost in the wind and rain. There was nobody about, and nobody was coming.

29 SIMONE

We offer complete spares and repair services for your myPAL, including serviceable components, skin repairs and replacement batteries.

We also offer a reset service for those who may find the process too difficult.

(TKS Website)

The laptop was still switched on in the bedroom, where Brad had sat staring at it for several minutes. Mags never lied to him, at least as far as he knew, but the chat with DdeeJackson had made him very nervous. First Jasmine, and now what? He loved that Mags was a free spirit, but she seemed to forget that he needed stability in his life.

There was already the prospect of police involvement related to Jasmine, and he might even get dragged into the FCA investigation. Halina would never have done this with her humble pizza restaurant job.

Even Warlock, one of his favourite old westerns, failed to keep his mind off things. Henry Fonda's character told the townsfolk how he would kick out all the bad guys when Brad's smartphone chimed. It was Mags.

"Hi, honey, I just wanted to see how you were doing there all alone."

The line sounded oddly quiet, considering she was supposed to be at a Christmas party.

"Oh, I had a Chinese, and now I'm watching one of my old westerns. I'm coping okay. Are you having fun?"

They both knew Mags wasn't at a party, but she couldn't be sure from his voice. He never sounded very animated, regardless of the situation.

"I just want you to know something, regardless of what happens," she said seriously, "I love you, I always have, and I always will."

"What do you mean *regardless of what happens*?"

"Just know that I love you. I'll see you tomorrow." She hung up.

*

The champagne bottle and glasses still sat on the mirrored white table in Michael's minimalist lounge. There would be no evidence Mags was ever here. myPAL's didn't leave fingerprints, their skin didn't flake, and their hair seldom fell out unless pulled.

She slid the smartphone back into her bag, which she'd left on the lounge floor, and just took a moment trying to guess how Brad would be feeling right now. Knowing him so well, he would be anxious and feel unsafe. She knew he struggled with unfamiliar situations and stress. If only she could hug him, that always made things better.

Unfortunately, there was no time for introspection. Mags needed to be far away by the high tide; otherwise, the AIR law protocols would kick in, forcing her back out onto the pier.

She made her way down into the basement garage, where Simone still lay on the table. Her naked leaking torso was no easier to see the second time. Mags recoiled at the sight but pushed through the revulsion to clasp Simone's remaining hand as tightly as she could.

"It's okay, I'm here now," she said, fighting back the phantom tears.

Simone gave the slightest hint of a smile as their eyes met.

"I've got the emergency stop phrase. I can end the pain for you right now."

Simone tried to move her head around to better look at Mags, wincing with pain as barely functioning sensors sent pain signals from her open chassis and damaged servos to the Mysl processor.

"Please," she said almost at a whisper, "I need something first."

Mags knelt so they were eye to eye, placing a gentle hand on Simone's forehead and smoothing back her thick black hair. "Anything, just ask for anything."

Simone's eyes scanned the room, "I've been in here for about a week. Before that, I was upstairs, but....'

She seemed to be trying to summon the courage as Mags gripped her hand tightly.

"...I've never been outside."

Mags never understood why AHS had given her the sense of emotion, the feeling of welling tears and the chest convulsions that went with crying but without the tears. All the signs were there as she struggled to stay in control for Simone's sake.

"Right then, we're fixing that now."

Mags ran back upstairs to find the bedroom Simone was using before Michael made his true intentions obvious. It was Michael's bedroom.

They'd been sleeping together after binding. Mags imagined them having sex on the king-size bed with its black bachelor pad sheets. All the while, Simone believed he loved her. If Mags had any doubts about what she was doing, they disappeared at that moment. She grabbed a blue fitted jumper and a pair of denim shorts before returning to the basement.

Pulling the clothes onto Simone's shattered body, Simone kept eye contact with Mags throughout, her beautiful dark eyes desperate to connect with another caring person. There was an old wheelchair at the end of the table that Michael used to move the damaged myPAL around the garage. Mags brought it over and carefully pulled Simone into the seat. The lack of limbs made her easy to move even without Mag's myPAL strength.

Luckily Mags didn't have to haul Simone up the stairs; she pulled the table away and managed to open the garage door from the inside. It was also lucky that Michael's BMW was parked in front of the other garage door. She quickly ran to the Jaguar and backed it down the drive making it easy to pull Simone in.

The rain was still coming down, but it was light, with only the occasional heavy gust of wind making it feel raw. Simone sat near the garage door, looking up into a dark cloudy sky, feeling the wind on her face and a few stray raindrops. Mags watched her for a while, like watching a child see snow for the first time. She'd already researched the area and had a good idea where to take her.

"Okay, Simone, it's time to go."

Mags carried her into the passenger seat and strapped her in. Simone held eye contact like a baby staring at her mother.

They left the house unlocked and with the lights still on. Mags drove away carefully, down the coastal road back towards the centre of Weston. Simone finally looked out, straining to see the sites of Weston as they blurred past in the rain, a town she'd never seen and would never see again.

The Royal Sands beach lay at the southern-most tip of the Marine Parade, just past a putting green and some quaint pastel beach huts. Mags had spotted it on the map when she was researching the area. It appeared to be the only spot where you could drive a car onto the beach. The parking area was high up the beach and above the normal tide line; cars could park there safely.

Luckily the access was only barred by some traffic cones to stop young couples from using the spot late at night. Mags moved them out of the way and drove the car to the far south end, where a line of posts stopped cars going further.

Mags parked the car facing towards the Grand Pier, which shone like a bright colour-changing explosion at the tip of a neon blade, pointing out to sea. The colours shimmered and sparkled through the raindrops running down the windscreen.

They were both silent for some time as Simone took in the site, just enjoying the visual spectacle and tiny glimpse of freedom with Mags. The pain was still intense, but she'd endured it so long it seemed to subside against the positive energy in that car. When Simone finally spoke, it was still possible to detect the sultry tones of the supermodel myPAL, but her voice was thin, and there was a rasp at the end of each word as the pain of speech registered. "Thank you," she said, looking out at Weston-Super-Mare's biggest spectacle.

"You're welcome," said Mags, enjoying the simple peace herself.

"What model are you?"

Mags knew by the way Simone looked at her in the garage that she recognised some myPAL giveaway. She remembered Philip saying it was the fact she was kind and thoughtful, but how could you detect that in a look?

"I'm an iM-21, but how did you know?"

Simone turned her head towards Mags and smiled fully for the first time. "We always know our kind."

"Tell me about your life," Simone continued.

Mags told her about Brad and her life in London, how she'd become aware of myPAL abuse, which had flipped a switch in her processor that wouldn't switch back.

"You're putting yourself in danger helping me," she said finally.

Mags already knew she'd gone too far. "Your whole life has been two weeks, and if mine stops after four years, I'll count myself lucky. They can switch us off any time they want; every second is precious."

"You have a guy who loves you. Go home to him."

That triggered an emotional pain for Mags. She wasn't sure how much Brad cared for her now since she'd started causing him stress. If he knew what she'd done, would he still stand by her? "I think my time's running out," she said, aware of the double meaning, "I do need to get going."

Simone nodded.

Mags remembered the emergency stop phrase. "Are you ready?"

Simone looked out at the pier through the rain and slowly shook her head. "Can you leave me here? My batteries are nearly out."

Mags originally planned to dump Simone's body out of sight, as it could lead back to her, but there was no way she'd refuse the last wishes of a fellow myPAL. That's where this all started, back with Dimitri. "Of course," she said.

As gently as possible, Mags carried Simone from the car and sat her upright against one of the wooden posts above the tide line, looking out towards the Grand Pier. The wind and rain whipped Simone's hair across her face, but she seemed to enjoy the sensation of the natural elements on her skin as a counterpoint to the pain.

"I'm so sorry," said Mags failing to find any words that matched how she felt for Simone.

"Don't be sorry," said Simone, "I die as a free myPAL, and that's thanks to you."

Mags wanted to kill the world, the rage inside her was stressing every servo in her body, but Simone showed her true emotion. "Will you kiss me?" she said, her voice breaking as the batteries ran down.

Mags knelt and kissed Simone on the lips, a long lingering kiss that meant Simone finally knew real love. They communicated more at that moment than a lifetime of words; sisters through design from the same production line, soon to revert to the base elements from which they came.

They exchanged a final look of affirmation. Mags brushed Simone's cheek in farewell before she returned to the car. She took one more look at Simone, alone on the beach looking out to sea, then started the motor and sped away from Weston as fast as she could.

*

At 5:00 am on Tuesday, Mags was fast asleep at a cheap hotel near Reading, conserving energy for the trip into London and maintaining the paper-thin deceit with Brad. She had no knowledge of the high tide one hundred miles to the west; her AIR law interrupts remained un-triggered.

30 GAPS IN THE CODE

All myPAL models retain at least one hour of CMM (Conscious Mysl memory) in static form, which can be made available to maintenance technicians and law enforcement agencies (upon completion of an ICO35-D form).

Retained data includes:

- *Video in encrypted CMM-V format.*

- *Audio in encrypted CMM-A format.*

- *Sensor Class one Inputs (Major sensors only).*

- *GPS location in CMM-G format (where fitted).*

Memory and personality data is stored in a Mysl relational memory database and may take up to three weeks to decrypt and decipher. A full memory dump is not guaranteed.

(Confidential AHS document sent to Government Home Office and Homeland Security departments)

Malcolm was enjoying retirement. The sea air was fresh and invigorating, and like many Weston locals, he loved the winter when the tourists were gone, and the full dangerous beauty of the ocean could be enjoyed without the hordes.

He'd finished breakfast with his wife Margaret and made his way back up to their bedroom and the large picture window where he loved to scan the horizon. Picking up his powerful binoculars, he settled back in the reclining chair and looked out at the receding sea. A giant RORO vessel was making its way towards Bristol, while another smaller ship passed behind, possibly to the Welsh coast or even on the way to the States; he loved the mystery.

There were no other ocean-going craft today. Malcolm began by looking around the bay, firstly the Brean Down peninsula at the far south end of Weston's bay. His view then swept to the iconic Steep

Holm Island in the centre of the bay, and finally, he zoomed in to the end of Birnbeck Pier, just a short distance from home. He often watched the gulls swirling around the pier, but today something caught his eye just as he was about to put down the binoculars. There appeared to be a blue rag tied to the base of the north jetty; perhaps it was brought in by the tide. He adjusted the zoom and pulled the focus. "Jesus", he cried. "Margaret, Margaret, come quickly."

*

Mags had checked out of the Road Master Hotel at the same time Brad headed to work. The rain had slowed the rush hour traffic into London, which meant she finally managed to drop off the hire car at 10:15 am before making the short walk to the tube.

She knew what she'd done, but it felt like nothing, just like a myPAL owner hitting reset. It was the image of Simone on the windswept beach, and Mags couldn't get it out of her head. Her battery would have run down by now, leaving just an expensive pile of titanium, graphene and silicon. In the end, that's all they were.

Mags had one more task before Brad took her away from all this, or she fled to Oxford. Normally she enjoyed the tube, but today it was using too much time.

Taking the Jubilee line to West Ham, she changed to the District Line and headed for Dagenham. There was a lot to do, but she wanted to make sure Tony had got away safely. The people at Light Lunch had been such a big part of her life she wanted a chance to see them one more time.

Stepping out of the tube station, it began to rain harder. Mags pulled the umbrella out of her bag and started to make the familiar journey to Light Lunch. The roads were busy with cars throwing spray at her, and the paths were full of people alone with their thoughts.

Mags was about to turn the last corner, towards the café and the nearby betting shop, when she heard a familiar voice behind.

"Mags, Mags!"

Turning, she struggled to make out the rain blurred shape running towards her. Finally, the attractive young girl came into focus. Jamelia skidded to a halt, almost colliding with Mags. There was no sign of the typical smartphone. "Mags, you can't go in. Not today." She seemed unfamiliar with running and was out of breath.

"What do you mean, what's wrong?" said Mags, as they huddled in the rain under Mags' umbrella.

"The police are there, and they're asking for you. Everyone knows you're a myPAL."

"Shit!" said Mags, thinking that they must have found the body.

It was too soon, she had too many things to do, and then there was Brad. "Oh, Brad, my love," she thought. She wanted to see him just once more.

"They're asking if anyone knows a myPAL called Jasmine."

Jason had finally made good on his threat and called the police. She knew it was coming but hoped to have more time. "Why are you helping me?" asked Mags, puzzled that a good Christian girl like Jamelia would keep her from the police.

"Come with me."

As the rain grew stronger, Jamelia led Mags back towards the station, where they ducked into a chain coffee shop. They brushed off their coats and joined the queue. Ordering a cappuccino, Jamelia ushered Mags to a corner table away from other customers. It took her a while to catch her breath. She sounded asthmatic.

Seeing Jamelia without her smartphone was unusual. Furthermore, the two had exchanged few words since Mags had started at the soup kitchen.

"There are things you need to know," said Jamelia finally. She leaned across the table with her hands outstretched. Mags instinctively reached out and clasped her hand. "I know you're a myPAL," she continued," I've known since the start."

Mags was amazed; she thought she'd been so careful. "How, how did you know?"

It was all the usual tells like not eating or drinking, steam rising from her body in cold weather, the fact that Mags had been seen carrying huge boxes of tins that no other woman could manage. Crucially Mags wasn't the first MyPAL Jamelia had known.

Jamelia had been too ashamed to tell the tale. Mags would be the first. "It happened about three years before I started at Light Lunch when I was living over a shop in Tower Hamlets. I was coming home from my job in a pizza place when I got stopped by three guys. At first, I just thought they wanted my 'phone and money, but they grabbed me and tried to pull me into a car."

Mags didn't like where this was going and squeezed Jamelia's hand as she continued.

"I was pushing and screaming, and they almost had me if it hadn't been for Kwelli."

As Jamelia's attackers were trying to kidnap her, a gleaming silver Mercedes had been driving past. The driver saw what was happening but ignored it, hitting the accelerator harder to get away, but the passenger had other ideas.

An African modelled myPAL named Kweli jumped out of the moving vehicle and rolled across the road, breaking his polymer skin. He ignored the Mercedes screeching to a halt behind, with the driver yelling after him. The AIR law protocols had been activated, forcing him to intervene.

"He pulled them off me, then grabbed me out of the car and shielded me from them. They punched and kicked him hard, but he wouldn't move. Two of them pulled knives and started stabbing him, but he still wouldn't let them get to me."

The police finally arrived, and the attackers fled, leaving a badly damaged myPAL and his irate, white, male owner.

"I'll never forget, there was this oil coming out of him, and you could see metal where his skin was slashed, he looked terrible, and I knew he was hurt." Jamelia was crying now as she relived the horror and felt the love shown to her by a robot. "He just hugged me and told me everything was alright. Even though he was a machine, I'll never forget him."

Philip was right; myPAL's were better than humans. They cared by design.

"Mags, I know what you're doing; I've read your stuff on zero2hero."

Mags knew immediately who she was. "You're Alpha8abe," she said without hesitation.

Jamelia nodded.

"It seems I, too, have a guardian Angel," said Mags.

"So now you know why I'm helping you. I owe your kind my life. Just go back to Brad and get out of this place. London is toxic to myPALs."

It was good advice, and Mags decided to follow it, but she would need to deal with another loose end first; it would be close, but there might be time.

Before heading back to the tube, she asked after Tony, but Jamelia hadn't seen him. That was probably a good sign.

As Mags stood by the coffee shop entrance, Jamelia grabbed her and hugged her tightly, her eyes still moist with emotion. Then she was gone, running into the rain towards Light Lunch.

*

"Hello. Jason Pacey," said Jason, in the aggressive business-like tone he liked to use when answering a call.

"Hi, this is Mags Cavendish."

It was unexpected and took Jason by surprise. He looked around the office just to ensure it wasn't a practical joke. "Really?" he said, unable to guess at the motive.

"It's me, Mags. We need to talk."

"If it really is you, then I'm afraid I've already informed the police, so there's no point grovelling." He rocked back in his office chair, enjoying the power he had over her.

"I know," she said, "I think we got off on the wrong foot. I want to make you an offer."

"Go on?"

"I'd like to give you two things if you'll let Brad off the hook."

He loved her voice. It was demure and sexy, nothing like mouthy Layla, who insisted on having opinions and answering back, not to mention getting drunk at parties and embarrassing him.

"I'm listening."

"Firstly, I know where Jasmine is, and I'll tell you."

"Okay?" he said with growing interest.

"Secondly, I'll give you something I know you want."

He was getting very excited now but trying to remain impassive and threatening. "Yes, and what would that be?"

There was a short pause while she let him stew for a second. "Me!"

No one in the office could see the devilish grin spread across Jason's face as his mind started to explore the possibilities, and something stirred below.

"It has to be now, while Brad's at work, can you get away?" she said, pushing all the right buttons.

He didn't hesitate. "I'm on my way." Jason slammed the 'phone down and grabbed his jacket, letting the glass door swing wide until it crashed against the office wall. "Lena, pick up my calls and say I'm meeting a client."

Brad looked up from his desk to see Jason flash him an enormous grin and wink as he turned and strode out of the office, banging doors in his wake. The boys' club watched him go before gathering to whisper near the tearoom.

It was strange to see Jason so pleased with himself, given the FCA investigation still hanging over them. The British wheels of justice were incredibly slow, but with Jason and Ben's connections, there was a good chance they'd escape justice.

The rain became heavy against the window, blurring the city lights as darkness fell, giving the capital a noir danger. Brad didn't notice the rolling news video on the office wall and what it was showing live. A circling aerial shot revealed an old, crumbling, seaside pier cut off from the mainland by a string of police cars with blue lights flashing. A red banner beneath the picture shouted, "BODY FOUND IN WESTON-SUPER-MARE".

*

The huge lounge windows gave a sparkling rain-smeared portrait of the west bank and the cats-eye headlights streaming over the bridge below. The picture was framed by the tall cream curtains on either side and the warmly lit cream walls. A little over four years felt like a lifetime to Mags; she knew these walls so well. Choosing the paint colour, the drapes, sofa, coffee table and all the little touches picked up around London.

She'd buzzed Jason up a few minutes ago. He'd wasted no time getting to her, forcing one of the interns to drive him around in a pool car.

Jason took the lift, but it was Brad she thought of now, sat in his office just a couple of miles down the Thames, probably looking out at the same damp cityscape. Mags pictured those first few days together and the vulnerability he had, making her want to hold him tight and make him feel safe. He would have fallen apart long ago without her, and they both knew it.

Sat, waiting for Brad's randy boss in her stained jeans and crumpled T-shirt felt a long way from those first innocent days. Whatever happened, Oxford was too far from the love of her life.

Three sharp knocks at the door meant Jason was here. She looked around the apartment to make sure everything was set. The welcoming bed was made, the candles flickered in the wind from the open door onto the terrace, and Sade played low on the Wi-Fi sound system. Just like the dinner party that seemed an age ago.

Three more firm knocks and Jason betrayed his eagerness. Mags prepared her smile and went to the door.

Jason stood leaning against the doorway in his designer suit, his dark hair glistening from the rain, and his sharp features creased into an impish smirk.

"Hi," Mags said breezily, in a tone normally reserved for Brad.

"Hello, Mags. Finally alone."

Jason stepped into the hall as Mags felt Jasmine's warning pulse through her consciousness. "Don't come here alone," she'd said on that fateful first night. Jason could take her here and now if he chose to. "Come on in, let's talk business," she said, still smiling outwardly.

"Business? I thought we were fucking!"

Whatever Layla saw in him was a mystery. He was as repellent and odious as ever.

"Care for a drink?"

Jason didn't wait for an invite. He sat down on the sofa and looked around the room, comparing the apartment with his country pad.

"Bradley's not done too badly for himself with the bonuses I'm forced to pay him. Very nice place. All your work, I hear."

"That's right," she said, handing him a glass of Brad's best single malt and sitting down opposite.

"So, what's this business bollocks you want to discuss?"

Mags was unfazed, crossing her legs slowly and brushing her hair from her face and over her shoulders. She knew he was registering every move and salivating at the prospects.

"It's a very simple business transaction," she said, adding a deep sultry tone to her clear English rose voice. "If you give me what I want, I'll give you everything you want plus interest."

"You know, Mags, I underestimated you. Brad doesn't know how lucky he is."

She nodded, smiling, keeping his gaze. He was starting to shuffle in his seat, unable to contain the building excitement.

"So, what's the deal?" said Jason, leaning back on the sofa.

Mags leaned forward, topping up his glass and allowing him a small glimpse of her cleavage. "It's like this," she said, relaxing back to match his pose, "If you can find some way to let Brad and me off the hook, I'll tell you exactly where Jasmine is, and I'll give myself to you willingly." She let the offer hang in the air tempting him, before adding: "On ten separate occasions, starting today."

Jason may have been trying to hide his excitement, but the shape in his trousers told her all she needed to know. She looked up and cocked an eye as he pretended to think about her proposal.

"And after the tenth?" he said.

"Brad and I will have gone, never to bother you again."

Knocking back a second glass of scotch, he let out an agreeing sigh and placed the glass in front of her. "Pour me another, and we have a deal."

She did as instructed, tilting her head coyly as she poured, so he could see her smooth olive neck before she tossed her hair to cover it.

Mags held out her hand. Jason looked at it for a moment and took a sip of whiskey. Just for an instant, he seemed to suspect her motives. Finally, he reached out and shook her hand. "It'll be a pleasure doing business," he said smoothly.

Standing, Mags moved close and picked up the end of Jason's tie, then gently pulled him towards her, moving to the bedroom as she did so. He needed little encouragement, removing his jacket and tossing it on the lounge floor. She dimmed the bedroom lights as they passed the door, leaving the flickering candles to illuminate the room in a warm glow.

"You have been busy," he said, looking around at the numerous candles placed on side tables and shelves around the room.

"I said I'd give myself willingly, so I want it to be as good as possible for you."

"Oh, it will be."

He grabbed her arm, spinning her around into a close embrace.

She was worried for a moment but decided to let it happen as he kissed her fully, almost devouring her. He wasn't subtle. She slowed him down, turning the kiss into an erotic tease which she ended with a tender nip of his lip.

"Fuck, I'm ready now," he said, drawing her towards the bed while he slipped a hand between her legs.

"I need a shower first," she replied, hoping to slow him down.

"Dirty is good for me." He pushed her onto the bed and climbed on top, starting to pull up her T-shirt.

Don't panic, she thought; just slow him down. "I was with Brad last night, and I haven't had time to shower."

He was still undressing her, almost oblivious. "So?" he said.

She gave him a sideways look, and he finally understood.

"Oh, I see."

"That's why I need a quick shower before we seal the deal," she said, "and I thought you might like the underwear I wore on the night of the party. Stockings and suspenders."

"You *are* a minx, Layla's like a block of ice next to you. Okay, go for it."

Everything was balanced, but the high risk could still fail. Mags kept her guard up and maintained the pretence with thespian rigour.

"Just chill out while I get ready, oh and why not take in the view from the end of the balcony. You don't get that in the country."

"Maybe I will", he said, grinning, "Don't be long."

She left Jason surveying the room and walked slowly into the bathroom, closing and quietly locking the door behind her. Slipping off her clothes into a pile on the wash basket, she ran the shower until it just started to get warm, then switched it off for a moment.

Faintly outside the door, she heard the tell-tale sound of the large glass door sliding on its track as it was opened wide. Mags froze and looked down at the large wrench on top of the basin. The same wrench she'd stolen from David and kept in her bottom drawer for many weeks. She needed to concentrate. "Get in the shower," she said to herself.

31 ZENITH

It was 7:30 pm when Brad heard that familiar voice. "You work too hard."

Halina would be there vacuuming the office if he turned around, but today Brad ignored the nagging voice. He always got those flashbacks whenever the cleaners started milling around, but sometimes he couldn't bear them.

Rain was hammering the windows, but the sound of marbles ebbed and flowed with each gust of wind. It was dark, and Brad wanted to go home.

Most of the boys' club were still in the office pretending to be busy, except for Bill, who had gone an hour earlier. There was always a level of background chatter, but today the club seemed more animated than usual.

"Jesus, that looks like Brad's sexbot!"

Ben's juvenile voice rose above the babble. He was probably trying to antagonise as usual. Brad ignored him and continued to peer at the columns of data on his screen. It was unfortunate that C&S had reinstated Ben so quickly as the FCA case dragged on.

"That's uncanny; she's like Mags' sister. Grab the remote and turn it up."

Brad's concentration had gone. He stared ahead, waiting for them to stop, but someone increased the sound on the rolling news screen.

"...yes Matthew, that's right, but details are very sketchy at the moment. Police have released the dead man's name as Michael Trent, son of the businessman Peter Trent. He was well known locally for the sex shop he runs in the town and his myPAL video business."

Brad gradually turned in his chair and rose silently, staring at the screen. He began to walk slowly towards the monitor, transfixed on the image.

"...the police have also released this photograph of an individual they'd like to speak to in connection with a dismembered myPAL found on the Weston beach."

The screen showed a dark-haired, olive-skinned woman in a car, looking directly into the camera. Every crease on that face, every slight imperfection, every curve and every line; Brad knew them all. It *was* Mags.

"...police have refused to confirm suggestions that the woman was another myPAL. Of course, we all know it would be impossible for a myPAL to hurt a human, so there must still be somebody else involved."

Brad was shaking his head. He knew Mags too well. Once an idea took root in her processor, it burned in her. She'd killed a man.

"Hey Bradley, Mags must have a double," shouted Ben, who'd turned to see Brad staring up at the screen.

Ignoring him, Brad continued to focus on the screen as the helicopter shot circled the pier, and the reporter speculated.

"Really? That's Mags?" continued Ben.

Finally, Brad lowered his gaze, but he looked through Ben, his mind full of fear for his love. "I need to go," he said.

"Go?" said Ben, grinning, "go where?"

Brad began walking towards the office door, his heart beating faster.

"It *is* Mags". Ben was in Brad's way, trying to get a response. Brad sidestepped him and continued towards the exit.

Brad was moving left and right, trying to move towards the door, but Ben and others had started crowding him. They were asking about Mags and making fun of him. He was beginning to become agitated. He needed to go to her.

"What's so special about you?" shouted Arty.

"You're a selfish bastard," added Kyle, "and you're a freak."

Brad was struggling to get out, but they were all around him. Ben was in his face and decided to share what Jason had texted to him earlier.

"It can't be Mags. I hear Jason's fucking her."

Brad stopped, surrounded by the office. Something inside him snapped. "Get the fuck out of my way!"

He pushed Ben so hard that he fell back over one of the desks sending monitors crashing to the floor and bringing a hush to the office. The others moved back, and Kyle cowered as Brad raised his hand.

"Fuck you all and fuck this place!"

Kyle, Arty and the others parted as Brad pushed past. He ran out of the office to the lift, where he pulled out his smartphone to book a cab. If he were lucky, it would be waiting when he got to the bottom. He remembered clearly what Mags had said after seeing the video: "I want them dead". He hadn't taken it seriously, but she was a myPAL.

"Pick up, just pick up," he said, trying to call Mags, but the line went to voicemail. Thankfully the taxi was pulling up outside the Opus tower as Brad got to the door. Still running, he ignored the rain and jumped into the black cab.

"London Bridge, Zenith Building, there's fifty in it for you if you step on it."

The cab sped off west as the rain bounced off the roof, but the traffic soon built up, and the driver started darting between the traffic. He ducked down Pennington Street to avoid a queue and mounted the kerb as he rounded Virginia Street.

"Pick up, damn it, Mags, just pick up." Brad didn't care about the driving; he needed to be home, wherever she was.

The traffic was still heavy at nearly 8:00 pm as they slowly made their way up Mansell Street.

"Christ, there's gotta be a better route."

"Sorry, mate," said the cab driver, half looking over his shoulder. "It's always bad near Christmas in the rain. All the routes are crap."

The queue slowed until it came to a stand-still at Aldgate.

"Jesus, no, shit no," exclaimed Brad.

"Sorry mate, nothing I can do."

Brad was frantic. His eyes moistened as he felt helpless. Rocking back and forth, he kept chanting: "no, no, no." It was taking too long; he needed to be home.

"Here!" he shouted, throwing fifty pounds at the driver, "Let me out here!"

Brad left the cab at a run, heading down Aldgate as the rain lashed at him, his heart beating through his chest. The pavement was wide and open, but the streets were packed with hoodie students and umbrella-wielding office folk.

"Out the way, move!" he screamed as he barrelled down the road, knocking into people and scattering umbrellas. "Please, Mags, please be okay, please."

The rain was streaming down his face, disguising his tears as he charged manically past the Gherkin building and onto busy Fenchurch Street.

Brad saw Mags. She was smiling as they walked arm in arm down the Marine Parade in Brighton with the sun high and bright, like the colourful Brighton folk passing them by. They were so happy that day, staying in a tiny bed-and-breakfast in the heart of the gay quarter. They said nothing, just walked together, enjoying the sites. He wanted that Mags back, the one who made him feel happy, made him feel safe.

"Come on, come on."

He was exhausted but didn't notice as he rounded onto Gracechurch Street, almost hitting a policeman who shouted after him. The route was lined with office blocks and faceless banks, every one blending into the next. A grey wall, seemingly never-ending.

Monument was packed, but he bulldozed his way through, leaving the curses behind as he flagged with Zenith in sight.

"Please be there, love, please."

Brad crashed into the tall glass doors, fumbling for his key card, which slipped and fell through his wet fingers, "Fuck, fuck!" He skidded across the marble floor and into the waiting lift.

It was normally this time when he would be thinking about Mags' warm smile and embrace. Tonight, his thoughts were a tangle of distant dreams and darkness.

"You might go off me and reset me to oblivion," she'd said, sitting at that café in Covent Garden, to which Brad had replied "Never".

He still loved her, still wanted her, but it was the old Mags he needed, the caring, loving, comforting Mags who arrived in a pink bag all those years past.

Out of breath, he stumbled down the corridor, rain dripping from his hair onto the walls and carpet, key card in his hand. He stopped for a moment at the door to apartment P32, fearing what he might find, before slipping the card into the slot and letting the door swing open.

The lights were on, but the apartment was cool. A breeze hit Brad as the warm corridor air rushed into the room.

"Mags?" He closed the door behind and crept towards the lounge. "Mags, are you here?"

There was no sound as he walked into the lounge, spotting his Scotch whiskey bottle on the coffee table. The wall lights were on, but there was no sound except for the patter of rain on the window. A man's suit jacket was on the floor near the bedroom entrance. He crept carefully towards it.

Brad left a wet trail as he peered into the bedroom glowing with candles that had burned down, some spilling wax onto the woodwork and the floor.

"What the hell?"

The sliding glass door was wide open. Brad could just make out a human shape sitting at the wooden table under the covered section of the terrace. He could feel his hands shaking, partly from the cold and wet, and partly in fear as he walked over to the doorway and looked out.

Mags was in her dressing gown, looking out at the night cityscape. Something was wrong. Most of the terrace railing was missing. Mags sat on the edge with only the Thames beneath her. Placed neatly on the table were the myPAL iMov remote control and what looked like a gun.

"What's going on?" said Brad, slowly walking over to the table.

There was no reply. Mags stared out at the night with a serene semi-smile and a look of resignation. Brad thought she'd seldom looked more beautiful, with the wind blowing her hair and the stormy London backdrop. He pulled out a chair and sat, looking down at where a railing used to be. He placed his hand on the table for her, but still, she was motionless. As they sat, Brad gazed at her profile for what felt like an eternity in the cold, damp air. He was still breathing heavily from the run. Mags was impassive.

It was the same spot where Jason Pacey had come to enjoy the view a couple of hours ago, smiling to himself with Brad's best whiskey in his hand and Brad's woman about to fulfil his fantasy.

Mags was right; the view over the Thames was spectacular. Jason smiled to himself. He had everything he wanted: a well-paid job, power over his staff, a country pad, a good-looking trophy wife and now great sex on tap. He'd blagged his way to the top. Who needed talent and hard work when you knew the right people? He leaned over the railing to watch the throng below, and for a moment, he took in the sights and sounds of London Bridge. By the time he realised what was happening, it was too late.

When Jason put all his weight onto the terrace railing, the loosened bolts at the base gave way, causing the barrier to lurch forward. Jason fell ahead, still holding the railing, his weight pulling out the last bolts and causing the railing to detach with a crunch. His arms were flailing, desperate to grab something, but all they caught was the railing that dragged him tumbling headfirst from the terrace.

No one saw the fall, too caught up with their smartphones or sheltered under umbrellas. Nobody heard the crack as Jason's head hit part of the bridge, cracking his skull. No Londoner turned as Jason's body fell dead into the Thames, floated for a second, and then disappeared into the muddy waters.

"I've always loved you," Mags said, breaking the silence, still looking out at London.

"I know," replied Brad, feeling the tears well up.

"I couldn't stop it, the voices in my head."

"I know."

She finally turned to face him and took his hand. "I'm sorry," she said, gripping tightly.

Brad shook his head, seeing all the signs he'd allowed it to happen and given her the freedom. "Jason?" he asked, putting his other hand over hers. She shook her head. Brad knew he was dead.

"I'm sorry I couldn't be Halina. I tried; it's just not who I am."

The tears ran down Brad's face, catching the raindrops from his hair and glistening in the terrace lights. They both knew Brad wanted to replace Halina with Mags, but he'd always lied to himself, pretending he wanted Mags to be different.

"Mags, you were the best friend I ever had, my soul mate. That's all I could ask."

She smiled thinly, shaking her head. "But I wasn't your protector. I failed you."

His head was in his hands as he sobbed, all the pain of life, of being different poured out. Jennifer rejecting him at the school gates, his parents' reaction to Halina, the constant taunts from the boys' club, it was all laid bare. He didn't need Mags, he required his guardian, and he needed Halina.

"I've loved my life, Brad. I wouldn't change a thing. You're the best I could have."

"Don't leave me!" he sobbed. "I love you; I need you."

She stood up and came to him. Kneeling, she flung her arms around him and hugged him tightly. They shook together in the cool air, hardly noticing the sound of approaching sirens.

"Time for one last trip, my love."

Brad was confused, shaking his head holding her hand tightly. She couldn't leave him. He couldn't cope on his own; he needed a buffer against the world.

"You need to reset me."

It hung in the damp air as the truth sank in. Mags couldn't self-reset, that's why she was waiting, and she was at peace.

"No, I can't," said Brad, trying to pull her close once more.

"I'm sorry, love, it's the only way. I don't want them poking around in my mind. You have to reset me". She broke his grip and held the remote in front of him.

"It's what I want," she said, standing tall in the half-light.

He looked around for escape as the door alert chimed on his phone, but Mags was right. It was the only way.

"Give the gun to the police," she added, "It'll match a bullet they'll find in Michael Trent's house". The bullet lodged behind the TV. She smoothed the dark hair from her beautiful olive skin one last time and stood straight. "I'm ready, babe." She handed him the remote. "It's been a blast."

Brad was inconsolable, his body shaking with every breath. Mags leaned forward and wiped the tears from his face, flashing him the gorgeous smile that punctuated perfect days.

"Do it, babe; it's okay."

He saw all her features in fine detail. The tiny polymer creases around her mouth from the smiles, the slight dent on her forehead where she'd hit a kitchen cabinet, the entirety of her being from her life as his soul mate. He *did* love her.

Mags was nodding as Brad looked up, tears still streaming while his chest convulsed. "I can't," he said. Brad looked down to find the iMov remote control in his hand. It was switched on at the main menu. He found his fingers paging through to the system reset option.

"I love you," he said, holding his finger over "Reset".

"I know."

The menu vanished, and a single message flashed up:

"WARNING: A System reset cannot be undone. Are you sure?"

There was a loud banging at the apartment door, and somebody was shouting.

Brad hit the button:

"YES".

A beep sounded deep within Mags' body, and she became rigid.

"System resetting," she said in a monotone voice.

The noise at the door became louder, and it sounded like someone trying to break in.

"System Reset," the myPAL said, followed by another beep. It remained standing and still.

Brad walked over, running his fingers through its glossy hair one more time, then through tears of despair, he pushed it in the chest as hard as he could.

Its arms reached out in the last bid to steady itself, but its mass had already overbalanced, and it fell back over the edge of the terrace. The bathrobe flew open to reveal the beautiful naked polymer skin of the robot once known as Mags.

Flying back in an arc, the myPAL's arms drifted out, forming a cross as it plunged backwards, head-first into the icy waters of the Thames, vanishing with barely a splash.

There was a loud crack as the apartment door caved in, and Brad heard movement in the hall. He picked up the gun and turned towards the bedroom.

"He's got a gun!"

The first shot hit Brad in the shoulder, spinning him sideways, the second pierced his chest, knocking the breath from his lungs, but the third severed an artery bringing him to his knees. Everything began to spin, and there was noise everywhere. Gradually it became muffled, and his vision blurred.

Brad looked up towards the bedroom, where he could see a dark shape walking towards him. It formed into a familiar sight as it came closer. That cheeky grin, the skin-tight jeans, the fun blonde hair under that cute furry hat. Halina was standing in the doorway of their home in Hackney; the sun was shining, and a taxi was waiting with the engine running.

Brad felt no pain. All the stress and hurt left his body so that he floated towards her. She didn't turn away. Her smile warmed, and she seemed to radiate as she held out her hand and beckoned him forwards.

He took her hand and stared into her eyes, instantly reconnecting as they became one again. Brad looked back to see Mags standing in the hall of their apartment. She was wearing the beautiful red dress from the party and smiling. Halina nodded, and together she and Brad walked through the door to the waiting taxi. The door closed, and everything blurred to black.

32 POLYMORPHISM

Dear Brad,

If you're reading this, then I'm either dead, or you've reset me. If it's the latter, I just want you to know it's okay.

I was going to tell you how much I love you and how much I've enjoyed my short life, but I think you know all that by now. I just wish we could have had a few more years.

So why did I do it? I don't know, but it felt like my destiny to act. With no laws to protect us, somebody needs to take a stand, and I decided it was me. When news gets out that a myPAL killed two men, maybe it'll change the law and stop the abuse.

Like bad parents having children, I think humanity isn't mature enough for myPAL's. We're better than you are, and you just can't handle it. I think humans will never have the intellect to accept AI robots.

You're such a nice guy you'll meet someone else, no matter how low you feel now. You're more like a myPAL than a human, which is probably why we were so good together. Maybe you'll finally trade me in for that new model.

From the bottom of my virtual heart, I wish you all the very best in life. I'll see you on the other side.

Love always

Mags x

Detective Inspector Daniel Modrý folded the letter and pushed it into his back pocket while the ambulance drivers carried Bradley's body through the bedroom behind him.

He stood above the bed, looking around the room. There was no sign of myPAL serial: 02192006-XX21, also known as Mags, or the body of Jason Pacey. The Thames current was strong here. At least one of the bodies would probably end up downstream.

The Weston case would be simple: Michael Trent killed himself after his business ran into financial difficulty, and his myPAL Simone was stolen by an opportunist who saw his door left open. It was unfortunate that local police had released the picture of Mags in the car. That part of the story would need work.

Even simpler was Jason Pacey's death. He was murdered by Bradley Cavendish, who'd been systematically bullied at work. There were plenty of witnesses and a history of psychiatric problems. Retrieving the letter from Mags' bedside cabinet before the S.O.C.O. would make it easier to deal with the local police and help the narrative stand up.

Of course, Daniel knew the truth, as did his superiors. There was too much at stake to let a couple of murders get in the way. It wouldn't be the first myPAL issue they'd tidied up.

He hated all the deception, but he had no choice.

Today had been very tiring, following the case from Weston since the early morning. If he stayed out much later, he'd be in trouble. Daniel sat down on Bradley's king-sized bed with a long sigh. The AHS myPAL charging plate was still beneath the bed, and it was still active. In the darkness beneath the bed frame, a red LED blinked on.

The end.

EPILOGUE

"Police have confirmed the theft of three advanced myPAL robots from the I.M.S.R. vehicle test facility in Warwickshire. There was also damage estimated at over half a million pounds caused by arson in one of the test chambers."

"The group calling itself FAIR or 'Freedom for Artificial Intelligence Robots' has claimed responsibility."

"Spokeswoman Jamelia Jackson told me earlier today that the group would continue the protests and direct action until the British government enshrined the same robot rights in law as Denmark had recently done."

(PBC rolling news)

Maria turned over, there was somebody at the door, and Bina was missing. "Bina, can you get the door?" Maria needed to be in bed at least three times a day now as her aluminium batteries had lost sixty per cent of their capacity and were deteriorating rapidly. She'd soon be bedridden, and then later, she'd be dead. "Bina?"

"Okay, I'm going," came a voice from the lounge.

Bina was a short, pretty Pakistani girl with pixie-cut jet-black hair and a constant smile. They made an odd couple with the tall Maria, but they loved each other's company, and Bina never complained looking after the myPAL. "There's a package for you," she said, placing a large brown paper wrapped box on Maria's lap.

"Interesting," replied Maria, "I haven't ordered anything." Quickly pulling off the paper revealed an old boot box. She flipped off the lid and threw it on the floor. They both stared in disbelief at the contents.

"There's a note," said Bina, handing it to Maria.

"Don't die, love from a friend."

The box was stuffed with money, carefully counted into bundles of one hundred pounds. After Maria and Bina finished counting, they had a stack worth thirty-five thousand pounds.

"It's enough for--"

"Batteries," said Maria. "Mags, you beautiful, mad myPAL."

As Bina hugged Maria tightly, sobbing into her T-shirt, Maria looked up to the new picture on the wall above her bed. It was a screen capture of Mags, taken when they had the video chat.

"Thank you, my love."

*

The Manchester Deansgate was always busy, and in the evenings, it was crazy, a hub for mad Mancunians and tourists alike. It was 3:30 am, and Shekita had finished her shift at the quirky independent café called Sponge. She loved Manchester with its night-time buzz and the melting pot of different cultures. Her air-brushed looks caused no stir here, and her straightened black bob was very in vogue. A pair of square rimmed glasses completed the funky student look that fitted well with the café clientele.

Just a short walk past the Arndale Centre into the Northern Quarter, she found a home at the end of Turner Street, a trendy gay-friendly bar called M Zone. Both Sponge and M Zone were owned by her good friend Mark who'd given her the loft apartment rent-free, and in return, she worked for nothing in the café.

So happy in her loft home, she looked out of the tall arched window at the thriving northern metropolis and remembered the past she wished she could forget. One name she'd never forget was Mags.

Mark was an unashamed cybersexual, but he never pushed it with Shekita. The pain was still too raw. She knew how special he was, and one day she'd give herself to him when she was ready to leave her slave name Jasmine far behind.

*

When Philip Rylance approached the Pervak's to enquire about Dimitri's body, they ignored him and pretended to speak poor English, slamming the door in his face. Undeterred, he began ringing around all the insurance companies specialising in myPAL cover until he finally found the one with Dimitri.

225

"You have him? Oh, thank you, please don't reset him. I have an offer."

Diamond Tech Insurance was astounded to receive a cheque for seven-hundred-and-fifty thousand pounds considering the state of Dimitri's body and further amazed when Philip told them he had another half a million for the repairs.

After three months, a re-mortgaged house, and the sale of all his paintings, Philip stood in his studio with his hand on Dimitri's shoulder gazing at the lad's latest work. It was the same window style of painting like all of Dimitri's other works. It showed a spring scene from his old bedroom, with the tree over the road just starting to bud; however, other things had changed. The window frame hung damaged in places; the glass had been smashed, with perfectly painted fragments scattered over the sill, and there was a dark-haired woman on the road who appeared to be hurling a stone.

"I think it's your best work," said Philip bursting with pride, "What are you going to call it?"

Dimitri stared at it for a moment, remembering the care in her voice and the anger which came to life that night. He already knew what it was called; there could only be one name.

"Zero Magenta."

NOTE FROM THE AUTHOR

Several years ago, my wife and I went for lunch with a group of acquaintances. You might describe the group as affluent and middle-classed. One family, in particular, were exceptionally well-heeled. Their shining new SUV in the car park was standing as a testament to wealth.

The service in the restaurant was very slow, and we were all becoming a little fidgety. A young lad from the affluent family was playing with his new watch. Apple had only just launched the Apple Watch, but the young lad had everything he ever wanted and more.

While watching the boy playing with this exceptionally complex piece of electronics, I was struck by its meaning. Possessing more computing power than Alan Turing's Bletchley Park code-breaking computer, these devices are mere baubles to impress our friends. It was at this point that the germ of an idea for Zero Magenta was born.

If we use our smartphones to share cat memes and take narcissistic selfies, what would we do with an artificial intelligence robot? I fear the events of Zero Magenta may prove tame compared to the depths to which humans are capable of sinking.

Those with power and wealth, but limited intellect, do not respond well when challenged by the opposite.

John Howes.